Rainbows and Unicorns

S.N. Moor

Contents

Hey Dad

HERE IS YOUR ONE page in this book to, as usual ((I know) *rolls eyes*), tell you this is as far as you can read. I know I said last time I would write a book you could read and I'm still working on it. Albeit very slowly... like super slow... like sloth slow, but hey... the people have spoken, and they want this series to continue... soo... I'm giving them what they want. I can quickly summarize this book for you though.

So here it goes, Evelee and her friends are hanging out having a super fun time. YAY fun time. And they have a Memorial day party. YAY party. Lizzy, that crazy chick, brings a fruit dish she melon balls, they play games and then they have another party at the club where they dress up as Rainbows and Unicorns. Magical. And... the end. Oh, and they plan a beach trip. Now it's the end...well, for now because you know... series continuing and what not.

As always thank you for your understanding XO

This book is dedicated to all of you good girls.

Now be a good girl and read this book and don't come until I tell you to.

Introduction

<u>Rainbows and Unicorns</u> is the third book in the series. It is highly recommended you read Cupid's Contract and Bunnies and Bowties first. If you haven't read those, stop here, because there are spoilers below (the title links will take you to those books).

In **<u>Cupid's Contract</u>**, Everlee meets her four delicious men who give her the time of her life and the confidence she lost after dickface, Rich, destroys her. The only problem is the men make her agree to only sleep with them two times before they part ways. By the end of the arrangement, Everlee gets attached but doesn't know how the men feel, so she honors the agreement against her own desires and leaves. She's scared of getting hurt again.

<u>Bunnies and Bowties</u>, picks up two months later. She's been absolutely miserable, and unbeknownst to her, so have the men. Lizzy, being the amazing BFF she is, gets her back out on the scene, but she runs into her men and things are as hot as ever. She wants to talk with them about a future, but she's already committed to visiting her family for Easter. We get to meet her eccentric brother, Beckett, and her mother and father. Her mother is hellbent on a marriage and grandkids for Everlee and uses every oppor-tunity to remind her, going as far as setting her up on a date with a lawyer. Everlee does her part but is missing her men desperately. The church her family attends is hosting a birthday party for one of their members and during the celebration Everlee comes face to face with her men (while on her date). They were all in foster care together a few towns over from Everlee growing up. Small world. As you can imagine, fireworks ensue, and Beckett picks up on all the sexual tension between them all and calls out she's in a poly relationship. Our favorite fivesome is formed and it is HOT! HOT! HOT!

EVERLEE – SHOULD HAVE WORN PANTIES

"LET'S GO, HOOKER!" LIZZY shouts, pulling me out of the front door.

"Calm down, it's your party, so we can't be late," I huff, trying to slip my shoe on while being pulled out of my back door. "If you make me fall down these stairs, then we'll definitely be late." I laugh.

She sighs dramatically, like a toddler whose sucker just got taken away. "I'm just so excited!" She clasps her hands under her chin.

"I know you are boo!"

"Are you both ready?" Callum asks, standing beside the car door holding it open.

He has taken the role of chauffeur tonight because Brady is out for the next several weeks on some sort of mission with their friend Michael Dufrey. He said that he couldn't really talk about it and wasn't even sure how long he'd be gone, so who knows? It's been a week and when I asked Jax this morning if he'd heard from him, his head fell to the side.

Then he continued explaining how we wouldn't hear from him until he's back. It's just the way these things go.

Jax was asked to go too, but declined this mission. Thank God! I don't know if I could handle it. Having him out there, doing something dangerous, and not knowing if he's ok. I couldn't do it with any of my guys.

"Yes. Lizzy was taking forever getting ready," I say, giving him a kiss before I climb into the car behind her.

He brushes his hand over my ass before he grabs my arm and pulls me back out with a scowl on his face.

I can't help but smile, knowing exactly what he's going to say.

"Everlee," he lightly reprimands.

"Callum," I repeat his name in the same tone, trying not to smile.

"You aren't wearing underwear," he growls. His eyes are like blue flames, narrowed on my face.

"I don't know how this still surprises you after all this time."

He shakes his head. "You'll be punished for this later."

A heat races through my body. "I hope so." I wink and press my lips to the corner of his mouth before I climb into the backseat.

"Thank God you two stopped. I was going to need an underwear change."

"Stop!" I smack her arm playfully.

"At least someone wears them," Callum groans from the front.

Lizzy shoots me a glance before she fans herself.

She was radiant. Absolute perfection, wearing a cream-colored dress with off the shoulder sleeves, that glowed against her light brown skin. Her hair was pulled back into a bun with a white and pink flower tucked just off to the side. "You look beautiful," I whisper to her.

She grabs my hands and I can feel the thin sheen of sweat on her palm. She's nervous. "Thank you. I'm so glad you're here with me."

"Are you kidding? There's nowhere else I'd rather be."

She doesn't let my hand go, instead only grips it tighter. When we pull on the street for Bo's, I feel her hand tighten briefly, before it relaxes, but still not releasing.

Her and Tony rented out the top floor for the party tonight and I don't know if she's more excited about the party or the fact it's at Bo's. She and Emmett are still ironing out the details on whether she can have her reception here. She had initially tried to get Vixen, but Tony and I talked her out of it. The only problem with Bo's is that she wants a DJ and a dance floor, but Emmett's not sure he can make it work within the space with enough tables to support her ever-growing list of invitees.

On nights he talks to her, he finds me at home and gives me extra long hugs. I imagine it's because he wants to tell her no, but he's trying to work it all out for me, even though I haven't, nor would I ever ask him.

"I'm sorry Beckett couldn't make it. Him and Will give their warmest wishes," Lizzy sighs.

"Yea. If we had a date, before I knew they were coming up a few weeks ago, they could have waited. Two birds, one stone."

"You mean two cocks, one mouth," Lizzy cackles.

Callum cuts his eyes in the rearview at me.

"Lizzy!" A blush tinges my cheeks.

"Everlee, I'm just kidding," she says louder than necessary while shaking her head no. She holds out both her fists, sticking her index and middle finger out and pointing them at her face. "Mouth yoga," she whispers, then freezes.

My gaze follows hers, and standing out front of Bo's is a handsome man waiting for his bride to be. Tony is wearing a dark blue suit over a cream-colored shirt, with a light pink rose tucked in his front pocket. His straight back and unwavering legs are a stark contrast to his busy hands in front of him. While they may be clasped, his thumbs are rubbing feverishly on each hand. If I was Lizzy, I may call out that he looks like a bundle of nerves because that is one of her favorite things to read in books, but I'm not. Obviously, because I'm much more mature, I laugh at myself.

When Callum pulls up front to drop us off, we climb out of the car and Lizzy grabs Tony's hand to give it a squeeze. Pushing past her own nerves and excitement, she is trying to calm him down.

They are perfectly matched. In both their strength and bond, as well as their attire.

If this is any indication of how their wedding is going to be, then we're in for a beautiful and over the top treat and I can't be more excited.

Callum walks around the front of the car and hands the valet his key before holding out his arm for me to take. "Such the gentleman," I mumble, casting him a side eye. On the streets, because he sure as shit isn't one in the sheets. A memory of Callum pressing me up against a wall and taking me from behind last night flashes through my head, causing a heat to race across my skin.

He turns and gives me a devilish grin, almost like he knows what I'm thinking. "We're going to have to do something about your wardrobe."

"If you think for one second, you can dictate what I wear, or don't wear, you have another thing coming buddy."

His other hand crosses his body and lays gently, but authoritatively, on mine. "Underwear. It's a simple thing."

"That gets in the way and leaves lines. And this dress is tight."

"Trust me. I know how tight your dress is," he growls, and a heat vibrates through me. "Are you wearing anything under your pants?" I retort.

"This isn't about me."

"Answer the question, Callum," I command defiantly.

He stops and turns to look at me, his face inches from mine, his eyes narrow and squinted like he's fighting with himself. "No."

"You..." Another flush sweeps across my skin. Mother's ass! I should have brought two dresses because I'm a hot mess. A hot, moist mess!

Lizzy calls over her shoulder, "I'm going to need you two to stop fucking for a few hours so I can have my party. I know. I'm a selfish bitch, but really, I'm looking out for my vagina. And when I say my vagina, I mean the one between Everlee's legs."

I laugh, and Callum is left speechless. It's rare that happens, but Lizzy has figured it out and has a knack for keeping him off balance. Keeping them all off balance. Emmett and Knox usually fall right in with her, but Jax and Callum... clams. Lips shut and eyes wide open in shock. Probably not an actual clam, but I'm envisioning some cartoon version with gigantic blinking eyes dangling off its shell.

Tony opens the door and the smell of fresh bread wafts through, swirling around us.

"Everlee," the doorman nods with a slight smile. He's probably closer to his seventies and has short salt and pepper hair, which stands out in contrast to his dark brown skin. His eyes are brown and hold a tinge of cloudiness behind them, but they always sparkle when he smiles.

"Fredrick." I nod and smile back. I make it a point to greet him every time I come here, which lately has been at least once a week, during the guy's Monday meetings.

"Your party is upstairs waiting for you, Ms. Lizzy."

"Thank you, kind sir," Lizzy says with an English accent, tipping her invisible hat.

Another thing she does when she's nervous. She talks with random accents, sometimes mixing several into one sentence. One time, I forget what we were doing, she went from a deep southern country twang to Russian and then Italian. And then my favorite time was in college when she gave her entire senior thesis presentation with a French accent.

She's never been to France.

Or studied French.

But one of the panel members she was presenting to was. So that was super awkward. She apologized several times throughout the presentation and would try to correct, but would eventually go back to the accent.

Fredrick looks at me with a furrowed brow and I just nod. He also knows Lizzy by name, since she's in here probably more than me, talking to Emmett about the reception and wedding catering.

The wedding is still a year away, not exactly sure of the date, but that's not stopping her.

We wave to the women at the hostess stand before we ascend the front staircase, and standing at the top are my men, looking so fucking delicious. Knox and Jax are standing on the left of the stairs and Emmett is on the right with a few of the head servers who are helping to cater for the event.

All three of them are wearing dark blue or black suits with white shirts and bowties. Their pants grip their thighs, making me feel like a lioness in the safari, while their jackets hug and flare in all the right places. Saliva floods my mouth like a broken dam floods a river. I'd never tell Callum this, but at this very second, I'm regretting not wearing any panties. The moisture pooling in my needy little pussy will prevent me from sitting down for at least an hour, if not more.

Callum and I pause on the stairs and let Lizzy greet the men first, then Emmett and the servers. Jax, Knox, and Callum are here as investors of the restaurant, not friends, even though Lizzy invited them as such.

While Lizzy is talking to the other servers, Emmett briefly looks me up and down, then tosses me a quick wink before he takes her by the arm and leads her into the party.

I greet Knox and Jax, giving them each a lingering hug and a kiss on the cheek, just off the side of their lips, inhaling their scent. It's only been a few hours since I saw them off this morning, but I simply can't get enough of them. I'm like a fucking cat in heat with these men.

Jax's hand slides down my back, brushing along my ass, then pauses. He pulls back and looks at me with *that* look.

"Don't start. I've already heard about it from Callum," I mumble, pressing my hand against his hard chest.

"Girl. You do you, because God I love it when you do," Knox defends, then leans in and whispers, "Plus, it makes it easier if I want to sneak you away during the party and show you how much I *really* love it." He winks, then spins away, sauntering into the party so proud of his exit. He looks over his shoulder, "If you need anything, Ms. Everlee, please don't hesitate to let me know."

A breath puffs out of my chest, because that's all I can do. Just like Lizzy has a knack for making the guys speechless, they have the same effect on me, but for a very different reason.

Jax moves his hand to my hip. "Did Callum also tell you that you will be punished later?"

"You know... you keep saying that, but I haven't seen anything I would deem worthy of punishment." I pat his chest and walk away. The sound of his low chuckle behind me makes me smile and causes a tingle to race up my spine.

Perhaps a promise of what's coming.

EVERLEE - LEAKY FAUCET OF AROUSAL

My stomach turns when I see no missed calls or text messages from Beckett. He and Will were supposed to land at noon, and it's just past four in the afternoon and there's been no word. I didn't want them calling me because I didn't want Lizzy to see and have the surprise be ruined, but a quick text would have sufficed!

A scream echoes out, followed by a shrill and then laughter.

Problem solved.

When I get through the crowd, Lizzy is screaming at Beckett, nearly jumping in his arms, and losing all sense of decorum. "You said you couldn't come, you little shit!"

He's laughing as he sets her back down. "We could come up for the day. We just got off our shifts this morning and then we fly back tomorrow evening."

She gives Will a hug, then smacks him on the chest. "We are supposed to be a team against the McKinleys. You and me!"

He laughs, grabbing Beckett's hand. "I'll keep that in mind next time."

"I'm holding you to it, hot stuff. Give me your phone," she demands, holding out her hand.

He looks cautiously at Beckett, who nods, so Will relinquishes his phone slowly. She taps away quickly, entering her phone number, then takes a selfie to attach the photo to the number.

"Careful, she's been known to make inappropriate ringtones before."

"Stop, that was only one time, and you left me alone for several hours. What was I supposed to do?"

"Not that."

"Pshh." She bats her hand in the air and hands him his phone back.

He quickly glances at it, then chuckles. "Nice." He smiles, but doesn't explain, and I'm dying with curiosity to know how she put herself in his phone.

"Hey Beckett," I say, moving in to give him a hug.

"Hello darling." He pulls me in, then whispers, "Your men are looking rather delightful this evening."

"Very delightful. Yours as well."

"I can hear you talking about... well, men." Will chimes.

"Good day, Will," I say, moving over to give him a hug. He's just slightly shorter than my brother, by like maybe an inch, but just as muscular.

Callum walks up behind me with his hand on my lower back and greets Beckett and Will with a handshake. "Beckett, Will. Glad to see you again."

"Callum," they both say in unison.

"Beckett! You handsome devil. Ooh-wee, you two boys clean up nice," Betty says, walking over with a short, gray-haired man behind her. She's wearing a black dress with black and gold sequins, while the man, I assume, is her husband, is wearing a nice black suit. The pants are about an inch too long and bundle just around his shoes.

"Betty! You sassy minx!" Lizzy shouts, throwing her arms in the air, walking over to give her a hug.

"Hello deary. You look absolutely radiant and Everlee, darling. Looking beautiful." She pulls her head to the side, like she's looking around me, then pumps her eyebrows before clawing the air. Yes. It's a tight dress! But it makes my ass look fantastic. So...

Betty continues, "This is my husband Gerald," she says, patting him on the chest.

Gerald waves meekly at the group. He's very much a small personality compared to Betty's boisterous and unexpectedly large one.

"Nice to meet you," the collective group says.

Callum rubs his fingers down my arm and excuses himself briefly from the group. Butterflies swirl in my stomach as I watch him walk over to Jax and Knox. Three of my men looking so devilishly handsome.

"I picked up your fine-looking brother and his beau today at the airport," Betty explains.

"You did?"

"I did." She nods, crossing her arms in front of her chest.

"She gave me her card when we were here a few weeks ago, so I figured why not?"

"I'm expanding my empire," she jokes. "I'm going to go private soon, then take over the world. Start a company and call it Betty's Bitchin' Rides."

Our group erupts in laughter.

"Thank you for entertaining her," her husband jokes.

"Entertaining her? Never. She's the one who does all the entertaining. A joy. A light in our dim lives," Lizzy sings.

"Well, aren't you sweet as pie."

"She's sweet as something," I mumble sarcastically.

"Sugar," Tony coos beside her, planting a quick kiss on her cheek. "Sammie and Davis want to say hello when you get a minute." He nods to a couple holding hands across the room, waving at Lizzy. They look familiar. Perhaps I've seen them at one of their more recent parties, but I don't know them.

Sammie is close to six feet tall without her heels on and has perfectly straight, jet black hair that reaches to her waist. Davis is several inches shorter than her, with short black hair and a nice body- strong, but nowhere near as muscular as my guys. The way he stands just half an inch behind her, and the way he looks to her -almost for permission- tells me she definitely wears the pants in the relationship.

Lizzy waves back before giving me a quick hug. "I'll talk to all of you later! A party just for me-" She starts to flitter away before Tony clears his throat, causing her to laugh. "For us, darling, for us. But mostly for me. You hate parties." She bats the air playfully before she continues walking across the room.

"He's going to have his hands full with that one," Betty says, watching them walk away.

"He'll get used to it," Gerald jokes.

"Darling," Betty's hand rests on Gerald's chest. "If you think you're used to me, then I have to mix it up a little. Variety is the spice of life."

"Don't I know it baby!" He pats her butt, and she lets out a squeak. "Let's get you a drink and go dancing, my Queen!"

Betty throws her hands in the air like she's doing the salsa or something, as they walk over to the drink table.

There's no one on the dance floor, but I get the impression Gerald is used to that and probably enjoys getting the party started, or even flaunting his lovely queen around for everyone to admire. He seems head over heels in love with her and, from what I can tell, she loves him big. He's quiet, but not shy. Quirky, but not in your face eccentric. He matches her crazy, beautifully - a perfect pair.

"How are your guys?" Beckett asks when it's just the three of us.

"Great."

"When are you going to tell mom and dad?"

"Never." They are so stuck in their ways, with their traditional thoughts on marriage and relationships, that me coming to them with this... I don't think they'd be able to process. I don't think they'd disown me, but it would be awkward. Tense.

Beckett laughs. "I bet they'd love them."

"We're not having this conversation."

He holds up his hands. "One last thing, and it's a serious question. How do you plan on having a long-term future with them when mom and dad are kept in the dark? Family functions, dinners, holidays? Have you thought about that?"

I nod, recalling we briefly talked about it last month after Easter. The talk probably required more in-depth conversation about those things, but I'd been thinking about it, them, for months and I knew I wouldn't leave again. I guess I sort of took the approach that if they're what I want, then we'll figure out the rest. I knew kids and marriage were likely not going to happen and I was ok with that.

If the marriage issue became a big deal, perhaps we could have a little ceremony between all of us. Plus, there's a trend where people aren't getting married anymore. Lifelong partners. That's what we are. If we had everything else but the piece of paper, then did it matter? Kids. I still don't know how I feel about that yet. I talked myself into not needing kids with them, and maybe part of me hopes they'll change and that will be one of the things we figure out along the way. I'm not in a rush for them, so who knows? Plus, I'm fairly certain I'll be an auntie in less than two years. Likely nine months after the wedding.

Holidays... we still need to figure that out. Easter worked out so well, and it will next year, but Thanksgiving and Christmas. Those will be the tougher holidays to avoid or participate in. Maybe for the first year or two I could just not be dating anyone? But that won't last forever and I definitely don't feel like having mom set me up every holiday. I could simply pick one to be my boyfriend in front of my parents, but I don't know... I'd feel bad for the others and wouldn't want them to think they are less, because none of them are.

It's not perfect, but we'll figure it out. I believe I'm meant to be with those men, so the universe will provide. Things happen for a reason, so I just need to wait and see what path this will take. It's going to work out because we are meant to be. Boom!

"Well, have you figured it out?" Beckett presses again when I don't answer immediately.

"I don't know Beckett, but I'll figure it out." There's a slight edge in my voice when I answer, causing his brows to perk up in defense.

"You always do," he answers softly, not wanting to push too hard.

"So when are you moving out of mom and dads?" I fire back, ready to move the conversation off of me.

"I don't know Everlee, but I'll figure it out," he repeats my words back to me.

Being the mature person I am, I stick my tongue out at him. "How's work going?" I look at Will.

"Great. The new house has been fantastic. I think they're just grateful I'm not Beckett."

"Har har. Hilarious."

Will shrugs and smiles. He's a good-looking man with a bright white smile. He seems wholesome and sweet, but still a little reserved. Definitely not as outgoing and in your face as Beckett, which is honestly the best thing for Beckett. He needs someone sensible to balance him out. If not, it would be total chaos.

I watch Beckett watch Will laugh and have never seen him so happy. He's almost glowing, which tells me it's something serious. And because he's never brought a man around to meet the family or to important events.

Beckett looks over my shoulder. "Looks like one of your men would like a word with you." He pumps his eyebrows.

My head snaps behind me and I see Emmett standing by the railing looking at us, so I wave him over.

"He trimmed his beard. Now he looks like a sexy lumberjack in the summer with it all tight around his face."

"He's sexy lumberjack every season."

"Who?" Emmett asks, sliding his arm around my waist, but keeping his hand at a respectable height.

"This hot guy I know."

"Hmm." He cuts his eyes at me.

I smile, winking.

"Are you enjoying yourselves?" Emmett asks the group.

"We are. Are you glad this party is finally here?" I inquire, and he looks at me knowingly.

Emmett's been stressing out about this event since they finalized the paperwork two weeks ago. Fortunately, Lizzy gave him creative control over the menu, which she thought would help, but it probably didn't. Emmett is a perfectionist and couple that with his baby and one of the first large events he's had... he's been an absolute wreck.

"It looks amazing," Will chimes.

Emmett looks up and sees a server walking towards him. "I'll chat later," he leans over and kisses my cheek. "Beckett. Will," he nods before moving to meet the server.

"He seems stressed," Beckett notes.

"He is. He loves this place and wants it to do well."

"I was looking at their menu while I was waiting for Beck to get ready and it looks like they have some amazing food."

"It's all very good. I've tried most everything and you really can't go wrong. Although..." I reach over to one of the tables and grab a card with the menu printed on it, then nod. "Yea, he has a select menu and this," I point to a sandwich named 'The Lizzy', "is a special gourmet sandwich he made exclusively for the event tonight. And judging by the fact she's not completely lost her shit, I don't think she's seen it yet." I grab another menu and slip it into my purse. I'll frame it with a nice matte and give it to her as a gift. A sandwich named after her, at her engagement party?

Emmett went all out for her. I'd like to think he would have done it anyway, but I think part of it is because of me. He knows how much Lizzy means to me, so he wants it to be absolutely perfect for her.

We move to the side of the party, so we aren't awkwardly in the middle of the dining room and they download me on everything that's happened in the last two weeks since they were last up, which isn't a ton. Beckett met Will's mom, who recently started dating a man that Will called 'fun'. He doesn't elaborate with his description and I don't dare ask after Beckett gives me *that* glance.

Beckett told me how mom's been in a panic the last several days in prep for their Costa Rican getaway- the only reason they aren't here. They've had it booked for months now and Lizzy forgot. My parents were bummed, but promised they would be at the wedding whenever it was and sent her a nice gift, she opened yesterday. A leather-bound vow notebook with their names embossed in gold foil on the front. Lizzy cried, then immediately video called them oohing and aahing over it, at which point mom started crying. It was a mess and the call wouldn't be complete without a little jab at the end about mother looking forward to getting me that gift one day soon... hopefully.

She's so wrapped up in the idea of marriage for me, even if it's not what I want. Although, I guess to be fair, I haven't told her that. Maybe I should start planting the seeds next time I see her.

Lizzy waves me to her side as she walks around the room talking to everyone. I love how inclusive she wants me to feel, even though this is her day. One of her many days. I can't help but smile as I watch her work the room.

Glowing.

She's absolutely glowing.

I'm so happy for her.

"You're smiling." Callum walks up beside me, hooking his hand around my waist.

"She's so happy."

He lets out a low hum. I know what he's thinking. What he wants to say.

But he won't.

We had an in-depth talk after my brother and Will left last time. He tried to convince me of everything I was giving up to be with them, but I shut him down. I told him I'd made my choice and I wasn't leaving, so I didn't want him bringing up weddings, kids, or my future happiness anymore.

"She's glowing," he agrees softly.

"What's going on?" I turn to him, slipping my hand in his.

"Nothing. I just saw you over here looking so fucking delicious and I wanted to claim you. Mark you as mine, and by extension ours, since we can't all claim you tonight. Men are looking at you in this dress and let's just say it's driving us all wild."

I look around the room and see Emmett flittering from server to server, checking and prepping food, while Jax and Knox are standing with their heads together near Beckett and Will's table, watching Callum and I.

"Well, you know I only have eyes for you four and no one else."

He smiles, "You better."

"Well, there was this one guy."

His hand flattens on my lower back and he pulls me in tight, our hips touching one another, his cheek pressed to mine. "If you so much as think of another man, I will find him and end him. You are ours and no one else's and if I have to fuck you right here in the middle of this floor to prove it, then I will," his voice is low, and lethal, but a second later he changes to light-hearted, "But that would most definitely ruin your friends party and we don't want that."

"We don't want that?" I mumble, my pussy clenching from his feral possessiveness. My mind was still stuck on him fucking me right here in the middle of the floor. I know other words were said, but they just sound like woo woo woo in my head.

If you would have asked me a year ago if I wanted a man to say those things to me, I would have said hell no, but when he does it. Fuck! It turns me on like a match in a gas can.

It's why I don't wear panties. Aside from the obvious, I don't need to feel like I've pissed myself constantly because my pussy has a freaking leaky faucet of arousal around them and two... well, there isn't a two, except for maybe ease of access just in case I find myself in a dark hallway with one of them.

"Ready to eat?" he asks.

"Now. It's about time for the speeches."

He smirks, shaking his head.

"Oh fuck. You said eat, like you and I go sit at a table for food. Like people food." Should have been paying better attention and not thinking about my pussy, so I didn't think he was offering to feast on me. Wishful thinking, I suppose.

His brow furrows. "So many questions..."

"Shut up. I'm not horny, you are."

"The latter is one hundred percent true, and you aren't horny? I can smell your arousal coming off of you in waves and I want to fucking taste it on my lips. Clean you up and make you come so fucking hard."

I whimper. I straight up whimper. Asshole. He's fucking with me on purpose.

"Excuse me," I growl at him.

He smirks and walks away to Jax and Knox, while I hurriedly make my way to the bathroom before I leak down my leg or through my dress.

EVERLEE - DOORS ARE FICKLE FRIENDS

- -

THAT ASSHOLE! I KNOW his little game. He's mad I didn't wear panties, so he's making me pay for it. That's ok, because the joke will be on him.

I push my hand on the ladies' bathroom door and start to walk in, but a hand grabs my arm and pulls me back into the hallway.

"Not in there," Knox says.

"I have to-"

"You *have* to come with me." His eyes are twinkling with mischief.

"If I want to live?"

"Not quite." He pumps his eyebrows and I nod, letting him lead me down the hall, through the kitchen, to Emmett's office in the back corner. He closes the door and presses me up against the door, lifting my leg to his waist as he presses against me. His lips find mine, his tongue pushing its way in. "You taste so fucking good."

"Knox," I whimper out.

"You should have worn underwear tonight."

"Why?"

"Because now my come is going to be leaking out of you for the rest of the night." He hoists my dress up and releases his cock in two quick movements and a second later, I'm moaning as he presses his hard length inside of me. My hands smack against the door, like it will hold me up when my knees get weak. The door is a fickle friend.

"Knox." My leg clenches tighter around him as my arms fight for direction - hold on to the door, or wrap around Knox.

"You're so wet. Remind me to thank Callum later." He takes my mouth again as he fucks me hard and fast.

There is no finesse to this fuck, it is raw.

Pure.

Hungry.

"I need you to come Everlee, because I won't until you do and I want to unload in you so bad right now."

"I'm so close."

He pulls out, drops to his knees, throws my leg over his shoulder and licks like I'm his last fucking meal. My hands smack on the door again as my back arches and my pussy thrusts into his face, taking what it wants. What it needs.

His tongue circles around my clit, going straight for what makes me come the quickest, as he slides two fingers into me and fucks me. He adds a third a minute later and the pressure, coupled with his mouth sucking my clit, sends me over the edge. My orgasm crashes hard and fast, sending wave after delicious wave pulsing through my body. My legs buckle, but he holds me up, wiping his hand across the back of his mouth.

"My turn," I say as he stands up and I drop to my knees.

"Everlee."

I grab his cock and suck it into my mouth without waiting.

"Fuck," he moans, pressing both of his hands against the door. "You're cheating."

My cheeks hollow out around his cock and I suck him until he hits the back of my throat.

"But fuck it. Cheat away." He presses me back so my head is against the door and rocks his hips faster and faster until he's fucking my face. I grab around his ass and pull him into me at the same time his balls tightened and his orgasm explodes down my throat. He raises on his toes as he gives the last two thrusts, then pauses for a second while his cock pulses in my mouth.

I wrap my hand around the base of it and run it up and down a few times, getting every last drop before he pulls out. "I wanted to come inside of you."

"You did," I say, wiping my thumb across my lip.

"Shit."

"What?"

"Your lips are swollen, just fucked lips."

I suck them in my mouth like I can suck the swelling away. "Hmmm."

"We can't go to the party with you like that."

"Well, you should have thought about that beforehand."

"I did! That's why I was going to fuck you."

I pucker my lips. "Oh."

"Yea." He bats his hand in the air like I should have thought about that.

"Well, fuck."

He walks out of the room for a second and I think he's left to go back upstairs until he comes back with a piece of ice. "Suck on this. Maybe it will help."

"I need something to wipe away the water when it melts."

"Shit." Knox stammers around the office. "Emmett's going to kill me."

"Why?"

"He's very particular about his office."

"Really?"

"About this place? Yea."

"Why did you pick it, then?"

"I wasn't really thinking."

"I couldn't tell."

He throws his beautiful fuck me smile over his shoulder. "Well, I blame you."

"What the fuck? I was going to the bathroom and you stole me away."

"To be fair, I sort of warned you when you first got here. You wear a dress like that with no panties and one, if not all of us, is going to steal you away."

The handle of the door rattles and we both step in one direction, then the other, not moving from the spot we're in.

Jax.

"You two having fun?" He stops and looks at me holding the ice and steps over, grabbing my wrist. The humor drops out of his eyes and is replaced by worry and concern. "What happened? Are you ok?"

"I'm fine."

"She ran into the door."

I look at him. Sure, if the door was a cock. I ran into it over and over again.

Jax nods. "And you were just being the concerned friend and getting her ice?"

"Exactly." Knox points in the air.

"Get the fuck out of here," he demands, not buying it. "Let me see." He tilts my chin up and smiles. "Not too bad." He presses his lips to mine and gives me a soft kiss. "Interesting."

"What?"

"The door you ran into tastes like Knox's cock."

I smile. "That is interesting."

"Fix your dress unless you want everyone else to see our pussy."

I look down and find my dress still hiked up around my hips. A downside to having a super tight dress. Bitch stays in place, either up or down.

"Let me help you." He grabs my dress and pulls down, letting his fingers linger over my ass. He sucks in a breath, pressing his cheek to mine, breathing in my scent.

"Jax," I moan.

"Lizzy is about to make a toast so we can eat."

"Fuck."

"It's ok. She sent me to get you because she had an idea you were..." he clears his throat and quotes her, "Getting her pussy pummeled."

"Shit."

"She seemed happy about it. So weird."

I can't help but laugh. I love that chick with every part of me.

"She did say to hurry and find you and then voluntold me to help finish you off if I caught you in the middle. She was stalling and threatened her last resort was to make up a song about meeting Tony and sing it for everyone. She really didn't want to do that."

I suck the rest of the ice in my mouth and follow Jax back to the party. When I get to the table, Beckett casts a knowing glance at me and shakes his head. I sit beside him then toss a head nod to Lizzy, who smiles at me then raises her glass, tinking it with her knife. It hits me in this moment she was waiting on me, holding up her party so I could get my "pussy pummeled". I feel equal parts lucky to have a friend like her, but also felt guilty as fuck. How selfish am I to fuck Knox at her party? I'll find a way to make it up to her and ignore her when she tells me there's nothing to make up.

"Friends, family. Thank you so much for coming out this evening to celebrate me and my main boo. Tony has been an absolute light in my life, a rock who supports all of my crazy ideas."

"Just a few," he inserts, garnering a few laughs from the crowd and a warm smile from Lizzy.

"And being a friend. I hope you can all find your person who makes you feel the way Tony makes me feel." She turns to face him, placing her hand on his shoulder, "I can't wait to do life with you and make lots and lots of babies!" She squeals before handing him the microphone.

"I don't know how to top that, so I will try to match it. Lizzy is my equal, my love, my life. She is the wild and crazy to my calm and collected. She pushes me and I try to tame her. Some. A little. Ok, really not very much, but I do try, so I feel like I should get some credit for that."

"You do babe. Get credit for trying." She pats his chest.

"I love you, Lizzy. You are *my* rock and the light in *my* life. Before you, I wandered around alone and now I have a best friend for all of life's crazy adventures and I can't wait to figure out what they are and do life with you." He gives her a big kiss, dipping her back.

"Wowzer," she says. "Everyone, if you haven't already, please find a seat and enjoy this delicious meal that my friend, owner and chef, and future Michelin award recipient, Emmett Monroe, has prepared for this evening. They are flights of all his best dishes and I can say that without even looking at the menu, because he is a master in the kitchen. You will not be disappointed. Enjoy and bon appétit."

The servers come out and place dishes on the table with such rapid precision it's mesmerizing to watch, like they've rehearsed it a thousand times. Moving this way and that, offloading trays of food. It's almost like they're robots on tracks the way they move, never bumping into anyone.

Our food is delivered and I grab a few of my favorites off the tray and see the one called The Lizzy. Just as I'm about to try it, she squeals out. She must have just realized it, because she's standing from the table and stomping across the room to stand in front of Emmett. "You're going to make me cry, asshole."

He laughs.

"I mean that in the most affectionate way possible."

"I know." He picks up her hand and kisses her knuckles. "Enjoy love."

She looks at me with her eyes set, and I know exactly what she's saying. *He's a good one. A keeper.* They all are. I nod and smile, taking a bite of 'The Lizzy'.

"Can we sit here?" Betty asks walking up.

I nod, since my mouth is full, then quickly swallow and say, "Yes, yes, please sit."

"Where's your hot date?"

For a moment I panic, not knowing who she's talking about since I've been bouncing between all the guys this evening.

"Callum," she clarifies. "Did you forget who your date is?" She chuckles.

"She's a lightweight and can't hold her liquor very well. She forgets her own name at least once a week," Beckett chimes in, covering for me.

I cut my eyes at him, but appreciate the help. "He's around here somewhere. He's part owner of this place, so I'm sure he's making sure all goes off without a hitch."

"Very good." She pats Gerald's arm. "I've been dying to come to this place for so long."

"Everything is fantastic, and the way Emmett has prepared everything is even better. You get to sample all of his top items!"

She picks up the first sandwich and moans, holding onto the table for support. "Hello!"

We all chuckle.

"Watch out baby, I'm coming for you tonight!" She shifts from side to side in her seat.

"I should have brought her here sooner," Gerald teases.

When I look across the room, I find my guys huddled in a corner talking and I desperately want to go to them, but that will come later tonight. Callum catches me looking and gives me a wink, then Emmett spots me and nods towards the sandwich in my hand. My eyes roll into the back of my head, to show him it's so good.

Callum signs to me, *Jax said you ran into a door earlier. Hope you're feeling better.* There's no concern on his face, only a slight smirk.

It's your fault.

He throws his head back, laughing. *I'll be your door tonight.*

We'll see.

His eyes grow larger and I can't help but laugh. God, I love these men.

EVERLEE - WHEN YOU WANT TO BE TIED UP, BUT ARE SHUT DOWN

Dinner was absolutely fantastic and the dessert was even better. Another flight of all his best desserts - cheese cake, chocolate molten cake, and mini crème brûlées, that were all the perfect size. Halfway through dinner, Callum walked over and sat beside me, planting a light kiss on my neck just under my earlobe. He knows that's one of my weak spots and was still trying to pay me back for not wearing underwear. If he keeps it up, I'll never wear underwear again. Or clothes. He'd really lose his shit if I started going out in public naked!

After dinner, some music starts and a few people take to the dance floor, but I walk over to check on Lizzy.

"Girl," she says, leaning back in her seat like a well-fed queen and slaps the table.

"Yes?"

"Your man." She kisses her fingers.

I look around quickly to make sure no one is close enough to hearing.

"I looked first. Give a lass some credit."

"Lass?"

"Fuck. I will be whatever. That was delicious."

"It was very good."

"Did you know he created one just for me?"

I smirk.

Her eyes narrow at me, causing me to chuckle.

"It may have been mentioned in passing, but he's been a mess these last two weeks. So stressed out. When I do see him, we don't talk." I smile.

"Queen." She rolls out her arm and bows her head. "Can you help me to the bathroom? I feel like I'm too stuffed to move."

"Yes, darling."

"It will be good practice for my wedding day. You will be my designated pee helper."

"Such a distinguished title. How did I get so lucky?"

When we get into the bathroom stall, I lock the door, then turn around to unzip her dress and pause. "What's this?" I say with a modicum of concern. There are marks across her back in an x shape and then one around her waist.

"What's what?"

"Were you tied up with rope?" I ask, rubbing my fingers along the marks.

"Oh. Yea. That." She laughs softly, then turns around to sit down on the toilet. I turn away, still stuck on the marks on her back. "So. When you told me about the sex club they used to own, I thought it would be fun to check it out. With Tony, of course."

"Of course." I was equally shocked and curious as hell. "Well?"

She laughed, "You kinky fucker. I'm surprised you haven't been already."

"Why?"

"I don't know. It just seems like something you'd do or have done already."

"That's where you got the marks?"

"Yes."

"So you were tied up with rope?"

"It's called Shibari. It's Japanese rope bondage."

"What the fuck?" I whisper.

"So erotic." She fans herself. At some point in the conversation, I turn back around to look at her. Not to watch her pee, because that's fucking weird, but to talk to her. I had to see her face to know she wasn't fucking with me.

"Yea?"

"We've been a couple of times and they have rooms where you can watch, or be watched and they have lesson rooms. So last week, we saw them doing a demonstration and when I tell you it was hot... I nearly came in my seat watching them and Tony didn't even touch me. He seemed to be turned on too, so for our six-month anniversary, I got us a private class on Shibari. We went into a private room where Madame Dubois showed us how to tie and rig and everything in between. She talked to us about safety and the art and the knots. She set us up, then let us fuck."

"With the ropes on?"

"How else? I was hanging in the air and the way he could move me around." She shimmies her shoulders. "I'm getting hot just thinking about it."

"This was at Allure?"

"Yes."

"So someone was in the room while you two were..."

"Well, kind of. She was there helping teach us how to perform Shibari safely, but once we were all good to go, she left. There was a button in the room in case we ran into trouble. Girl. When I tell you it was hot. He could literally fuck me while I was swinging."

My thoughts began to drift on how it would be with all four of them in the room with me. "Is it discreet?"

"Totally. That was one thing I was concerned about. You have to submit to testing if you plan on having relations with anyone internal. Lighting is dim. There are membership fees, background checks and contracts. Also, no phones or pictures."

"Makes sense."

"You should totally check it out."

"I might. I know the boys have a room with all sorts of toys and stuff in it, but they've never used it on me."

We wash our hands and continue our conversation.

"Have you asked them?"

"No. I've always been too scared, although I have been getting a little more confident, so asking them to go to a sex club shouldn't be weird at all." I laugh, slightly embarrassed. "I didn't know you were into these sorts of things..."

"Ehh... variety. Tony had mentioned it a couple of times and bought us handcuffs and it sort of slowly escalated. I think he has a larger fetish that he's working me in to... I've asked him, but he doesn't really say much."

My lips twist. "Well, who knows? Maybe you can find your kink and his, at Allure."

"Well, if at first you don't succeed, try, try, try, try, try again. And then maybe once more for good measure."

"At that point, it sounds like you like it and are just scared to admit it."

"Oh, I like it a lot. They have other rooms with other types of activities, but they still look a little too intense for me. But who knows, maybe I will see a demonstration on it and want to try it."

When we walk back to the party, tables have been cleared and moved out of the way for dancing. The music isn't too loud since people are still enjoying a nice meal downstairs.

"Your boy did good."

I smile at her.

"Tony was a little concerned about sandwiches, but halfway through dinner he was raving about it. So now, I just have to work out details with Emmett about reception and renting out this place so we can have the DJ and then get Tony to agree to the price. Maybe I will have a few more sessions with Madame Dubois. Not going to lie, being a domme interests me very much."

"You would want to be a domme?"

"If we had a sex room at our place, we would call it the Lizzydom. Or queendom. See what I did there?"

"Oh, I see."

She pumps her eyebrows at me and turns to walk over to Tony, who is talking to Sammie and David. No, that doesn't feel right. I know her name is Sammie, and his starts with a D.

"What are you looking at?" Knox asks, walking up beside me.

"Just watching Lizzy."

"How are your lips?"

"Which ones?" I cringe almost immediately. I don't know why I said that.

He chuckles, "Touché."

"Sorry. That was weird."

"Don't be sorry, love. I love weird."

"Speaking of..." I grab his arm and pull him to the side near the banister by the stairs. "You all used to own Allure?"

He looks around. "We probably shouldn't talk about it here, but we'll talk when we get home. I don't know what we're going to do yet, but we wanted to talk to you first."

I try to hide the confusion on my face and simply nod. What in the hell is he talking about? Talk to me about what? Surely Lizzy hadn't said anything to them about our conversation. My gaze drifts to her across the room and she's still talking to Sammie. No, there's no way.

Now I want to leave so we can get home and talk about whatever it is Knox is talking about, because clearly something else is going on. I was going to ask if they had an interest in going... is that what they're going to ask me?

KNOX - WHEN YOU HAVE A SPITFIRE, WIND HER UP

JAX IS WATCHING EVERLEE from across the room and I can tell by his white knuckles, he's clenching his fists pretty hard into the palm of his hands. He's always so protective of her. I mean, I am too, but let a woman breathe a little. Damn. People don't like being smothered. Shown you care, yes. Smothered. No.

She's dancing with Lizzy and has a huge smile spread across her face that makes me feel warm inside. She has that effect on me. It's what makes me so scared of losing her. The last time I felt that feeling was with Sophie, and then she left.

My heartbeat flutters for a second.

Jax nods at me, then walks over to stand at my side. "You good over here?"

"Yea. Just watching our girl."

"Me too."

"I know. Let me see your hands," I command softly.

"No."

"Jax. You need to relax. She's not going anywhere." I hope I'm not lying.

"I know. It's that freaking dress."

"You would still feel this way if she were wearing a potato sack and let's be honest, she'd pull that off too."

He cuts his eyes at me and growls, causing me to chuckle.

"She looks good. But not just like hot, but good. Happy."

"Yea." I stare at her, and let her joy and light fill that piece inside of me that battles for control, pushing the darkness away.

"You seem like you're doing good." He nudges my arm.

My lips flatten into thin lines. "I am." He knows about the darkness and for a long time we would talk about it, not with the others, just the two of us. They wouldn't understand. They would say they do or may even want to, but they wouldn't. They can't. Not unless you've been through it. Jax has his vices, his memories of things he holds on to, and I have mine. Although lately, I feel like I'm doing better. And not just because I want to, but because I actually feel it.

I know it's Everlee. She tells us we saved her, but the truth is she's saving *me*. When she left us, I took it hard. I hid it from the guys because I didn't want them to worry, but I was drinking more. Going to bars and letting the booze make me numb to memories and feelings, and the thing about it was I hated myself for it. With every drink I finished, I felt like my father. One step away from some asshole, laying his hands on a woman or raising his voice, and I'd unleash. Unleash all this rage that was building up.

But now I'm good. I haven't had a drink in eight weeks and not because I'm giving them up, because I miss our Old-Fashioned's, but because I wanted to prove to myself I *could* do this.

No. *Needed* to prove to myself I could do this.

That I'm not him.

My father.

My drug has been Everlee, good, bad, or indifferent.

She is it.

Earlier tonight was my want, my need, for my drug spilling over.

It's a weakness, but I don't care.

On top of the fact that Callum came walking back over with that look on his face. He hates when she does things like this to spite him, and I can't get enough of it. He's always had girls bow to his every request. He says jump and they ask how high. But not my girl - our girl. He tells her to jump and she says fuck you.

And I. Love. It.

Have I tried to plant seeds in his ear to get him to ask her not to do something, because I really want her to do it? Abso-fucking-lutely. It's a win-win for me. Fuck with Callum and watch Everlee shine like the spitfire she is.

"So she came to me with a question. I shut it down for now and I swear I don't know how she found out since it was just brought to our attention, but she was asking about Allure."

"What?" His head snaps in my direction.

My shoulders shrug, but I'm still watching our girl move on the dance floor. She's a siren and her hips are my song.

"What did she say?"

I tear my eyes away from her briefly to gauge Jax's level of worry. He's gotten good at hiding infliction and feelings within his words, but I can still read him like a fucking book. Call it years in the trenches together being shot at. "She didn't really ask anything, but more made a statement. 'You all used to own Allure'. I shut it down and said we shouldn't talk about it here."

"She doesn't know Sammie, does she? I saw her talking to her earlier, which surprised me."

"Not that I know of, but Sammie wouldn't disclose any information unless she had expressed consent from all of us. She takes confidentiality very seriously. Probably more so than Callum. Which is saying a lot."

"That's what I was thinking."

"Well, we need to talk to Everlee about it tonight before she hears it from anyone else."

He nods without speaking, no doubt wondering the same thing I am. How in the fuck did Everlee find out about Sammie and what does this mean for our relationship?

EVERLEE – EXHIBITIONIST UNLEASHED

A HAND SLIPS AROUND my waist, causing a tingle to run up my spine. It's amazing how my body reacts to them, like it knows them without even seeing them. When I turn around, Callum is looking at me with a smile on his face in the dim glow of the remaining lights.

"You know, Lizzy paid Emmett a pretty penny to have his team here clean up."

I scrunch my nose. "I know, but he's still here and not coming home until this place is spotless and I want all my guys tonight so," I shrug and stuff another cup in the trash can.

He grabs my arm, spinning me towards him, and the look in his eyes makes my hands weak. The bag drops to the ground and I'm fairly certain all the napkins and plastic cups I've picked up were for naught.

"Shit."

Callum chuckles and rubs both his hands across my fore-head, pushing the loose strands of hair out of my face. "You are pretty wonderful, you know that?"

"Because I'm cleaning up trash because I want all your dicks tonight?"

"When you say it like that, it doesn't sound as nice."

"What if I say it like this..." I lower my voice to a sexy temptress, "Because I'm cleaning up trash because I want all your dicks tonight?"

He rolls his eyes at me, smiling. "You're a dumbass some-times. You know that?"

"Keeps me young," I say, patting him on the chest.

"Your brother seemed to be doing good. Him and Will looked great."

"They did, didn't they?" I wrap my arms around his neck and slowly move my lips to his for a soft and quick kiss. "They leave tomorrow, just a one-night trip to surprise Lizzy, but I'm glad we got to see them again. I wish they'd move up here, but they won't. At least not anytime soon with Will's gran."

"Things will happen when they are meant to happen."

"How prophetic of you."

He grabs under my chin and holds my gaze, causing a tightness in my stomach. "These lips." His teeth scrape over his bottom lip. "I can't wait to get you home and punish them."

"Promises, promises."

"I know," he sighs. "Now, be a good girl and show me where the bags are."

"Yes, sir." I pump my eyes playfully at him. He wasn't in dom mode right now, just simply flirting. I point across the floor. "There's a big box that says TRASH BAGs in big white letters."

"Keep it up and see what happens."

I bend over, letting my dress ride up high enough to where I know hints of my pussy can be seen if he tries hard enough.

"Fuck Everlee." His words are short with a lust filled rage.

He's behind me a second later, one hand on my hip and the other positioned right at my entrance. I throw my head back and plant my hands on the table, ready for him, but he doesn't move.

"There are people around Everlee." His warning is like silk, gliding over my body and making my nipples hard.

I slowly push my hips back and slide onto his finger. The sound of his breath sucking in causes my stomach to tighten. "They're closed," I whisper back, before biting down on my bottom lip. I'm so fucking wet right now.

"There's still staff here." He pulls it out slowly, but leaves it at my entrance, daring me.

I don't know if he's trying to warn me away from what I want to happen, or trying to turn me on more. I push back again and notice he's added a second finger. "Skele-" A puff of air escapes as my pussy clenches around him. "Skelton crew." I press back onto his fingers, taking more. "And they're all downstairs."

He bends over so his cheek presses against my hair and his lips are gently brushing my ear, sending shivers straight to my nipples. "You want me to fuck you right here?"

"Thought crossed my mind."

"You're too loud."

"I can be quiet."

He laughs, a deep and throaty laugh because we both know I'm lying.

"You feel so fucking good. So wet." His thumb brushes over my ass and I let out a moan.

"So quiet," he teases. "Perhaps tonight we will test your limits. Handcuffs and a ball gag to teach you how to be quiet."

I look over my shoulder at him. My eyes have to be a cross between excited and nervous.

"Now be quiet while I fuck you."

I moan quietly in excitement.

Holy fuck. Shit. Mother's ass!

We're doing this! We're doing this!

Fuck.

Be quiet, Everlee. Don't make a fucking sound.

My dress lifts higher, just before I hear his zipper sliding down. A second later, I feel the head of his cock at my entrance, pausing.

Teasing.

Impatience threatens my muscles. I want to push back and take him, but he's toying with me. Testing me. His hand slowly glides his cock in and a shiver races through my body as I stretch around him.

Fuck me, he feels so good.

I suck in a breath.

"Not a fucking sound or I stop." His voice is rough. Commanding.

I nod eagerly as he pulls his hard cock out slowly before pressing it back in again.

A moan almost escapes, but I swallow that bitch back down.

My hands grip to the table as he picks up speed, pushing into me faster and faster. He grabs my hair and pulls it back, arching my face up to the ceiling. "Do you like this?"

I nod.

"You like me fucking you in public? Does it get you off knowing that at any second someone could walk up those stairs and find me fucking you from behind with you bent over a table?"

My eyes cut to the stairs, fear quickly replaced by something else. Something more. A tingle in my stomach.

"You do like it. The thrill and excitement of it all. I had an idea the first time I fucked you on the bed for the boys. The way your pussy dripped all over my cock when you saw them watching you. I saw the way you performed for them, grabbing your breasts, touching yourself."

A deep breath blows out of my nose. It was the only thing I could do not to moan out. His cock and his words are driving me crazy. Driving me into a state of sweet oblivion.

Heels tap on the floor below at the base of the stairs, and my heart stops for a second. I realize in a flash it's not because I'm scared they're coming up, but I'm scared they're not. I want them to see me getting fucked by Callum. I want them to know who I belong to.

Who he belongs to.

Who they all belong to.

"Goodnight," a voice calls from downstairs.

"Answer her," he commands, letting my hair go.

"Goo-" My words get stuck in my throat.

"Try again," he commands, pumping into me faster and faster.

"Good night," I squeak out at the same time his fingers move around to my clit.

I growl out a sound, rocking back into him, pressing my arms against the table.

"You're so fucking wet for me, my little exhibitionist. That's what you are. Did you know that?"

I didn't, but it doesn't surprise me. The first time I had experienced anything like that was the first time I was with Callum. He was right. Having those guys watch me unleashed something inside of me and then when I left them, I still searched for that feeling. Which is how and why I turned to living room masturbation with the windows open. I wanted my neighbors to see me. I wanted them to watch me.

That sounds a little fucked up, but also so right.

His hands drop to my waist as he grabs both sides and fucks me. I can tell he's getting close by the way he shifts and the breaths he takes. As the orgasm pushes closer, so does the need to bring it there. My body begins to take over, taking what it needs. Willing to do anything to get to the finish line.

I hear footsteps behind us, and again, I freeze. My stomach twists into knots and then something else happens. I'm so turned on at the thought of someone else watching me and I know Callum heard them, because he pauses for a second, then continues.

They don't move. They don't leave.

They're watching us too.

Fuck, this is so erotic.

I hope it's one of my guys, but also hope it's not.

How fucked up is that?

Callum leans over, his chest brushing against my back. "Are you going to come for me?"

"Yes," I breathe out.

"Remember. Don't make a sound."

Is that even possible? To be silent having an orgasm? A real one. Sure, when you're faking it, you can be as loud or quiet as you choose. But I've never had to fake it with these boys and I've also never been quiet because they are usually some of the most intense I've had. Which, as many times as we've fucked, I don't see how that's still possible.

He slides his hand back around to my clit and circles. Lighting up all the lights inside of me like I'm a fucking Christmas tree without a single burned-out bulb. Rare, but oh so fucking beautiful when it happens.

I press back into him, wanting to feel his cock so deep my lungs are bruised. I want him to grind into me and take. Fuck, I want him to explode in me.

His other hand slides up my back and around my neck. Why is this so fucking hot right now? Maybe all the talk of Lizzy at that club has unleashed something inside of me. It's been on my mind all night and when I tried to bring it up to Knox, he shut me down, which only made me think about it more.

Callum inches his finger around to my mouth. "Suck," he commands.

I suck his finger into my mouth as his other finger works my clit and his cock works into my pussy. Tears are seeping out of my eyes because I can feel the orgasm building inside.

A small moan escapes and I panic. Terrified he'll stop. He's done it before, granted at the time he wasn't balls deep in me on the verge of his own orgasm.

It's coming.

A tsunami building.

Sucking out all the water as it builds higher and higher. A wall of sex and pleasure growing.

"Come for me Everlee, I know you're close." He grabs my hair and pulls it back, taking my lips in a rough and needy kiss.

My orgasm hits me and I'm moaning into Callum's mouth as he swallows them down.

A moment later, he's moaning back and I take them. What I would give to sit on his cock right now and drive it into me.

He thrusts a few more times, then stops. He pulls away from our kiss and it's like the world comes whooshing back.

I remember someone is watching us and turn to find Jax there, his eyes on fire. I'm equally turned on and angry that he didn't come to join, but we were in the middle of the restaurant.

Fuck.

We're in the middle of a nice restaurant. Not that I'm classifying the types of restaurants it's acceptable to fuck in, and those it's not.

I can't believe we just did that.

"Now you have to deal with my come running out of you the rest of the time you're cleaning up all this trash." I cut my eyes over my shoulder and watch him zip up his pants and walk to Jax, but not before he sucks my arousal off his finger.

"Asshole."

I thought I whispered it, but I guess not because he throws his head back laughing. A few moments later, I walk over to the table that has a hoard of napkins on it and wipe myself clean, tossing them in the trash with everything else.

The weight of the trash bag pulls down my arm as I watch them talk, Jax's eyes never leaving mine.

What are they talking about? Are they talking about me?

Callum looks over his shoulder and winks.

Smug asshole.

I glare back at him and he laughs again. God, what a beautiful sound.

They finish their conversation a few seconds later and he takes to the tables, cleaning up trash. Another moment later, Jax is doing the same.

My guys are with me, cleaning up trash.

I can't wait until we get home.

CALLUM - OUR LITTLE BLANKET

EVERLEE, KNOX, AND I climb out of the car and walk inside, falling onto the first couch we see. Emmett and Jax are on their way home. Emmett just had to lock up behind us, so it should only be a couple of more minutes.

"I'm so tired," Everlee moans. "You know... just mentally exhausted?" She yawns.

"It was a long day for you, I'm sure." Knox chimes in from the couch across the room.

A car door closes and seconds later, the back door is opening. "Oh, thank God. I thought you all were going to be up and wanting to chat and party and I was going to have to be the jackass who wanted to go to bed," Emmett says, walking in and heading straight for Everlee.

She lifts her feet and lays them back on his lap when he sits. Emmett tilts his head back, resting it on the couch as he absentmindedly rubs along her legs. After a moment, he pops his head up and looks at me. "You let her wear this outfit tonight?"

Before I can even answer, Everlee is sitting up on her elbows. "Let me? You think he can control what I do?"

"He controlled you enough tonight when he had you bent over a table fucking you and wouldn't allow you to moan."

She sucks in a breath to defend herself, but realizes there's nothing she can say, so she flops back down to the couch. "He can't tell me what to wear."

Emmett laughs. "No, *that* he can't do."

She sits up and crawls onto his lap, straddling him, and lays her head on his shoulder. "How do you think tonight went?"

I've noticed recently this seems to be their thing - the cuddling- and while I'm not a jealous man, I want to be the one she cuddles into, but I suppose I can't have it both ways. She looks at me as the domineering one of the house- the one in control. Which in most ways, that's what I feel too, but occasionally I want the tenderness.

His eyebrows raise when he looks at her. "Great," He looks at the rest of us, "I want to make some tweaks to the upstairs area to make it more conducive to parties. I feel like that could be a good revenue stream for us if we do it right."

"More of these?" Jax drones from against the wall.

Knox throws a pillow at him, which he quickly bats away.

"I'm getting a drink? Anyone want one?" Jax asks, walking out of the room.

"No," Everyone chimes, nearly in unison.

"Fine. But I'm not sharing... Everlee," he says pointedly to her, since she always wants to nibble off our plates, or taste our drinks.

"Jax," she chastises, sitting up from Emmett's lap. "Sharing is caring."

"Our family motto." Knox sits up, pointing a finger in the air.

Everlee laughs while Jax chimes in from the kitchen, clinking glasses around. "I'm still not giving you my drink."

She lifts her dress up off her legs, exposing her ass. "Sorry. It was pinching around my lips. Legs. I mean legs. Fuck I'm tired."

"Never apologize," Knox says, licking his lips, watching her.

I've been watching him over the last several months and feel like he's in a good spot now. I was worried about him before and was trying to give him his space to process and deal, but he was getting close to me inserting myself. I'm glad I didn't have to, because when it's happened in the past, it creates a weird dynamic between us. One I'm not super fond of. I know he and Jax dealt with a lot of shit and they both process it in different ways. Jax lets his out in pulses, while Knox tries to push it down and pretend like nothing is wrong.

Knox leans forward. "Please say we're getting a show."

Emmett's hands at some point had slid around to Everlee's hips and I could tell he wanted her, even though he said he was exhausted.

"No. Knox. I'm exhausted."

She must have whispered something because he's laughing a moment later and lifting her dress up higher so he can rub her back.

"Fine," he says, unzipping the back of her dress and pulling it over her head. He admires her breast before she lays back down, nuzzling her face into the side of his neck.

Minutes pass and neither of them move and Knox looks from me to Jax, back to them. "Well, this is fucking awkward." He hops up from the seat and walks over to them slowly, leaning over to see Everlee's face. "They're asleep. They fucking fell asleep."

I can't help but laugh for two reasons. One, because Knox was so ready and two, because that girl can fall asleep nearly anywhere with a speed unlike anything I've ever seen.

"I'll carry her to bed," I say, standing from my couch. When I bend down to pick her up, her phone falls from her hand just as a message comes through.

Lizzy.

"Jax. Lizzy just texted. Can you make sure she's ok?"

Jax is walking over to the couch at the same time I'm walking out of the room with Everlee in my arms. She lets out a soft moan and turns into me, and whispers my name. A tingle shoots down my spine, and my heart tugs as I watch her sleep.

"Callum," Jax says with a layer of concern in his voice. My foot rests on the bottom step as I wait for him to walk over to me, Knox following.

"What is it?"

He holds the phone up for me to read.

Lizzy: *Let me know what they say about Allure...*

"How does she know?" Knox asks.

"I don't know. We'll talk to her about it tomorrow morning." I shift Everlee's weight in my arms. She's not heavy, but right now she's dead weight and I'm exhausted.

"Do you know what we're going to do? Say?"

"I don't think we have a choice, do we? I mean, technically we do, but..."

"How do you think she's going to react?" Knox asks, concerned. His question isn't really how she's going to react, but if I think she's going to leave.

"I have no idea. I don't think she'll leave, but she may not like it."

He nods, but doesn't speak, the worry clear in his eyes. "I call dibs lying beside her tonight."

I smile at him. "I figured you would."

Some nights are worse than others for Knox and those nights he needs her. Needs to feel her. Wrap his arms around her. I don't like the fact she is the equivalent of his soothing blanket, but I also don't want to take it away from him right now when he's trying to work through things. My hope is that he can stand on his own feet over time.

"I'm going to shower up, then come back in here," Knox says. "I'll be quick."

I nod. "I'll lay in here with her until you come back."

She lies on her side; her fists balled up under her chin, so I find my place behind her and let her melt into me, fitting to her like a puzzle piece.

The bed is shaking a few moments later, only it's probably been longer because I feel like my head is in a daze and Knox smells fresh.

I roll out of bed. "I'll be back in a little."

"Take your time," he says, snaking his arms around her, taking the place I just left. He buries his nose in her hair and closes his eyes.

I probably should have put a shirt or something on her, but I didn't want to wake her and she sleeps naked ninety-nine percent of the time. She says she gets too hot otherwise and we don't mind.

EVERLEE - THE PROPER WAY TO WAKE UP

MY SKIN IS MOIST with a light layer of sweat, and the room is dark. There's an arm wrapped around my waist and I'm naked. It takes me a minute to remember what happened and how I ended up here. I had so many plans for when we got home, but then that couch called my name and then Emmett came home and I passed out. I remember telling Emmett to take my dress off, because I was going to put on a little show for the boys, specifically Knox, since he asked, but then I closed my eyes for one second and here I am.

When I slowly sit up in bed, I see Knox to my right and Jax to my left. Emmett and Callum are on the other side of the bed, above me. They all look so delicious, with their tattoos and cocks on display. If I was artistic, I would draw this. Four men sprawled on a bed around me with their cocks out.

A wicked thought passes through my mind.

Not really wicked... just... not *not* wicked.

I mean really, it should be quite enjoyable for everyone...

The bed shakes softly under me as I move over to Knox. He would appreciate this the most and would probably want to watch me wake up the others. I have no idea what time it is and I don't care. Our new room has windows now, but the one downside is that it's no longer connected to the enormous bathroom, but they're still making changes so it's ok.

Knox mumbles something and shifts just a bit when I climb over the top of his legs to straddle him. I'm careful not to touch him too much, because I don't want to startle him. My idea is to slowly wake him with pleasure and then he can watch me wake the others the same way.

I lower my head close to his cock, blowing a warm breath over it. He must have taken a shower before bed because he smells like his body wash, which is one of my favorites. The lavender and eucalyptus is an intoxicating combo. His cock is still soft, so I slowly run my tongue over his head. The idea of getting him off while he sleeps is something that I've been wanting to try for a while, just haven't had the chance.

I slowly take his head in my mouth and suck softly. He moans out and shifts all the way onto his back.

Yes. I'm getting closer.

His cock gets harder and harder in my mouth, so I suck him in further and further until he's hard enough for me to wrap my hand around. I'm still moving slowly, not wanting to rush this at all. I just want to enjoy him like this.

After another minute, he's fully hard, but still not awake. Or maybe he is, and just faking it. I slowly climb up his body and line my pussy over his cock, and gradually lower myself onto it.

Fuck, this feels so good. The first thrust in, the feeling of being stretched, sends chills racing across my body. I have to bite my lip to prevent the moan from escaping.

My hands move to my breasts as I slowly raise up and lower myself again. I can feel my orgasm slowly spooling, feel my arousal coating Knox's cock with each time I press down. Knox's hands sluggishly move to my hips as he wakes up, so I watch his face, waiting for the moment his eyes open. When he does, a smile stretches across his lips and my chest swells.

"Well, good morning, Ali."

I pump my eyebrows, then lean over, pressing my hands on the bed on either side of his head. "Want to watch me get the others up?"

He smiles, "In a minute." His hands firmly grab on my hips, holding me in place.

"You have to be slow. I don't want them to feel the bed shake."

"Oh, I can be slow," he whispers, raising his hips off the bed, thrusting up inside of me and rolling his hips around.

Fuck. Me. What did I just get myself into? I suck my lips into my mouth and clamp down to prevent the moan from escaping. His hands cover my breasts as we slowly rock on one another, his size filling me completely. Jax shifts and we both freeze, looking at Jax, then at each other. He twitches his cock in me a few times, teasing me with that delicious smile of his.

After a few seconds pass and we determine he's not waking up, we continue. I don't think we've ever fucked this slow, but goddamn, it is sexy as hell. There's more feeling. More intention. I feel more connected to him.

His hands freeze and he looks at me, so I stop. He sits up and wraps his hand around the back of my head and inhales the air around my neck before he says, "If you want a group fuck, then you need to climb off me now."

Our eyes lock for a second while I contemplate what I really want. I know what I wanted before, but feeling him move like that inside of me. A shiver moves up my spine, causing my nipples to get hard.

He kisses my neck, breaking me from my trance.

"Ok," I whisper, as I slowly climb off. "Who should I go after next?"

His eyes perk with excitement and he nods at Jax.

"Yea?"

He nods and I climb across the bed, using the same methods I used on Knox, but Jax wakes up as soon as my hand clamps around his cock.

He starts to speak, but Knox is right there and puts his hand over his mouth. "Shh." I don't stop bobbing on him, my hot mouth sliding down his shaft, while my hand works his base.

He grabs Knox's wrist and moves it off his mouth. "What's going on?"

"What does it look like?"

I run my tongue up the length of his cock, before swirling it around his head, then suck him in hard. He hits the back of my throat and his next words are cut off and his hands move to my head to hold me in place.

"Don't move too fast. We don't want to wake the others."

Jax turns his head to the side and while I can't see it, I feel like he's glaring at Knox with a *what the fuck* expression plastered across his face.

Knox taps me on the shoulder, but I don't stop. I love sucking this man's cock. All of them really, but Jax… I don't know if it's the energy he puts off or what, but it makes me hot for cock.

I laugh on the inside, picturing a hot for cock shirt. Only it would have to be safe for the public, so maybe a picture of a rooster. A little on the nose, but fuck it. It's my shirt.

"Angel love. If you keep doing that, he's going to come in your mouth and then I will have to take you and fuck you the way I wanted to a moment ago and I can assure you, that the boys will rise from their miserable slumber then. So unless you want that, you need to stop."

I can taste Jax's come on my tongue and know he's at the edge of his release. Fuck, I want to taste him so badly. I want to swallow him down, but I can't. Not yet. I groan, then pull off his cock.

"Thanks a lot," Jax grumbles.

"You're welcome," Knox snipes back.

"Now, who?"

"Emmett. Callum won't likely have the self-control to stop," Jax says.

My bearded teddy bear. I start to climb over to Emmett and get too close to Jax. He grabs my hips and pulls my pussy to his face, so I'm sitting on it, right at Emmett's head.

"Fuck, Jax," I moan out, arching my back up.

He wraps his arms around my legs and pulls me down further onto his face, spearing his tongue further inside of me. I don't know if he can breathe the way he has me on him, but damn.

"You have to stop," I regrettably whisper.

He pushes me back a little and raises his chin. "No."

His one word startles me. "No? Are you two?"

He dives back in between my legs.

"Well, fine then, slide back some so I can reach Emmett's cock," I whisper-yell, through a moan.

He pushes his feet into the bed and slides us back, so his head is by Emmett's stomach. I feel like a bunch of four-year-olds playing hide and seek from adults. Running around in the dark, whispering loudly and wondering how everyone keeps finding us. There's no way Callum and Emmett are still asleep. I watch Emmett for a moment, trying to focus as my orgasm edges closer, then finally act when Knox clears his throat.

Admittedly, I'm not as delicate as I was with Knox, because I'm losing the will to wait. I want them all awake and I want them all fucking me like yesterday. I run my tongue along Emmett's semi-hard cock and suck him in my mouth. He's either pretending to be asleep, or the sounds of Jax eating my pussy out right by his ear stirs him. Either way, he's hard in no time with eyes wide open moments later.

"What?" he asks groggily, then turns his head to his right and sees Jax munching down on my pussy.

He hums in appreciation, while I continue to suck him in my mouth. "Let me," he moans and with ease, Jax lifts me up and passes my bottom half to Emmett like I'm a fucking platter you pass around the table. Which gets me thinking about Thanksgiving. Perhaps a little costume on the table with an apple stuffed in my mouth. I could let them eat off me.

Yes. This would take some more thought and planning, but not right now. Right now, I needed to focus. I have three of my four guys awake. Now it's Callum's turn.

When I look at him, he's staring back at me with a smirk on his face. "What's going on here?"

"You aren't supposed to be awake," I whine.

"How do you expect me to sleep through all the whispering, moaning, slurping, and fucking?"

"It wasn't my fault," Knox throws his hands up.

"Well, now that you're all up. Want to have some fun?"

"Sounds like you've started without me."

"Save the best for last?" I smile.

"Hey. I'm right here!" Knox teases.

"And first, and second, and oh God," I cry out, "third." Emmett just inserted two fingers inside of me, sending my mind and body reeling.

"I'll accept that," Knox smiles with satisfaction, scraping his teeth over his bottom lip as he watches Emmett finger fuck my pussy.

"I was talking, Emmett. You can't simply-" A moan comes out, as my orgasm slams into me. My pussy pulses around his fingers and tongue as he continues to drink down my orgasm.

"Be a good girl and drown him with your cum," Knox moans, spanking my ass.

"Fuck," I pant out. "I need you all." Not waiting for an answer, I grab Callum's cock and suck it into my mouth while my hand glides up and down. I don't know if it's that point in my cycle or all the talk of weddings and babies, but I desperately want their come inside of me. Everywhere. I want to bathe in it. I want it to be dripping out of every hole in my body. I want them to claim me.

Now!

"Jax!" Callum commands.

"Already on it." The bed shakes as he rolls off, then moves across the room to the drawer with the lube in it.

"I call bottom," Knox says, laughing. "Literally, not... well... literally."

Emmett releases my hips and slides up the bed only enough to suck a breast into his mouth as they dangle over his face. His teeth scrape across my nipples and he bites hard enough to elicit another moan out of me. He's been getting rougher over the last several weeks, but I love it.

He added more piercings to his cock, so now he has a Jacob's Ladder and My. God. The way it feels inside of me... and I can't help but wonder what Jax feels. While they've never done anything on their own, I sometimes wonder if they would... if I asked. I'd love to see Emmett suck Jax's cock, and would love to see Jax's face. Watch him thrusting into Emmett's mouth, losing himself in the feeling of it all.

Emmett admitted to being bi a few months ago and said he's been in a threesome with Jax, but Jax has never come out and said how he feels.

Seconds later, Knox's lubed finger is pressing on my tight hole, causing me to moan out with excited anticipation. He slips a finger in slowly, prepping me for his cock, while Jax finger fucks my pussy, stretching it with two, three, then four fingers. I love when he and Emmett fuck me at the same time. The tightness and the way I can feel their cocks rubbing against one another inside of me... It's erotic as hell, and just as hot, if not hotter, than fucking them. Almost like I can give them- Jax- a reason to take what he wants. I love to watch him when he's under me, while Emmett is fucking us. I say us, because when it's happening that's what it feels like and...

I breathe out. If I don't stop thinking about this, I'm going to come before they even get inside of me.

A moment later, Knox's cock is at my back entrance. He slowly pushes in and holds it there for a moment, letting me get used to him. I stop sucking on Callum, so I can concentrate on everyone getting into position.

Emmett slides back down so he's under me, but still not inside of me, while I straddle him. He gives Jax a look and I'm dying to know what it means. Perhaps I'm reading too much into it, because it's what I want versus what is actually happening.

Seeing what the eye wants to see, or something like that.

Knox pulls out so his tip is at my entrance, squeezes some more lube onto his shaft before he pushes back in. "Yes." I say, collapsing onto Emmett's chest, but only for a second. Knox moves quicker and quicker and when I slam back onto him, he grabs my hips and pauses.

"That's my cue," Emmett says, driving into the hilt with one thrust.

"Fuck me," I moan in, sensations spiraling through my body. His beautiful, pierced cock rubs and grinds perfectly in my needy little cunt. The balls of his piercings providing the perfect ribbed sensation.

"You're so fucking wet for us, Trouble."

I am wet, so fucking wet. I moan out, "More," pressing onto Emmett's chest, fighting the urge to rock back and take both him and Knox as far as I can take them.

He presses in a few times and Jax gets on the bed beside Knox and coats his shaft in lube before he slides it along Emmett's, pressing it at my entrance.

I watch Emmett's face and we share a moment, like he knows I know how excited he is to feel Jax glide along his cock, sliding into me. His eyes roll into the back of his head before his hand grips around the back of my neck and he pulls me towards him, pressing our foreheads together.

"I love you," he whispers.

The emotion in his voice is thick.

Real.

Raw.

It robs me of my breath for a moment. I press my lips to his and fight to hold back the tears in my eyes. "I love you," I whisper against his lips.

Seconds later, my back is arching up as Jax eases into me, the pressure tight and delicious.

"Yes," I moan out.

Jax pulls out slowly, then pushes in again, while everyone else is frozen. I hear him grunt out as pleasure unfurls around each of us, his cock sliding against Emmett's, feeling the small metal balls lining his cock. Even though he hasn't said the words, I know he loves the way Emmett's cock feels now.

When Jax pulls out this time, Emmett does too, then pushes in with him. They sync up, pulling and thrust together and then Knox joins in.

I don't know why in this particular moment, but row, row, row your boat plays in my head, but in rounds. That's what I feel like this is. First Emmett, then Emmett and Jax, then Emmett, Jax and Knox, and last, me moving to suck Callum.

Pleasure builds through me, like a fire ravaging a dry hillside, engulfing all it touches.

Grunts and moans fill the air as we all move without speaking, feeling pleasure course through us, taking and giving what we want and need.

"Everlee," Callum warns.

I clamp my hand around his balls and suck harder. I've been experimenting lately with their balls, to see what they like and what they don't, and how they react. Before them I never played with men's balls, I always found them to be...weird. Like two little soggy walnuts just hanging out in a hammock.

But now...

Now, they're like two little love sacks for me to play with. Like a tactile fidget. Like a squishy or one of those toys, that's like a rubber balloon with water in it and you can squeeze it to move the beads around. It's like an adult sexual fidget.

Fuck.

Focus, Everlee!

I hollow out my cheeks around him and let him punch into my mouth. My throat clenches around his cock and tears run down my cheeks. Callum's hand clamps into my hair and he pulls. Pulls hard.

"Yes, Everlee. Fuck. You suck my cock so good. You take all of our cocks like such a good fucking girl."

"Her ass feels amazing, taking my cock." Knox continues the praise. "I can't wait to come inside of you. Fill you up." One hand rests on my ass, while the other glides up my spine.

My stomach tightens with his words and while I don't want babies now, I would love for them to fuck me to get me pregnant. All of them unloading inside of me.

Shit! What is wrong with me?

I think I've been reading too many books with the breeding kink in it, although it's usually the guys. But their words, it's like they're right out of some of my books.

Callum unleashes with a restrained ferocity, fucking my face and bringing me back from wonderland. He grunts out just as His warm release explodes in my mouth and I swallow him down.

My arms collapse, burning from holding up my weight, and I fall onto Emmett.

"Such a good girl," Callum says, brushing my hair back.

"Kiss me," Emmett commands.

I can still feel some of Callum's come on my lips, but Emmett licks it off before he takes my mouth in a hungry kiss that breathes life back into me. It's a kiss that sends my head to the clouds. His tongue swipes and rolls in my mouth, pressing harder and faster, matching his cock thrusting into me.

My body starts pulsing, and my pussy starts clenching as another orgasm is on the horizon.

"Yes," Jax moans. "She's getting close."

Knox reaches his hand around to my clit and begins rubbing in circles, and seconds later, I'm bucking backwards as my orgasm rips through me.

"Oh, my God. Oh my God," I scream out, probably the loudest I've ever screamed out before.

Knox unleashes a second later. "Fuck. I tried to hold on, but her ass was pulsing and clenching around my cock, sucking it in."

Once he finishes, he pulls out and rolls off the bed to clean himself up while Jax and Emmett continue. "Fuck me. Hard," I say, making eye contact with Emmett.

He smiles at me and reaches up to wrap his hands around Jax's ass, bringing both of them further into me.

"Oh," Jax moans out.

My stomach clenches tightly, like butterflies are swarming inside of me. I don't know if butterflies can swarm, but these are. The pleasure these men get from their cocks inside of me turns me on faster than a hot knife through butter. My pussy is pulsing as my body spools up again. I shift and Jax grabs my hair, pulling me backwards towards him, causing pain to burn across my scalp before it turns to pleasure. He claims my mouth with his, sucking on my bottom lip. Emmett grabs my nipples between his fingers and rubs, sending a shockwave pulsing straight to my clit while Callum pushes through and wraps his mouth around my breast. Licking and flicking my nipple.

"Yes," Emmett cries out, pulling me back down.

My hips are rocking back onto them, their cocks gliding along one another, sending shivers down my spine, making the walls of my pussy throb.

"Boys," I moan out.

A plea.

A sheen of sweat covers my body as the little hairs around my face stick to me. My orgasm builds again, and I don't know if I'm ready for it. These are the ones that take me for a ride. The feeling is so good it sometimes hurts. Like every muscle in my body seizes and forgets how to work.

"This feeling... it's incredible," I mumble out.

"Show us, baby," Knox urges from the side of the bed, watching us. He loves to watch the men fuck me. He's every bit the voyeur to my exhibitionist.

I close my eyes and let the feelings take over, the pulses, the sensations, the tightening of the stomach. It's coming.

The storm.

The orgasm.

I feel like I should name her because when she comes... when I come, it feels like an out-of-body experience.

"Oh fuck. Oh fuck. Oh, fuck." It hits me like a freight train barreling over an ant. My body is rocking back and forth like I'm riding a rodeo bull. My brain doesn't know which way is up or down, or back or forth.

A grunt echoes in my ear and then, a second later, another. Both boys nearly come at the same time, filling me with their come. I can feel the slickness inside as they slow their thrusting. Jax is the first to pull out and immediately my pussy misses him, but also welcomes the change. Emmett pushes in a few times slowly and the ridges of his cock rings rub along the inside of me and I just close my eyes to savor the feeling.

He slowly pulls out and I flop onto the bed like a wet, fucked, hot mess express.

"Well, this is how I need to wake up every morning," Knox says a moment later.

"Shut the fuck up," Jax snaps, shaking his head.

"What? Tell me you'd rather be woken up by an alarm. How boring. Nope! Not me. I want a super sneaky blow job to wake me up."

"I'll buy you a blow-up doll."

"Nope! Won't do."

Jax throws a pillow at Knox, which he bats away, causing it to land on my face. I don't move. I can't. My body is still calming down from the orgasm - scratch that. Orgasmssss I just had.

Knox is lifting the pillow off my face. "Why is it that most times we have sex, I'm always scared we broke you?" He pokes my cheek.

"You satiate me."

"Satiate," he repeats, elongating the s. "How sexy."

"You're an idiot," Jax chimes in, lifting me from the bed. "Not you, of course." He kisses my forehead. "Let's get you cleaned up."

He carries me across the hall through the old voyeur room into the bathroom where Emmett and Callum are waiting. Emmett looks up at me from the bath with a curious expression on his face. Is it because he said he loved me?

My heart swells and I have this overpowering need to climb onto his lap and wrap my arms around him. He's the first to have said it, and the first one I said it to. Even though it's how I feel about all of them. I just didn't want to come across as too much, so I've been biting my tongue, but this morning.

In the moment.

The way he said it.

My skin tingles just thinking about it.

"Special delivery," Jax says walking over to the tub.

"I'll sign for her," Emmett says reaching up to grab me.

"Hey there," I say, curling into his chest as he lowers me into the water.

He brushes the hair away from my face and kisses my forehead. "Hey there."

We sit in silence for a moment, soaking in the hot water, letting it soothe away all the aches while we wait for the rest of the guys to get in the tub. They wash me and completely spoil me. Emmett and Knox taking my upper half, while Jax and Callum take my lower. Emmett takes extra care when shampooing my hair, to the point I almost fall asleep, while Knox rubs and massages soap into my neck, chest and back.

Do I moan?

Yes. That's what I do. It's like my off-switch in that department is broken or something. Has been ever since I met them. Or perhaps since it was never used before, it's like this new toy my body keeps using. Like when a toddler says fuck and everyone reacts, so it goes around the house and out in public yelling fuck, fuck, fuck, fucking diaper. My moan is the equivalent of a fucking diaper.

I lean my head back on Emmett's shoulder and let the lavender and mint smell swirl around me. With the hint of eucalyptus mixed in, it really opens the senses.

EMMETT - PERFECT DAY

<hr>

WE'RE OUT OF THE bath thirty minutes later and while Everlee is in her room getting dressed, I walk downstairs to get breakfast ready. It's almost six, so I have plenty of time to create anything I want. Rifling through the pantry and fridge, I land on homemade cinnamon rolls, grabbing all the ingredients and setting them on the counter. I don't think I've made these for her yet, since I only make them a few times a year. I don't know why, because they aren't too hard to make.

Ten minutes later, a small set of hands slip around my waist from behind me. I turn around and see Everlee standing there in one of Knox's shirts and a pair of my joggers with her hair slicked back, still wet from the bath. I don't know why we keep buying her clothes because she rarely wears them around the house. She just goes into our room and scavenges through our drawers, picking what she wants.

Which I don't mind at all. She can do anything she wants. She has my heart. To be fair, she's had it for a while, but now she knows she has it. I wasn't intending on telling her

I loved her this morning, it just sort of came out in the heat of the moment. It felt right.

In that moment she saw me. The real me. The one who loves her fully, but also has feelings for Jax. She wasn't upset or jealous, but hopeful and supportive. Almost like she wants to be the conduit for us, to guide us together. Not away from her, because that could never happen, but just to one another. When my eyes landed on Jax, there was a different look on his face, one that I hadn't seen before, or let myself see even. He was excited, but almost like he was excited for me... It nearly took my breath away.

We've never talked about his feelings or what he wants. We've never experimented or even talked about experimenting. We've simply never talked about it, but it seems like lately, he's seeking my cock during DVP. I know he likes it, because lately, while we're inside of her, I watch his face and goddamn. It takes everything in me not to explode. He loves the way his cock feels against mine and Everlee senses it, too. I think it turns her on.

She is so perfect for me, for us.

"What can I do?" she asks in a singsong voice.

Over the last several weeks, she's been helping me more in the kitchen and I've been teaching her a few things. She knew the basics before, but I'm teaching her the more refined and technical side of it.

The why behind the cooking.

I turn in her arms and brush a flour covered finger across her nose. "Good morning, love."

She looks cross-eyed at her nose, scowling, then her eyes meet mine. "Good morning, love." She presses up on her toes and softly presses her lips to mine.

"Do you want to make some glaze for the cinnamon rolls?"

"Yes! I actually used to make some growing up and would add a little orange citrus to the glaze." She peeps, smiling.

"Ok, sure. Make two batches. Knox can be a baby sometimes when he doesn't have his normal glaze."

She nods and pulls her arms out from around me and plants her flour covered palm on my cheek.

I huff out a breath, laughing. "You're going to get it."

Her eyes sparkle with mischief as she darts around to the end of the counter, hands gripped on the edge, waiting to see what I'm going to do.

"What about me?" Knox asks, walking into the room, grabbing her and dipping her into a kiss. He's completely unaware of what's going on.

She laughs when he stands her back up. "That you're wonderful."

"Oh. Of course." He grabs a pitcher from the cabinet and a dozen oranges. "Dude, why do you have flour all over your face?"

I roll my eyes and ignore his question. "Making fresh squeezed orange juice this morning?"

"It's been a while and we're up early enough."

"Sorry," Everlee mumbles.

"Never! And I mean never! Apologize for that kind of wake up. I feel like nothing can go wrong in this day now. Am I walking on clouds? Maybe." He looks down at his feet, jumping up and down.

Jax and Callum walk down a few minutes later.

"Good morning, boys," Everlee says, whipping up some glaze, while I pop the cinnamon rolls into the oven.

"Good morning, dear," Jax says, walking over to slip his arms around from behind. "What are we working on?" He asks, rocking her from side to side.

She looks over his shoulder and gives him a quick kiss on his neck. "I'm making some sweet glaze with a hint of orange zest for the cinnamon rolls." Knox looks up from squeezing oranges, so she quickly adds, "But I will have some plain for those who want it. Although I would hope *those* people would also try *my* orange glaze one."

Knox smiles. "*Those* people will try anything you touch."

"What the hell, man? I ask you to try things and you say no and shrivel up into a ball, and she hints at asking you and you're like ooh la la oui oui mon Chéri."

"I don't speak France."

"France?" I roll my eyes, but Everlee is laughing and Knox just winks at me like it was his plan all along.

"Here. Taste," Everlee commands, holding her finger up for Jax.

He sucks her finger into his mouth and gives a moan. When she tries to pull it out, he grabs it and holds it in for a second longer, then kisses the inside of her hand, then her wrist, up her arm to her lips. A flush sweeps across her body and I love it. How responsive she is to us.

"Now, now," Knox says. "My turn."

"No." Jax lifts Everlee and turns her away, who is laughing and screaming. She looks so tiny against his broad chest.

Knox tries to grab at her, but Jax deflects and within seconds the kitchen has turned into a game of keep away between Jax and Knox. Callum is standing with his foot and back propped against the wall watching the scene unfold.

This. Today. Is perfection.

Once Jax and Knox naturally calm down and Everlee is free to move about on her own, she walks over to her glaze and dips her finger in for Knox.

When he tastes it, he moans, but then his face contorts.

Everlee laughs again, "Stop. It's not that bad."

"I'm just teasing. It's actually quite good. The orange isn't overpowering. More like a hint."

"Such a refined palate you have," I tease, pulling the rolls out of the oven.

"I've been working on it." Knox does a little shimmy of the shoulders and dances a little jig.

I think I speak for everyone when we say we could listen to her laugh all day. One could also say I'm just head over heels for her, so that may have something to do with it as well.

"Want to eat on the roof? Watch the sunrise?" Callum asks.

"Yes!" Everlee squeals, clasping her hands together.

"Perfect. Everlee, Knox and Jax can take the plates, juice, and glaze up, and I'll help Emmett with the rolls."

They each grab their dishes and head upstairs. I can't ignore the fact Callum watches them, which tells me there's something he wants to talk about in private before breakfast.

"What's going on?"

He looks at me and smiles. "I heard what you said to Everlee this morning."

I roll my eyes, "So? I know you all feel the same, but are just too chicken shit to say it."

Callum chuckles. "Maybe so. Maybe I was going to say it this morning too, but then heard you and didn't want her to think I was only saying it because of you."

"Whatever." I finish scraping the last roll onto the plate. "Do you want to tell me what this is really about? Because I'm fairly certain it isn't about me telling Ev I love her."

"No. It's not."

"This is about Sammie's offer?"

He nods.

"You think she's going to get mad?"

"I don't know. I feel like we're in a great spot right now and this might put a wrench into everything. It just makes me nervous."

"Knox mentioned something last night about her asking about Allure. Do you think she already knows?"

"I don't know. It seems too coincidental Sammie brings this offer to us the same night I see her talking to Everlee, who then she mentions something to us."

"I wish Knox wouldn't have freaked out and gotten a little more info before he shut the convo down."

"Well, I want to talk to her about it today."

"I think that's best. Sammie needs a decision pretty quickly, right?"

"Yea." Callum grabs a small pile of napkins and some silverware and leads me up the stairs to the roof.

The weather has a slight chill in the air, but it looks like someone has turned on the hot tub because it's bubbling with its colored lights flashing. Everlee is rearranging the small bouquet she insists on keeping out here to provide a little more color, especially *since it's spring*. Our main dining room has two larger vases at the ends of each table, while the front room also has another arrangement.

I love the fact we can leave for Vixen's or Bo's at night, then come back to find something has changed. A little Everlee touch. It's almost turned into a game for the guys to see who finds what she's changed first. We don't mind. In fact, we love it. It means she's making herself at home, which puts us all at ease.

We've talked about her leaving, and what our future looks like several times. She seems to be ok with all the constraints and says that marriage isn't all that important. *The commitment is more important than a piece of paper*, she says. Which none of us can argue with. The only thing I think, rather, we think, she's not being completely honest with is kids.

I think she's still holding out hope we'll change our mind and part of me, and possibly all of us, is that we will too. Collectively. But it's one of those topics that's so hard to discuss, because we all agreed long ago that marriage and kids were out of the equation, but that was before her. Before someone who melds into our life so perfectly.

Who knows what the future holds, but I know I can't wait to find out.

We all sit at the table, with Queen Everlee at the head. It's her favorite spot out here, because she says she can see all of us, but really, I think it's because she likes to be the head of the table. I used to think it was to fuck with Callum, and maybe it started out that way, but it's morphed. She's grown more confident in her skin and in the bedroom. She asks for what she wants and she's not afraid to try anything.

We used to be a little more taboo, but that was when we handpicked individuals who were up for the task and lived that lifestyle. Everlee didn't. She was new to everything, but again, who knows what the future holds. But I'm very excited.

"Bon appétit!"

EVERLEE - "YOU ARE OURS, WE ARE US"

Breakfast was delicious. Emmett's handmade rolls were heaven in my mouth, to the point I was licking my fingers and picking all the crumbs on the plate when it was done. I thought licking it would be a little too much, so I decided on the sticky finger approach. I probably could have eaten at least two more, although I would have been absolutely miserable and after the morning I was having, I didn't want to ruin it.

"There's something we need to talk to you about," Callum says, and all the guys look at one another.

My arms get heavy and my stomach tightens. I don't think it's anything bad, like relationship wise, but it's something they feel guarded about.

I stand from the table. "Can we talk about it in the hot tub? I have a bit of a chill right now." As I walk over to the hot tub, I pull off my shirt and slip off my pants. Since being with them, I've worn fewer clothes. One, it's more comfortable not having to wear bras and panties, but two, it's less to remove when I need some special attention. Which being around them is all the time. I would have never thought of myself as one who loves sex, but with them... I literally can't get enough.

"Nooo. Can't do it. Ok. Yes, I can," Knox teases, jumping up from the table.

The water feels like fire against my skin when I step in, causing me to suck in a breath. I walk around on the seats to the opposite side so the others can climb in and then slowly ease down, letting the warmth of the water act like a blanket.

The men remove their clothes, leaving their boxers on, so I'm left with their beautiful tattooed torsos sinking into the water. Once we're all in, we sort of just look at each other for a moment.

"Well, hit me with it." I had an idea this had something to do with the conversation I had with Knox last night, or tried to, before he abruptly shut it down. Although I feel like we were talking about two completely different things, because there's no way they would know I was interested in checking out Allure to up our bedroom game. Although it really needed no help, because damn.

Can one go hoarse from orgasms? Who knows, but I feel like I'm trying to test the theory. Extensively.

Callum speaks up, "You are... we are... hmm." He stops.

"What is it?" My voice drops with concern.

"We want to include you on... things that involve us."

I nod, still unsure what's going on.

"As you know, we used to run Allure, a sex club."

I nod. "Look. If this was about last night, I can explain."

Jax chimes in, "That would help."

"I thought you all may be interested. And if you're not, it's totally ok."

"Wait. So, you started all of this?" Knox asks, utterly confused.

"Well…" I didn't want to say Lizzy, because that may make them a little uncomfortable. "It was just an idea. And I don't want you all thinking I'm not happy."

"That would make you happier?"

"I have no idea. It seems interesting and I would like to explore it."

"What will your boss think?"

I choke on the air I'm breathing. Tell my boss I want to be tied up in ropes and fucked. No thank you. "Well, obviously, I wouldn't tell him."

"I don't know if you could do both."

"Both what?"

"Jobs," Knox says.

"Jobs? I was thinking more about recreation."

"Everyone stop!" Callum commands, holding his hands out. "I think we're talking about two different things."

I push out of the hot tub and sit on the edge to cool off a little.

All the boys look at me, their eyes bugging out of their head briefly as they stare at my exposed breasts. I smile, loving the fact of how easily I can turn them on. "Sorry. I was just getting hot."

"Please stop apologizing for doing things you shouldn't be sorry for. I will make a list for you," Knox says.

Emmett winks at me.

"Let's start over," Callum suggests. "Last night, we were approached by the club owners of Allure. They're allowing us to put in an offer to buy the club back from them. They have some personal things they're working through with family and have to go back to Texas. And managing the club for the last several months with the travel is simply too much."

"Oh."

"When we saw you talking to Sammie and then later came to us asking about Allure, we thought you knew somehow," he pauses a moment, "but judging from the look on your face, I would say you have no idea what I'm talking about."

I shake my head.

"So then, what *were* you talking about?" Knox asks.

"I had heard the club was doing Shibari demonstrations and thought it would be fun if we tried that."

"Shibari?" Knox asked.

"Yes, it's Japanese rope bondage."

"Oh. I know what it is."

"Oh."

"And you want to do that?"

I shrug. "I thought it could be something fun to try." I can feel the blush on my cheeks and suddenly I'm self-conscious, so I slide back into the hot tub.

"Don't," Jax commands. "Don't retreat into the shell you used to live inside. Knox isn't pressing because it's a silly idea. We all love how sexually confident you're becoming. How comfortable in your own skin you're becoming. You're transforming in front of our eyes-"

"Like a butterfly," Knox interjects, flapping his arms.

"Shut the fuck up."

"What? I'm trying to keep it light because you're getting too serious. Making me itch."

"I'm simply trying to convey she never needs to feel bashful around us or ever feel like she can't ask anything."

"Well, convey it in a more upbeat tone."

Jax lunges across the small space and tackles Knox, pressing his head under the water.

Once Knox pops back up, Callum regains control of the conversation. "Boys."

All of their eyes are on me.

"So you want to know if I would have a problem with you buying back Allure?"

"Yes. A sex club, specifically."

"Will I get a free membership?" I pump my eyebrows.

"You can have whatever you want there," Emmett says, scooping me onto his lap.

"So you've already talked about it?" I wrap my arms around his neck and cross my ankles, laying them on Knox's lap.

"No. Well, not no, but not yes," Callum says.

"Clear as mud," Knox chimes and then flinches when Jax makes a move towards him.

"Sammie brought the offer to Jax and Knox before we arrived last night. Emmett was busy with the event, so the extent of our talking was Jax and Knox telling me and then me telling Emmett."

"And then me wondering how in the fuck you found out." Knox's voice ticks up an octave. "Which I can see now, you didn't know anything about, and I may have jumped the gun on our conversation."

"Shocking," Jax snipes.

Knox retorts by sticking out his tongue.

"Sammie? She's the owner?"

"I assume you knew, since you were talking to her last night."

Puzzle pieces start clicking into place. Sammie could definitely be the owner of a sex club. I bet she was a domme too. An image of her in a black shiny leather outfit with large metal loops hanging around her waist wearing a cat mask and holding a whip pops into my head. Very Halle Berry cat woman look.

"No, but this is all starting to make a lot more sense." Feeling the situation needed a more formal approach, sans the entire conversation taking place in a hot tub, I sit up and climb off Emmett's lap, ignoring his slight groan. "What do you all want to do?"

"We want to talk with you about it because if you have any qualms, we won't pursue it further. You're our priority."

My stomach tightens. "Ok. For the sake of this conversation, let's say I have no qualms. What do you all want?" I feel like we're in a very precarious situation in our relationship. They don't want to do anything that will upset me and I don't want to do anything that will upset them, with neither of us having the courage to say what we really think or want.

They look at me without speaking.

"Guys," I huff. "This can't work if we aren't open to having conversations about the tough things. Ignore how you think I will react or what you think I want. I don't know what I want right now, so I doubt you can figure it out. Scratch that. What I want is to have a conversation about this with you. An honest conversation. That's the only way we'll truly know if this is a good decision."

Knox puckers his lips and stares at me. "Well, then." He claps his hands. "I... I want it. I would like to take this conversation to the next step with Sammie. We loved Allure when we had her before. We sold to Sammie, because it wasn't where we wanted it to be and because it gave us the money for Bo's, Vixen and Loveuz. But... I do miss it." He quickly turns to me. "Not because of all the sex and debauchery, but because it allowed us to explore questions we had, and I loved being able to do that for others." He pushes out of the water and sits on the edge, looking at the guys. "Hell, Everlee's desire to try Shibari is a perfect example. Without Allure, she may be tempted to search it up online and find some freak with a fetish who doesn't know what he's doing and she could get seriously hurt."

"Simmer down there hot stuff," Jax teases. "Weren't you the one telling me earlier to keep it light?"

Knox rolls his eyes, but doesn't speak.

Callum adds, "We have Knox's point of view. Anyone else?"

"How would you run it? Where would we fit in? And I'm not asking to be selfish, just to have understanding."

Callum thinks about it for a moment. "We'd probably use a lot of the same staff that's currently in place, but I believe Sammie plays a large part in finding and vetting teachers for demos. We'd have to be there quite a bit, at least at the beginning, to ensure a smooth transition and make sure all proper measures are being taken. We will have to build trust with the team and get to know them better. It's been almost three years since we sold it, so I imagine there's been some turnover."

My eyebrows perk up.

He smiles, "I know, I know. I'm thinking."

Jax presses out of the hot tub, palms pressed onto the edge, causing his biceps to tighten. I try to contain myself, but fuck, it's hard. "Assuming the hours are the same at Vixen, we'd have to split our time. You take Vixen, Knox can take Allure, I'll keep Loveuz, and Emmett has Bo's."

"I can help too."

"Where?"

I shrug.

"Weren't you the one saying we needed to be open and honest?" Jax presses.

"Fine. I would… have an interest… in Allure." I squint one eye.

He reaches under the water and gooches my side.

"Do you want to be part of this, Everlee? Like included in conversations, ideas, the whole business piece of it?"

"Really?"

"Yes. You are ours. We are us," Callum says.

Knox claps loudly. "I'm getting us all shirts made that say that! You are ours, we are us!"

"Seriously. Shut the fuck up." Jax splashes water at him.

The heat of the water is making my heart race, or possibly it's Callum's words, so I push out of the water and sit on the edge again. "I don't know how you boys withstand the heat."

"I work in a kitchen," Emmett teases.

"Wait, are you saying… are you saying, if you can't stand the heat, then get out of the kitchen?" Knox asks, pushing out of the water sitting beside me and waves his hand at Jax. "I know, I know. You don't have to say it. Shut the fuck up." He rolls his eyes and presses his palms onto the edge of the hot tub.

Without thinking about it, I lick my lips.

"Insatiable," Knox says, winking at me.

I shrug. "And to answer your question. Yes. I would love to be part of the process."

What I didn't want to be part of was the conversation with Lizzy when I tell her I've gone from wanting to possibly take a class and visit it to having a shared ownership. Is that what it would be? Would I be part owner? I guess not, since I wouldn't be putting up any finances. Would I be working there for free? The more I think about this, the more questions I have.

The bubbles cut off and the guys climb out. Emmett grabs a few towels from under the cabinet in the outdoor kitchen and tosses them at us. While I'm bending over to dry my legs off, I feel a towel whip on my bare ass.

When I pop up, Knox is running away laughing with his towel between his legs like it's a broom horse.

"I'll get you!"

"I can't wait, love!"

Emmett, Callum, and I grab all the dishes on the table and carry them downstairs, while Jax opens all the doors.

Emmett and I wash the dishes and clean up the kitchen and decide we're going to completely veg the rest of the day and watch movies on the couch.

EVERLEE - SHUT THE BACK DOOR

- -

THE REST OF THE weekend passed with little excitement. Emmett and I watched movies all morning and afternoon. Callum and the others joined us around lunchtime and made some sandwiches, so we had a makeshift picnic. It was the best day I think I've had in my entire life, but that's how it's been lately. Every day is literally better than the last, which I don't know how that's possible, but it keeps happening.

Work has been fine, same as usual. Meetings and reports, reports and meetings. I'd be lying if I said, since our initial miscommunication fiasco about the Shibari and the club, I hadn't wondered what it would be like to work there. I know when it was mentioned about my boss and how I could work at both was all confusion, but now... what would it be like?

I laugh. Am I really considering leaving my comfy corporate job to work at a sex club?

No... right?

This is your boo calling. Pick up the phone.

This is your boo calling. Pick up the phone.

Lizzy!

"You changed my ringtone again?" I ask as soon as the call connects.

"I would've thought you learned after the last time not to leave your phone around me. I'm getting quite good at it now."

"Lizzy," I groan.

"You should be thanking me. That was the second option. The first was... well, I don't want to tell you. I may use it again in the future."

"You won't."

"Never say never, darling."

"What do you want?" I huff.

"I wanted to see what your plans are for lunch."

"Going out with my new best friend."

"Hark! Don't say such hurtful things."

"Where do you want to go?" I sigh.

"That's the spirit, lady love. How about Clemmie's?"

"Burgers?"

"They have superb fries and milkshakes."

"Superb? Can you give me fifteen?"

"I will give you fourteen and a half and not a second more."

"Thank you for your generosity."

"You're welcome."

I fire off a few more emails and save the report I'm running before I head for the door. I've had a productive first half of the morning, although Mondays usually are because that's when all the reporting needs to go out.

When I walk into Clemmie's fourteen minutes later, Lizzy is standing by the door looking at her phone.

"Everything ok?"

She holds her phone to my face. "So close. I tell you, since you've been hookering it up with those men, you've been living life a little too close to the edge for my taste."

14:29:37 was displayed on her phone.

"You were timing me?"

"How else could I give you shit for being late?"

"You have issues, you know that?"

"Ehh." She shrugs her shoulders.

"And what the fuck? I'm living life on the edge because I had mere milliseconds to spare on a time you set? Not you, who is getting fucked while hanging from rope?"

"It's an art."

"Call it what you want." Do I dare tell her about the conversation we had yesterday with the boys, or the meeting that's planned for later tonight at Bo's?

Not yet. But I'm not going to lie. I really can't wait to tell her if the deal goes through. I love her reactions when she loses her shit. It's actually something I've come to look forward to now.

"So anything new and exciting happening?"

"No."

"No more weird positions you want to share?"

"Nope."

"Well, aren't you a Chatty Cathy today?"

"Yep." That was on purpose because of what she said.

She glares at me, then walks up to the register and orders fries and a milkshake.

"You aren't getting a burger?"

"No. I just wanted fries and a milkshake."

I shake my head and order a burger and a milkshake. With the amount of fries she ordered, there will be enough for me to pick off her plate.

She found a table near the back corner of the restaurant and stuck our table number in the metal stand. When I sit down, I stare at her for a second because she looks like she's about to burst with glee.

"Oh. Ask me already!!" She's flapping her hands around and bouncing up and down in her seat.

"How was your weekend?"

"No!"

"How's Tony?"

"Not that either."

"How are your parents?"

"No," she whines.

"Your parents finally got a dog?"

"You are no fun, you know that?"

"That's not what the boys say," I smirk.

"Ooh feisty." She wiggles her fingers at me in approval.

"Fine. What is it you're so excited to tell me you are nearly bouncing out of your seat?" I slap the table. "You aren't pregnant, are you?"

"Lord help me. No." She scrunches her nose. "At least I don't think."

"Lizzy!"

"What? We had an oopsie a couple of nights ago."

"That's why you take the pill or something else."

"You know I'm too much of a spaz to remember to take a pill every day."

"They have other options, you know. Like IUDs."

"You remember when I did it the one time, and I was in god awful pain for months? Doctors said it couldn't be the IUD and then I take it out, and voila! No more pain?"

"Yes, but there are still other options."

"Condoms. That's pretty much it and the one a few nights ago busted, but I just had my period, so I don't think I'm pregnant." She shakes her head. "Why are we even talking about this, anyway? That's not what I wanted to tell you!"

"Oh. What is it you want to tell me?"

"We almost have a wedding date!"

"You are so excited because you *almost* have a wedding date?"

"Yes!" she squeals.

"How excited will you be when you actually have one?" I tease.

"Oh, shut it!"

The server brings our food over and before her basket of fries hits the table, I grab one. I also pay for it because they're hotter than Satan's house cat.

"Serves you right," she says, taking a sip of her milkshake. She lifts a french fry and dips it into her shake.

I've never understood why she does that. Who dips a fry in their milkshake?

"So how are your BOBs?"

"I haven't used them in weeks."

"No! Even the green monster?" She throws the back of her hand across her forehead. "Say it isn't so."

"I have four men. They keep me busy enough."

"At least they have their shrine, although I suppose it's more of a memorial. Perhaps I should come over this week and say a few words."

"I think you are coo-coo loco."

"Probably. So tell me. When is Vixen going to have another themed party?"

"What do you mean?"

"They had one for Valentine's Day and Easter. I'm thinking... next month. Rainbows and Unicorns."

"Why?"

"Pride month?"

"A bit on the nose?"

"Whatever. How fun would it be? Plus, I have a super cute rainbow skirt and silver sequin top that would look totes faboosh."

"That good?"

"Yes. Now don't you have some sway with the planning now? Word on the street is people are looking for a themed party. It's been a while."

"Word on the street?"

"Well, you know. But seriously. Vixen has a fairly big following on the socials and people have been asking about the next party."

"Seriously?"

"Would I lie to you?"

My eyes narrow at her.

"Ouch." She stabs herself in the chest with an invisible knife. "I'd never lie about something this important. Plus, you can get your brother and his beau to come visit again."

"They've been visiting a ton lately."

"Twice. And it's only for a day or two each time."

"Flights are expensive."

"Will's mom is a flight attendant."

"How do you know this?"

"Because. Like I told him. We have to stick together against the McKinleys."

"Fine. I will talk to the guys about having a pride party."

"Rainbows and Unicorns."

"Fine. A Rainbows and Unicorns party."

She claps her hands together and stuffs another milkshake covered fry in her mouth.

"So, what are your maybe dates?"

"April 20th, June 9th, June 22nd, or August 24th."

"Four dates?"

"Yes."

"What's the holdup?"

"Well, you have April 20th, which is four twenty," she snickers. "And four plus twenty equals twenty-four." She bobbles her head back and forth, "And next year is 2024..."

"Solid choice."

"Then there's June 9th, which is obvious."

"Six nine."

Lizzy taps her chest with her fist, then throws a peace sign. "Special tribute to my boo."

I blow her a kiss.

"Then Tony wants June 22nd. Boring. Nothing special at all. And then August 24th. It's just later in the year and it's cool to say eight twenty-four twenty-four."

"So really it's between April 20th and June 9th."

"Yes."

"Where do you want to get married? Do those venues have those dates available?"

She scrunches her nose. "I don't know where I want to get married." She runs her fingers through her hair and groans in frustration.

"What about Tony?"

"He doesn't care."

"Ok. Let's start here... do you want it in the States or not?"
She pulls her lips.

"Ok. How about this... how many people do you want at the wedding? Do you want it big or small?"

She looks out the window.

"Lizzy. You've been planning this day since you were little."

"I know! The pretend version. But now it's real and I'm freaking out. I want it to be perfect and that's preventing me from making any decisions at all."

"No matter what you choose, it will be perfect because it's you and Tony."

She fake gags, "Just kidding. Say it again. Really, just the I'm perfect part."

"But I don't think that's what I said."

"See, that's what I heard."

"I love you. Shit!"

"What?"

"I forgot to tell you."

She taps her fingers rapidly together like she's ready to gossip or just cast an evil spell. It could really go either way with her. "Tell me, now."

"Emmett said he loved me yesterday."

She inhales a large, loud, dramatic, over the top, lean back in the chair, hands flying in the air, breath. "Shut the front door. Rather, the back door."

"Back door?"

"For some reason, the front door reminds me of the pearly gates and heaven... and well... you know." She shrugs. "So I think back door fits better for you... opposite... plus you like the backdoor." She winks.

"So, the back door of hell?"

"You said it, but really, why are we still talking about this? He said he loves you!!"

I smile.

"Ev. That's exciting. When's the wedding?"

"Ha. Too soon."

She snarls. "If you get married, then I can just plan yours and ignore mine."

"You know I won't be getting married."

"Ev. You know, that I know, that you know there's a chance."

I take in a deep breath, but like a normal person. Quiet like a church mouse, not an overly dramatic elephant in water. "It's ok though. Marriage is your thing."

"Did you tell that sexy mountain man you loved him back?"

"I did. Before he fucked me. With Jax."

"You dirty hooker. Tell me more."

"No. That's all you get."

"You clit tease! My vagina just barely started to tingle."

"I have to get back to work."

We throw our trash away and she walks with me down the sidewalk back to my building. "Did you talk to them about..." she looks over her shoulder, "the new art classes you want to take?"

My brow furrows before I remember what she's talking about. "Yea."

"And?"

"Is this your backdoor way of trying to get me to give your pussy butterflies?"

"Backdoor is your thing... and front door... and side door? I've run out of door analogies for all the holes you like plugged."

"I'd like to plug your hole."

She starfish stands in front of me, legs spread, arms out in the air with her head back. "I thought this day would never come! Plug away!"

"People are watching and I was talking about your mouth, you perv."

"I thought you liked people watching." She makes an o face and places her hand over her mouth. "And you say perv, where I say wishful thinking."

"Too. Much."

"Love. You."

"I'll call you later."

"Hey. Let's talk weekend deets! It's Memorial Day weekend. I'm thinking a little par-tay? Low key, cook out at your place. Boy toy one can cook something special." She claps her hands. "I know what you all can be for Halloween."

"I'm scared to ask."

"They can be thing one, two, three and four and you can be that sexy cat with a hat."

Why did I just get images of the leather cat woman domme outfit again?

My watch buzzes to remind me of my meeting in fifteen minutes. "Need to run. I'll think about the costume."

"XOXO love bug. Go do adulting!" She shouts after me, loud enough to be embarrassing.

JAX - GOING TO A SEX CLUB

My nerves are about shot as our old world and new world are about to collide. Everlee says she's fine, but she's sitting beside Emmett at the table instead of at the head, which tells me she's feeling insecure and that makes me want to take her away from here and erase all of those feelings. The plan is to meet Sammie and I assume her boy toy, David, or whatever his name is, at Bo's to talk about the business. She's going to bring us the financials since she took over along with memberships, projected future growth, and any immediate opportunities or causes for concern she sees. Then we're all going to head to Allure and see for ourselves.

I've heard she's added a few rooms and a bar. I like that, but I'm interested to see what Callum thinks. He was adamantly against it whenever we first opened, because he was scared of the liability and risk of someone getting sloshed and behaving in a way that would involve intervention.

I catch Everlee's eye and give her a quick wink. She smiles back, but it doesn't reach her eyes, so I nudge Emmett under the table with my foot and nod towards Everlee. He bends down and whispers something to her before kissing her on the neck, which makes her smile and blush. She looks at me knowingly, so I blow her a quick kiss and this time she smiles and means it.

Her eyes dart to the stairs as the click click click echoes and bounces around the walls. Sammie appears a moment later with her jet-black hair pulled back in a high ponytail, wearing a pair of tight leather pants, Louis Vuitton heels and an oversized crop top sweater. I continue to watch for Daniel. I think that's his name, but he never comes.

"Oh, it's just me tonight, boys." Her gaze lands on Everlee and she smiles, "And Madame." Her voice drops an octave in approval, and I don't ignore Everlee's sigh of relief. She walks behind us and takes a seat at the other end of the table; the one Everlee usually holds. She reaches to her right and grabs Everlee's hand, and says in a slow and calculating tone. "This is an unexpected, but welcomed, surprise."

Everlee looks around and her eyes land on Callum, clearly looking for guidance.

Callum sits up in his seat, leaning forward just a little. "Good evening, Sammie. I hope all is well." She nods, sliding her hand off Everlee's. "Everlee is with us and I can trust you to be discreet?"

"Of course," she nods, then looks over at Everlee and mouths, "Well done."

Everlee smiles, but I can tell she's still uncomfortable, which makes me uncomfortable. I want to wrap her in my arms, then fuck away all her doubts and worries.

"So," Sammie clasps her hands together, "How should we do this?"

Emmett speaks. "We will enjoy a nice dinner and then we'll head to Allure. I assume the documents for review will be there?"

"Yes. Davis is finalizing them."

Davis. A plain name. One I will probably forget again.

"I've also reserved a private tour to walk you through the club. Much has changed over the last several years. Assuming that's ok?" She looks pointedly at Everlee.

Everlee sits up, back straight. "I can't wait." She does a good job hiding her nerves, but I know her. I see her. And I can tell she's a little uncomfortable. Later tonight, we will have to figure out if that's because of Allure or because of Sammie.

"Good," Sammie says, watching her for a moment.

The servers come out a few minutes later and take our orders. Emmett was going to create a special menu for tonight, then decided to let everyone choose what they want. I think mostly because he's still mentally exhausted from Lizzy's event.

Knox has been noticeably quieter this evening and I have a feeling it's because there's something he wants to tell us but is scared to. I already know, but he doesn't know that. When Everlee left, he spiraled a bit, going out more and staying out late. It wasn't all because of her, but it seemed to be the latest trigger.

He started going to bars, and then one night he ended up at Allure. I don't know why. I followed him until he entered the gates and then I parked on the street and watched him walk inside. I didn't go after him because we all had memberships, even though we hadn't used them since we left, and once you enter, they scan your card and register your name. I didn't want proof I was following him, because it would likely piss him off. If he did something stupid, I would have stepped in, but he was processing his way and wasn't getting reckless, so I kept my distance.

Dinner was nice. There was small talk about Sammie's family and why she's having to leave. She seems to really love Allure and put a lot of thought and work in to growing it, and is sad she has to leave. I know it was doing well when we sold it and I'm interested to see where she's taken it to, in terms of annual revenue.

Sammie used a ride share to get to Bo's tonight, so we take her to Allure. Knox and Everlee climb into the third row of the vehicle while Callum and Sammie take the second row and I drive with Emmett in the passenger seat. Talk is still very casual and Everlee seems to have relaxed some. The several times I look at her in the rearview, she has her head on Knox's shoulder and they're murmuring about something, passing whispers back and forth.

We arrive at the three-story tall brick building fifteen minutes later. From the outside, you would think it's an old mill shop that has long been out of business, with blacked-out windows and ivy growing up the exterior. There are no banners, no signs, nothing indicating a business exists. Very much a speak easy, although in this case, one could call it a fuck easy.

We pull around to the back, where there's a guard gate and a low brick wall surrounding the parking lot, making it very private.

A nice touch.

Sammie leans forward, handing me a gate access card. When I swipe it, the arm lifts, allowing us through.

"What do you do if you don't have a card?"

"Every card comes with a pin. You can either swipe the card or type in the pin. If it's your first time, there's a button you can press that goes directly to our front desk and they'll verify your paperwork has been submitted, along with a passed background check and medical check. It's on the website."

"Website?"

"Yes," she chuckles. "We maintain a high level of privacy, but have a small website with key information - forms, application, upcoming events."

Everlee's face glows in the back and I assume she's looking up the website. Knox's arm is casually draped across her neck, pointing at the phone, while whispering something in her ear, causing her to giggle. She whispers something back and he grabs her chin and presses his lips to hers.

"Are you going to pull through?" Sammie asks, pulling me away from them.

"Yea, yea." There are several cars here. More than I expected, actually.

"We have a fairly steady clientele; however, tonight is demonstration night. We have recently started doing demonstrations, tapping into the teaching piece of this lifestyle. When you all started Allure, I know education was important to you, so I've taken your ideas and implemented them. After doing exhaustive research, of course. I wanted to find the best of the best, so I scoured the country and even made a few trips out of the country to see what else I could find."

"Wow."

"Yea. I really hope you like what I've done with the place. Like I said at dinner, I really love Allure, but with me needed back home, it's just not a good fit anymore."

"I think Ev and I are going to watch the Shibari demo tonight while you all talk business," Knox chimes in from the back.

"Oh. I've built that into the tour so we can all watch it together. We usually pick volunteers from the audience. However, if it's something you're interested in, I can let the teacher know you'd like to be on stage."

Everlee's eyes nearly bulge out of her head before they lock on mine in the mirror.

After several awkward moments of silence, Sammie continues, "You can think about it if you want."

"Would I be naked?" She peeps, intrigue layered into the question.

My cock twitches at the thought of seeing her tied in ropes on the stage, but the other part of me is enraged at the thought of other men looking at her.

A Cheshire grin spreads across Sammie's face. "Only if you want to be. It's a demo, so I'd recommend bra and panties at the most. But really, whatever you're comfortable with. Allure is all about consensuality and comfort."

"If only you wore panties," Callum chides.

I have a feeling he's feeling the same things I am. Possessiveness.

Before she can say the words, the shit-eating grin on her face gives it away. "I'm wearing them tonight."

My eyes lock on Callum and I see the jealous rage peek its ugly head out for a second. "Of course you are."

Knox claps. "Should I wear my boxers?"

"Honey, you can wear whatever you want. Everyone will be looking at her. Though some ladies may watch you, too." She bites her bottom lip and I see Everlee's eyes flicker for a moment.

Good. At least when she goes through with this- because why wouldn't she? She's our little exhibitionist coming out of her shell- she'll at least know how we feel. I guess it would ruin the business deal if one of us killed someone, though. So there's that.

It will have to be a game time decision.

Callum's eyes meet mine and we both nod in silent agreement before I catch Emmett's. "This is going to be fun," he mumbles under his breath.

He's a lover, not a fighter. But I have a feeling if push came to shove with Everlee, he'd use his knife skills for a completely different reason.

Sammie directs us to a parking spot labeled VIP, and informs us it changes monthly. It's an incentive for members and randomly drawn every month. When we climb out of the car, Sammie loops her arm around Everlee's and walks with her. Everlee is not a short girl, but standing beside Sammie, who is also wearing six-inch-high stilettos, she looks so tiny.

"Can you keep it together?" Callum whispers.

"Can you?" I retort.

He shakes his head. "I think there will be a lot to discuss tonight."

"Hopefully not while we're sitting in a jail cell."

EVERLEE - SMUT BOOKS COME TO LIFE

- -

WE WALK THROUGH THE set of aged-oak double doors with large black knockers. Burned into the wood is a symbol I've never seen before, but it reminds me of a secret cult or something forbidden.

"After you all," Sammie says, waving her arm out.

The room is dark, and loud music pulses from the other side of the interior door, but it's like a slow beat with a lot of bass and high-pitched sounds. Almost like if electronic dance music was played with a didgeridoo, then slowed down. It's weird, but oddly satisfying. It makes me want to just move my body around in slow motion like I have no bones.

Did I accidentally ingest some drugs? I hold my hands out in front of me, staring at them.

Nope.

"We play the music at a level that reacts with your brain to provide a sense of calm and easiness."

"You can do that? Well, I guess you can because it's working. Wow." I turn to look at my guys who are watching me. They don't seem happy.

Not mad, but not happy.

Worried?

"Do you have your cards?" the woman behind the desk asks.

All the guys present a card and she scans them in. I should have known they had cards. They used to own the place, but still the idea makes me feel weird. Jealous?

"She's my special guest tonight," Sammie says, then asks, "Unless you want your own card?"

"She's fine, for now," Callum chimes.

Sammie ignores him and waits for my response, and that simple thing sends a pulse of electricity through me.

Power.

She doesn't let a man answer for her, or for anyone else, it seems.

"I'm fine right now. I don't want to slow us down, but I will go online and finish," I pause to look Callum, "filling out the form."

Yes. Finish. I already started.

Allure was something I was interested in before potential ownership came about, so I definitely want to explore it. With the guys, of course.

"Very well," Sammie casts an approving look over her shoulder at my boys before the lady behind the desk hands us a basket to put all of our electronic devices into. She stores them in a locker wall behind her and gives the key to Callum. "You can retrieve these once you leave. We have a strict no electronics policy."

The set of double black gloss doors buzzes and Sammie pushes them open. "Welcome to Allure," she says, holding her arms out wide. "There are complementary masquerade masks by the door here, for anyone who may want to remain anonymous in the public areas, or if that's their kink."

I look at the small tray and see an assortment of masks lined up. Mostly silver, some gold, some purple and some black. I choose not to grab one because we're only here observing and the room is dark. Slightly darker than the other room we just came from, but you can still see shadows and silhouettes of people moving around. I imagine we'll see better once our eyes fully adjust. I do like the fact, however, the main walkways are illuminated with green strip lighting on the ground.

We stand here for a second and take in the sight of this large room while our senses adjust. The music is louder in here and flows through my body like silk moves through the wind. Like a massage from the inside out.

Hips press up behind me as a hand slips around my waist, pulling me towards them. "Remember, you are ours and no one else's." Callum's words are low, and the promise hidden within makes my pussy pulse with desire.

I turn my head to look at him and take his lips in a quick but passionate kiss. There's something about this place that gives me energy. Makes me feel alive. I feel like here, I can be anyone. Like *we* can be anyone. Like we don't have to hide.

"This is the main room, with the bar on the left side. We have rooms to our right, as well as down the hall there." She points to the right side of the room. "We also have rooms upstairs. Fifteen total, plus two demonstration rooms."

The second floor is open to the first and people are walking along the halls with rooms lining the wall behind them. To my left, on the second level, is what I assume is a woman with bunny ears, leading a man behind her who is only wearing a tie around his neck and a cotton tail on his ass.

I try not to react, because until this moment, I didn't think about all the other kinks I may learn about here. Like books come to life.

Holy fuck!

I just got the best idea!

If we, they, we, I don't know. Anyway, if we come to a deal and own Allure again, we could have a smut book room.

Oh my God!

Where's Lizzy? She would totally freak out. Fuck. What if she's here tonight? Double fuck, what if she's watching the Shibari demo?

Panic turns to laughter. Her face. She'd fucking lose it.

I digress. Get back on track, Everlee.

Smut book room. Where all your book fantasies come to life. We could have themed book nights. Book clubs. I laugh at myself. A sex club, book club. SCBC! Each month we can theme the books. Monster, paranormal, tentacles, dom/sub, daddy.

Triple fuck!

This is a great idea! I'm so excited right now that I'm almost bouncing up and down where I stand. Grabbing the hand closest to me, I squeeze and can tell it's Jax.

Seriously, this place is like a horny drug. I just want to fuck like a rabbit.

Was there speed in my food?

No. I'm just really excited about my idea.

Jax leans down, his other hand sensually slips around my neck to grab it, causing my nipples to go hard. "Are you ok?" His lips gently brush against my ear, which sends a tingle down my neck, down my arm and across my body.

Is he fucking with me? Why am I so turned on by everything right now?

There had to have been drugs in that food tonight.

"Can we rent a room? Is that what happens here?"

"Honey, we will buy this place if that's what you want just so we can fuck you everywhere in it."

"Don't say that to me right now."

He smiles against my skin. "Why is that love?" His words are knowing and flirtatious.

"Would you like to stick your hand down my pants and find out?"

"Don't ask a question you don't want the answer to." His words are soft like velvet, but hot as fire.

Shit. This conversation turned quickly. Like veered off the fucking road and is now careening down an embankment about to hit fuck town. The little village that is always on the edge of the road I'm on.

I can't help it.

I push.

"Find out," I turn and whisper against his lips.

A low chuckle rumbles through his chest. His hand falls from my neck, his other still gripping my hand, and drags it over the top of my breast, between them, across my stomach. He pauses at the top of my pants for a second, then slips his hand under the waistband.

Fuck me. He did it.

Sammie is standing just in front of us, talking to Emmett and Knox about the changes she's made, along with the rooms and other things. Her words fade away as Jax's hand slides down and his finger grazes over my soaking wet pussy. I squeeze his hand tightly when I feel him pause and let out a breath.

"Oh baby," he purrs quietly.

A second later, Callum is pressed up behind me again, his hard erection pressed into my back. "Having fun?" he whispers, burying his nose in my neck as his hand glides up to grab a breast.

I look around and while it's very dark in here, you can obviously still see... things.

Like getting felt up and finger fucked in the middle of the floor.

Callum's hand glides down my chest, to my pants where he slips his hand in under Jax's and presses his finger to my pussy, curving it in slightly.

"Goddamn," I breathe out.

"We can get you all a room if needed. Free of charge, of course," Sammie says, watching us.

I hadn't even noticed she had turned around because while my eyes were open, they were sure as fuck not seeing.

"Perhaps. We will let you know later," Jax says as he and Callum slip their hands out of my pants and suck my arousal off their fingers.

"Yes. She looks quite tasty," Sammie says, turning around. "Follow me then and I will show you around. Perhaps Everlee would like to see the voyeur room."

"I want to see it all." The tone of my voice came out more like a kid asking to try all the flavors at an ice cream stand, where rainbows and unicorns are dancing just off the horizon. Or maybe a woman from the nineteen twenties stepping off a boat in a musical, seeing a new place for the first time. That sweet innocence that dances on the air.

"Well then, we must show her all of it," Sammie chuckles softly.

We pass by several doors off the main area that are private, rentable rooms, for general kinks and pleasures. She shows us one that's currently not occupied and said they're all set up the same. There's a bed, a bench, a few chairs, a swing, a pole, and several dressers full of various toys, gags, and whips. We travel upstairs where there are more rooms that are kink specific. They are set up like the rooms downstairs mostly, but each has a little something extra and the symbol on the door indicates what's in the room. The one we looked in had a large crib and baby bottles and accessories.

After we tour the top floor, we walk back downstairs, discussing where we should go next. The voyeur room, Shibari demonstration, or Eden. While we're waiting, I hear a familiar squeal and turn to see someone walking by in a bunny outfit, holding hands with a man in a mask. The woman is looking at me and then she hop-steps with excitement. I'd recognize that move anywhere, and that ass. I've seen it enough times growing up.

Lizzy.

She keeps walking, though, down a hall to the right of the room.

"Was that?" Knox whispers.

"I think."

"We have a strict no socializing in public spaces rule with members not in your party. It's to maintain a level of privacy for our guests. However, there are special areas designated for socializing. Bars, lounges, private rooms. These are all places people can speak with whomever they want. But public areas such as this are off limits."

"That had to be killing Lizzy, not to come over and talk to you," Knox whispers.

"Probably. I'll get an ear full later tonight or tomorrow."

Likely at lunch where she can be loud and inappropriate in front of lots of people.

The Shibari demonstration still has another thirty minutes before it starts, so we decide to go to Eden. She walks us down the hall Lizzy just disappeared into, passed several rooms and stops inside a large round room. The walls have four floor to ceiling mirrors in the corners, with water trickling down them distorting the reflection in the mirror. The floor is black, the walls are black, but the lights are a soft green.

"Here are the gates of Eden." She holds her arms out to two large black doors with card access off to the right. On the left door is =D and on the right is =N. Together, spelling =D=N in large golden block letters.

"This is a new area we recently finished. It's been open about four months now and very popular among some of our... clientele."

The way she paused before she said clientele was interesting. There's something layered into her words that I'm not picking up on yet, but the guys did. Or so it seems.

"This is our super exclusive section."

"Membership fee?" Knox asks in a serious tone. It's a little weird.

"Fifty thousand a year."

I choke on the surrounding air. "Sorry." I hold up my hand. "Parched," I say tapping my throat, embarrassed about my uncomfortableness around large amounts of money.

Sammie smiles. "Fifty thousand per year, grants them access to this area, as well as guaranteed tickets to special events and soirees. They also have the ability to purchase a private room in Eden and stay up to two nights, if desired. Upon entry into Eden, they are also given a personal butler who will see to their every need and endless champagne." She pauses to look at us. "This is really my baby and one thing I'm going to miss the most. Are you ready to see Eden?"

"Yes," we all say in unison.

She scans her card and the doors open slowly and I wait for music to start playing or something and then I'm hit with it.

Eden.

Wow.

Simply, wow.

We walk through the doors and pause to admire its beauty. In front of us is a large two- or three-story room, with warm lights and a large tree planted in between two rectangular shaped areas inset into the ground. The front one appears to have water in it, perhaps only half a foot deep? The back, while I can't see much around the trunk of the tree, appears to be dry and a little deeper.

"Our pool is ten point eight inches deep and heated to eighty-three degrees. There is a strict no sex policy in the front pool. However, the dry pool behind the tree is fair game."

"Sounds like someone is enjoying themselves," Jax says as echoes bounce through the room.

It's like we're in a completely different place. Whites, golds, and greens are the color choice of this area.

"Madame," a man says with an Eastern European accent, appearing out of thin air, holding a tray of six champagne flutes.

"I will not be needing your services tonight. I'm just show-ing some friends around."

"Understood Madame." He nods and waits for us to grab the champagne before he retreats.

I tilt the bubbly up to my lips and nearly moan. That's some damn good champagne. Holy shit. And I'm not one who likes a lot of champagnes.

Bertha appears, floating on her back, blowing water out of her trunk, swimming around the pool. I have no idea how an elephant is floating in that little of water, but I guess it helps she's not real. She's been appearing less over the last month or two. I don't know why I started seeing her or why I'm seeing less of her now. The only thing I can think of is that she helped me process some of my less comfortable moments. Some sort of weird as fuck coping mechanism?

I shake my head to clear it and refocus on Sammie and the room. There are three rooms on the left and on the right of this open space. All white, with gold handles. Judging by the space between doors, these rooms seem to be two, if not three times, the size of the rooms in Allure.

"These are our rooms that members can purchase for overnight stays." She walks down the right path. As we pass the large tree, there is a man wearing a mask with large golden curved horns atop his head watching two women sixty-nine, while he strokes himself.

I can't help but watch too, sucked in by their movements and moans.

A hand slips into mine and squeezes. "Ours," the voice whispers.

Callum.

"Yours." I wink back.

We pass the people in the dry pool and enter a set of other doors, and I can't help but wonder how long this building is. We have to be coming to the end soon. Why am I thinking about the length of this building? Because it's better than thinking about the man with horns jacking off?

This room has about ten or so people in it, with three wearing masks and is decorated in golds and reds, a stark contrast to the room we just left. In the left corner is a small bar, while on the right are two large doors.

Sammie must see me looking and answers my unasked question. "Those are viewing rooms for our voyeurs and exhibitionist." She pumps her eyebrows, and a blush tingles my cheeks. "Upstairs are Eden's private rooms."

When I look up, I see four rooms, two on either side.

"Two are setup like your standard rooms and the other require a two-hour lead on reservation so we can customize to their specifications. Swings, St. Andrew's Cross, ropes. Whatever their heart's desire."

"It's beautiful here."

"It's Eden."

"That it is…"

"Shall we get ready for the Shibari demonstration?"

I nod and we follow Sammie and sit our empty champagne flutes down on a table. In less than thirty seconds, someone appears from behind another hidden wall and carries them off.

"Are they robots?" I ask, half teasing and half serious.

She laughs and says no, but does not elaborate.

When we get back to Allure, we follow her down another hall on the other side of the main area. There are two large rooms, one that appears to be closed, and another that seems to be standing room only, with the exception of ten blocked off seats in the front.

"Those will be our seats tonight, usually reserved for our upper tier members."

We take our seats in the front row, and I can't help but look around the room. There are about thirty or forty people here, some sitting and others standing in the back.

"Seems to be a popular demonstration," Emmett asks.

"It's one of our newer ones and yes, it has been quite successful." She turns to me. "Have you decided if you want to demo?"

My teeth scrape over my bottom lip as I look between the guys, looking for any clue as to how they feel. I want to scream yes! Yes, I want to demo, but I also don't want to step out of line.

"Go ahead," Callum encourages.

I look at Jax whose lips are pinched in a hard line, then to Emmett who shrugs and lastly to Knox, who is as giddy as a squirrel in a nut shop.

I nod. "Yes. I would like to demo."

A smile spreads across Sammie's face. "Excellent. Once you're done. I will show you the downstairs. Something tells me you will like that area even more."

EVERLEE - KNOTTY THOUGHTS

THE LIGHTS DIM, AND a figure walks onto the stage, pausing under the center light. Her hair is pulled back, and she's wearing thigh-high boots and an inch wide leather strap that is crossed all over her body, covering her nipples and her vagina. She's stunning.

"My name... is Madame Dubois and I'm here to teach you the art of Shibari." She continues to talk, laying out ground rules and safety precautions. "Now. I believe we have two volunteers." She turns to face Knox and me, then smiles. "Yes. They will do nicely."

We walk on stage and the nerves that are turning my stomach are slowly being replaced by something else. There's an electricity flowing through the room and it fills me. Gives me life.

Knox's hand wraps around mine and squeezes. Is he nervous too, or can he sense my anxiety? He drops my hand and slips his arm around my waist, pulling me close to him.

"If you don't want to do this, you say the word and I will whisk you away," he whispers in my ear.

"Have either of you practiced Shibari?" Madame Dubois asks.

I quickly shake my head, followed by a nervous laugh, then turn to Knox, surprised when he admits he has.

"My nickname... used to be Knots."

His nickname in the SEALs? I glance at my guys and a warmth flows through me when I see their eyes laser focused on me instead of the dominatrix bombshell in front of me.

"Excellent. This will be fun. I will ask, for this demonstration though, you let me lead you?"

"Of course, Madame Dubois," Knox says, dipping his head.

She smiles. "You may undress to your comfort level."

"I expect you to call me Madame McKinley," I whisper to Knox while I remove my pants.

"As you wish, Madame McKinley." He tosses me a wink, then rubs his hand up my leg and over my ass.

"Lovely," Madame Dubois says, looking over my nearly bare body.

I may have told the guys I was wearing a bra and panties however, I left out the part that it was lace and a thong. If anyone tried hard enough, they would be able to see my nipples and pussy through the fabric. I glance at the boys and Jax and Callum are leaning forward slightly in their chairs with furrowed brows, Emmett has a grin spread across his face, and Knox is giddy. He loves when I test the boys, and this was a big fucking test.

Knox looks at the guys and they slowly shake their heads. I don't know what he asked or inferred, perhaps asking if they wanted him to take me off stage?

Madame Dubois speaks again, drawing the crowd in with her sultry voice. "We will work on the diamond harness this evening."

"Oh," Knox mumbles and glides his hand down my back. My body reacts like it always does and my ass shoots out like a cat being rubbed, or possibly looking for a fuck, because I'm pretty sure that's what I'll be doing after this demo. My stomach is already tightening with excitement, I just don't know what from yet. Is it the ropes, the fact

I'm about to be tied up, or is it because I'm standing nearly naked in front of a room full of strangers? Some are wearing masks, others are not.

The lights are dim in the crowd, so I can't see all of their faces, but the ones I can see... their eyes are filled with sex. A few men and women have their hands in their partners' laps, while some standing against the wall, have their hands tucked behind them. They are getting off on watching me. Watching us.

Fuck.

Madame Dubois hands Knox a bright pink rope, and he immediately starts running it through his fingers. Like a lost friend he hadn't seen in a while. I'm curious to know what he feels when he touches it, because there is something so erotic watching him handle the rope and pull it.

Madame Dubois continues, "I see you already have the rope doubled. Good. Now, what I want you to do is from the back, wrap it around her chest crossing it over. Keep it high because we're going to come back around the other side and cross it back up. We want the cross to be just above the sternum."

Knox lays the rope on me and it feels different than I expected. Hard, but also smooth. He crosses it over my chest, his fingers running along my skin, causing my stomach to tighten.

Madame Dubois walks around me, keeping her distance, and stands behind Knox, watching every move he makes. "Perfect. Can you create a quick release?"

I hear Knox mumble an agreement and seconds later she's explaining to the crowd and me the purpose of a quick release and how to tie it. With rope bondage, safety is key. Quick releases and rope shears are always important to have on hand.

Once she's done explaining, she walks behind me and checks Knox's work.

"May I check the rope?"

I look over my shoulder and nod.

"Words. I need your verbal consent."

"Yes. You may check the ropes."

Her fingers brush along my back. A foreign feeling. "Very nice," she says, then takes a step back. "Now that we have this done, we want to create some cross tension, so let's loop this around and back up, creating a cross at the top. But here we want to use the Munter's Hitch." She walks the crowd through how to create the knot while Knox demonstrates looping and pulling the rope through and bringing it over my back and creating a half hitch for cross tension. She has him loop it back around the front and start working on the diamond pattern, creating a half hitch on the front before running it through my breasts. His hands grazing my skin with each pass is driving me crazy. My nipples are hard and pressing against the fabric of my bra, while goosebumps erupt on my skin, a wake following his touch.

"Are you good?" he leans down and whispers, looking at my breasts, which are being squeezed into two rope dia-monds. It's a weird feeling. Somewhere between pleasure and pain, leaning more towards pleasure.

"Very good," I whisper back.

His teeth scrape over his bottom lip and a low groan vibrates within his chest.

I can tell by the look in his eyes he's turned on. Like a lot. When Lizzy told me about Shibari, I was interested, but never thought Knox would have been the one who had practiced it and been so turned on by it. His eyes look almost feral, but his breaths are controlled and evenly spaced, unlike mine. I'm panting like a dog in heat on the stage in front of everyone. If I wasn't so turned on, I'd be embarrassed.

Madame Dubois continues to instruct him, looping, wrapping, knotting, hitching, until my torso is covered in a beautiful diamond design with knots going down the center of my sternum, from just above my breast to below, cinching them in between. It's a beautiful design and the knots look amazing. Even Madame Dubois gives a smile of approval.

"Stunning." Her eyes are focused on me, rather than the knots, and a heat courses through me. I've never been aroused by a female before, but I imagine she has the knack for getting women and men to color outside of their lines. She has a way she carries herself that sweeps you up.

"Ours," Knox whispers, sliding his hand around my hip and gripping.

Ours seems to be a popular word amongst the boys tonight. I have so many ideas for this place to take it to an even higher level, although Sammie has done a phenomenal job already. It's easy to feel lost and free in here. Which I suppose is the idea.

Madame Dubois asks me to turn around so the group can see how Knox *beautifully* finished the knot. I feel slightly exposed with my ass on display, but the other part of me doesn't care. In my head, I'm showing my guys and that's it.

She waves her arm up towards the air, and a bar lowers. This is what Lizzy was talking about. My guys' faces are blank, but their eyes are wide and the erections in their pants are evident. They are as turned on as I am.

"The great thing about some of these harnesses is they are great for dominating and control." She looks at me. "Do you like to be dominated?"

Knox answers for me, "Not hardly. Though I suppose it depends." He winks.

My eyes dart over to Callum, who sits up in his seat a little further, his eyes gliding over my body.

"Well, you may like it more after this. I'm going to show you a face down suspension with this harness. It can be one of the more restrictive in terms of asphyxiation, so communication is key here." She looks at me, "Is this ok with you?"

"Yes." I'm learning. Words.

"Don't think because you are the bottom that you are not in control. I would argue that you have the most power. You say the word, we stop immediately and let you down. If you are having a difficult time breathing, or feel too much pain, you need to tell us."

"Ok."

She grabs a rope and walks Knox through attaching me to the bar. He's done this before, I can tell with his movements, but he's allowing her to lead him through the demonstration like he agreed to.

"Now here, we can choose to do several harnesses or cuffs to suspend her. The higher up the leg you go, the more pressure it will take off your bottom."

Me. I was the bottom. At first, I thought she was talking about my ass, which was confusing.

She continues, "Closer to the foot will allow more bend of the back, which over time could get very painful for your bottom and cause issues with their breathing."

My wide gaze turns to Knox and he winks. "I've got you, love. Nothing is going to happen to you."

"Love the communication," Madame Dubois cheers. "Now, can you spread your legs? He's going to run a rope around the upper part of your thigh and suspend you."

Knox's hand slides between my legs and his outstretched finger brushes over my pussy, and my legs buckle for a second. A low growl vibrates out of his chest, only loud enough for me to hear, and I swear it makes me even more wet. The tension and electricity flowing between us are palpable. Part of me wants to end the demo and fuck him on stage, while the other part of me wants to learn more. When I look at the crowd to see if they can see how aroused I am, I notice several couples who are... into this demonstration. One couple in particular. The man is watching me intensely while a woman is on her knees sucking his cock. No shame.

Knox gets the rope tied, his hands pausing and gripping on my legs before he stands. Madame Dubois talks the class through suspension and the next thing I know, my left leg is being pulled off the ground, so I'm making a sort of T shape with my torso bent at the waist and my leg horizontal in the air. He bends down, his hand taking a moment to slowly run up my leg and I tilt my head down further to look at him.

"Enjoying yourself?" I whisper so only he can hear.

"Immensely," he says, kissing just behind my knee. He knows that's one of my weak spots.

His hands glide between my legs again as he wraps and ties the rope around my other thigh. As Madame Dubois continues to talk about suspension and safety, he lifts my other leg and attaches it to the pole, so I'm now fully suspended.

"How are you?" he asks, bending near my face.

"Good."

"How is your breathing?"

"Good."

"Pain?"

"Not too much." I wasn't lying, but it was in that place between pleasure and pain. My weight was pressing into the ropes, causing them to bite into the skin a little. Which, had I thought about it more, I would have realized that.

"Great communication, you two." Madame Dubois walks around the stage and continues talking about how liberating and freeing these positions are, about the trust dynamic and the taking and giving of power, and the beauty of it all. She rattles off a few more types of maneuvers and suspensions, before she somewhat abruptly walks back over to me and begins instructing on how to take me down and untie the ropes.

My eyes sweep across the room and the handsy, rather mouthy, couple in the back has now switched. She was standing with her leg tossed over his shoulder while he feasted on her lady bits. I felt those blue eyes penetrating into the side of my face and forced myself to look away.

I was entranced and maybe a little jealous if I was being honest with myself. Not because of him, but... Fuck, it was hot in here.

I was hot.

Temperature and general need to fuck my guys. I was horny. Like horny with a capital H-O-R. Too horny for just a capital H, that bitch was nearly screaming!

My legs come down and they feel weird, my whole body feels weird, as weights shift and blood moves normally.

Knox moves in front of me and runs his hands over my face. "Are you good?" He presses his forehead to mine.

"I need you to fuck me so bad."

He laughs and then stops when his eyes land on my face. "Are you serious?"

"So serious."

"Now? Here?"His eyes are flashing in confusion, of wanting to strip down and fuck me, but not doing it in front of everyone.

I hesitate for a second. "Not in this room, but we need to check out another room before we leave."

"I fucking love you," he says, taking my mouth in a kiss.

Did. Not. Help.

"Take these ropes off of me," I command in a heady voice.

"Yes, Madame McKinley." He spins me around and pulls the quick release rope, releasing tension, and then makes quick work of getting the ropes unwound, dropping them to the floor.

"Goddamn Ali." He pants out a breath as his eyes rake over my body.

My fingers trace the pink rope marks softly etched into my skin.

"Beautiful artwork," Madame Dubois chimes.

Madame Dubois asks for a round of applause for us while I'm getting dressed and the room erupts. Knox bows, then grabs my hand and pulls me off the stage.

"Wow," Sammie notes when we get back to the group. "That was amazing. Probably our best demo yet."

"Are we close to wrapping this up?" Knox asks, twirling his finger in the air. His words are rushed, and the innuendo is woven throughout every word.

A sly smile curls on Sammie's lips. "We can, but there was one more thing I wanted to show you first. I think you will enjoy it." She tilts her head down. "A lot."

"Well, lead on MacDuff." Knox hops.

Sammie turns to leave out of a side door and we follow her down a hall, then down a set of stairs.

Jax grabs my arm, his voice raw. "Did you enjoy yourself?"

"I did. Did you enjoy the show?"

"Not as much as I will later."

"Promises, promises," I tease.

"Oh baby. I don't make promises, I don't intend to keep. And I promise you will cry out with my cock so deep inside of you, you'll be able to feel it in your throat."

My stomach clenches as tight as my pussy and I stop walking for a minute.

"That even made me wet my pants," Knox peeps, walking by.

"Shut the fuck up."

"We're here."

A large sign was etched out of metal above the door. INFERNUS.

KNOX - INFERNUS

"WELL, THIS GOT DARK fast," I tease, looking at the gloss black double doors in front of us.

INFERNUS, is etched in metal above them.

Hell.

I was proud of my little quip, but as usual, Jax did not appreciate it by way of a punch in the arm.

"Ouch."

"Boys," Everlee commands, linking her fingers in mine and pulling my arm in for a hug.

"This is... our play area for some of the darker kinks," Sammie says before turning to use her card to open the doors.

"Private membership?"

"Yes, this one is only thirty thousand a year. It doesn't offer as many perks as Eden."

"Makes sense."

She looks at me and nods her approval.

"I will preface this with everything is consensual. It may be consensual, non-consensual, but we take security and privacy very seriously. There are cameras up in the main hallways and then throughout the rooms. There are several signs noting the use of cameras and members also have to sign a contract."

"Good to know," Callum says, cautiously looking around.

"We also allow members to traverse the realms, if you will, once a month with their membership. If they want more, we require them to buy both memberships. We offer a ten-thousand-dollar discount if they purchase both."

Everlee looks at me with wide eyes. Her innocence is so fucking cute.

"There are only four private rooms down here, as well as a bar and a social area at the end of this hall. The rooms are large and really meant for group play."

"Group play?" Everlee peeps, a hint of apprehension in her voice.

Sammie smiles, "Let me show you. I have reserved a room for you all to enjoy for the rest of the night."

"I would have preferred Eden," I tease.

"Something tells me you have a bit of darkness in you, though."

I swallow, but don't speak. Her assessment hits a little too close to home.

"All four rooms are set up the same, however, two are building or room play while the other two are outdoor woods play."

"Which did we get?"

"There was only one available, so the outdoor woods room."

We follow her past one room and stop at the entrance of a second. The bar and social area are just a little further down to the left, I assume, because a tail just disappeared behind the corner. If Everlee isn't scared away after tonight, I'm going to marry her.

Change the rules.

Go rogue.

I don't give a fuck. Hell, after the Shibari demonstration, I wanted to marry her. She was perfect.

Shit.

She is perfect.

I can't believe I told her I loved her. She didn't say it back, but there was a lot going on. It wasn't really planned and the way it came out could have sounded like a jovial expression versus my feelings.

And that's what they are.

My feelings.

I love her. Deep.

Bone aching, deep.

I didn't want to. Fuck, I tried not to. But I can't help it. She's my siren song.

"This is your room for the evening. Stay as long as you like. We close at seven in the morning. I will have all the papers you requested in your locker at the front. I will give you all a week to discuss. If you have a decision made before then, you're welcome to reach out to me."

"Thank you for everything," Callum reaches out to grab her hand. "You've done some pretty amazing things with Allure."

"Thank you. Really. That means a lot to me."

"There are condoms, lube, towels, handcuffs, ropes, and more in the drawers of the room. You can adjust the light level of the woods with the switch on the main wall. Beds, bathrooms, and showers are also in the room for your use. There are also spare clothes in the drawers if needed. Your cards are your key. All four of you should be able to get into the rooms and on all the floors for tonight only." She winks.

"It was so nice meeting you Sammie," Everlee starts, then rushes to continue. "I mean, I know we've met before at parties, but now I feel like I know you." A blush tinges her cheeks and she laughs.

"Nice to meet you, too. And all the members signed NDAs regarding the discussion of other members. In fact, if you see another member on the street, it is encouraged you do not engage in conversation about Allure, unless both have expressed consent."

"How do you express consent to something you're not allowed to talk about?" Everlee asks, with that cute little dip between her eyes she always has when she's deep in thought. Usually, her tongue pokes out a little too, but that's only if she's concentrating on something.

Sammie laughs, "We greet members by saying Volitus, if we can speak freely. If not, then we have a normal conversation."

"Like a secret society!" I say, trying not to bounce. My balloon is immediately deflated when I look at Jax, who should just get the words 'Shut the fuck up' tattooed across his forehead.I snarl at him, then look back at Sammie and Everlee.

"Oh, and one more thing," Sammie says before leaving. "If you find yourself lost in the woods, you can either find a button on a wall or shout out *exit* three times in a row and a light will illuminate your path out."

"Get lost?" I ask.

"Are they watching us the whole time?" Everlee asks. It's hard to tell from the tone in her voice if she's concerned or turned on by the thought.

I will definitely say her sexuality has gotten infinitely more... just more. She's confident and I love she's wanting to explore what really turns her on. This is why we wanted to create Allure to begin with. Give people a safe space to find themselves. What Sammie has done with it is amazing and I can't wait to hear what Everlee thinks. I know she has some ideas in that cute little head of hers.

"No. The cameras pulse and watch the social areas to ensure all are behaving. The rooms are recording but are not actively being monitored with eyes until exit is called the first time. They assess the situation and determine if you are saying it in conversation or if you need assistance." She clasps her hands together. "I think that's everything. If you need more, please feel free to also call out Sammie three times and I'll be here as soon as I can."

"Thank you," Emmett says. He's been quiet most of the night, so I would be curious to get his thoughts on everything, too.

We walk into the room and all stand there for a second, taking everything in.

"I expected woods or something," Everlee says.

"There's another set of doors over here," Emmett calls from across the room. He opens them, then closes them quickly.

"What is it?" Everlee shouts, running over to him. He blocks the door and won't let her open the handles. "Let me see," she whines.

"Not yet."

She tries to pull his arm away, but it's futile. He's too strong for her. She's like a kitten hanging on the arm of a gorilla.

Not. Going. To. Happen.

She leaps on him and tries to crawl over his shoulders, but Jax runs over and grabs her around the waist, pulling her off. She's kicking and screaming and laughing. "I don't want to hurt you," she warns through laughter.

"Oh baby. You can't."

"I'm a black belt, lest ye forget?"

"Ne, I forget not."

Jax carries her over to the bed and throws her down, but she springs off it and runs back over to Emmett. "What's in there?"

"Jax and Knox's wet dream, that's what."

"Ooh now I want to see," I chime in, walking over, but he doesn't move.

"What are you doing?" Callum asks.

"I'm thinking."

"About what?" I ask, holding my arm out to grab Everlee and spin her in front of me, wrapping her in my arms. "Hold tight, babe. We'll get you in there," I whisper into her ear.

Her body relaxes in my arms, her hands holding onto my forearms, as her head lays back on my shoulder. "Should we team up and take him?"

She's spunky and full of energy, and so turned on right now. It's rolling off of her in waves and electrifying the room. Or maybe it's just me.

"I'm going to let you in. Calm down, Trouble. I just... there's an opportunity to make it fun."

"It's woods, isn't it?" I ask, and the expression on Emmett's face is all the answer I need.

"Have you ever been hunted?" I whisper to Everlee. Goosebumps erupt over her arms, and she turns to look at me, her eyes wide with excitement.

"No."

"Do you want to be?"

She looks around at all the guys. "Let's make it interesting."

"A wager?" Jax asks, surprised.

"You realize you're going against two SEALs," I remind her.

"So, are you scared you're going to lose?" She taunts, nibbling on her finger.

I spin her around so she's facing me and rub from her ass up her back, lifting her shirt. I lean in and kiss just under her jawbone. I know all of her special spots, the ones that drive her crazy and I love torturing her.

Her legs buckle a moment before she recovers. "You aren't playing by the rules."

"Does that upset you?"

"No." She rubs her hands up my chest, under my shirt, then down the front of my legs, cupping my cock. "I can play dirty too."

"How dirty?" I whisper back. She's about to see how far out of her depth she is, but if I know her, she'll adapt quickly and... God, it will be so good.

"So what's the game?" She turns back to look at the boys. "Hide and Seek? Chase? I'm at a bit of a disadvantage because there are four of you and only one of me."

"You get ten minutes to hide. The goal is to make it back to this room without being caught," Emmett says.

"That's unfair. You can just man up by the door."

"Fair point. We have to constantly stay moving and can't hover by the door," I add. My skin is getting tingly with excited anticipation.

"Fine. I get ten minutes." She moves towards the door. "Wait. What do I get if I win?"

"Love. You aren't going to win," Jax says confidently.

"Love." She walks over to him and stands on her tippy toes, and lets her arms dangle over his shoulders, her face an inch from his. "I plan on taking your ass down."

"Did she just say go down on my ass?" I toss out.

"Dibs." Emmett chirps.

"Fine, Squirt. When you win..." he rolls his eyes. "What do you get?"

"I don't know. I need time to think about it. I want it to be something good."

"Better than us?" I snatch her around her waist and pull her tightly into me so she can feel my hard cock pressed against her back. Yes. I'm hard. The idea of chasing her and fucking her against a tree or whatever the fuck is in there has me so hard. A tall fucking oak in my pants right now, kind of hard.

She turns to face me. "Never!" Her teeth latch gently to my neck and it takes everything I have not to take her to the floor right now.

"Does everyone agree to the terms?" Emmett asks.

"Wait, what happens if you win?" she asks, spinning around. I can feel her excitement pulsing through her.

Jax answers, "We get you, love. Any way, anywhere we want, when we find you. And we will find you. I can smell your arousal. Feel your heat."

Everlee crosses her legs.

"I will find you, and I will fuck you," I say, imitating and tweaking the scene of that one actor who was trying to find his lost daughter.

"This sounds like a no-lose situation for me."

Jax smiles.

"Will you yell out when you come in, so I know?"

"Yes," Emmett says.

"Go?" she asks, walking towards the door. "And you better not cheat."

"Never." Emmett says, grabbing her and bringing her in for a kiss, before he opens the door.

As the door closes, all I can hear is, wow.

EVERLEE - HIDE AND FUCK ME

MY PANTIES ARE SO fucking soaked right now. Tonight has been everything and more than I wanted and expected. Shibari with Knox and now this. I don't know what this is, but it's amazing.

Emmett closes the door behind me and in front of me is woods. Like actual, legit woods. The ground is covered in a thin layer of soft dirt, and there are loose twigs and leaves scattered around the floor and near the base of the trees and bushes. The air smells of pine and there is a whisper of bubbling water in the distance. How is this real? Alive?

The nearest tree is only a few steps away, so I walk over and rub my hand against it, and feel the roughness of the bark. It's dark in here, with a makeshift full moon in the sky above, which is casting a soft glow across everything. The attention to detail in this room is unbelievable.

Not wanting to waste time, I move further into the woods and toy with the idea of climbing a tree and perching out like a lioness. Do I want to go deep into the woods and work my way back, or do I want to stay close to the door in a great hiding spot? I have ten minutes to decide, well, less now, and my heart is racing. This is better than sardines at their house.

The idea of being hunted and chased. I would have never thought that would have turned me on, but I'm literally shaking with anticipation. Part of me wanting to let myself get caught, but the other part wants to win.

Tonight, I plan to win.

There's a clear path around these woods, so I follow it for a while, then veer off to the left, slipping out of my shirt and dropping it just off the trail. Breadcrumbs to nowhere.

I continue to run through the woods, but still heading towards the back, which I should be getting to soon. I still have to make it to the front and climb a tree, but I don't think I have a ton of time left. Pausing only for a moment, I slip out of my pants and put my shoes back on, which will be the last to go.

I push towards the right and curve back to the front and find the small, little bubbling brook. There are a few large stones stacked on top of one another with water trickling over them into a small round area about seven feet in diameter. I peek inside and see seats around the edges and dip my toe in the water. Warm. It's like a waterfall hot tub. Genius. The water continues to flow into a small stream about three feet wide and maybe an inch deep. It goes along the back wall and I have to imagine it curves back in a large loop to feed the waterfall.

I'm getting distracted.

I drop off my pants behind a bush, so it looks like I'm trying to hide them, but still leave them visible enough to be found. They have to be getting close to coming in. I should have set a timer or something.

Shit! I just realized I have my watch on and it's glowing.

How badly do I want to win? I stare down at my watch.

Pretty fucking badly.

I'm competitive by nature and the fact Jax and Knox are both SEALs makes it even more exciting. I tuck my watch in my pants and dart off towards the front. There's a tree there I can climb and watch.

"Ready or not, here we come," a voice echoes from the front of the building.

Shit! I'm not ready.

My heart is pounding out of my chest with a mixture of fear and excitement. I need to change my plan and hide somewhere back here.

KNOX - I'M A HUNTER, NOT A GATHERER

"READY OR NOT, HERE we come!" I yell out, stepping into the large room.

Emmett was right. This is my wet dream. The feel of the dirt under my feet, the smell of pine in the air, and water? There's water in here?

The sights, the smells, the sounds and the idea that Everlee is out there waiting for me somewhere... hiding. My cock is pressed tight in my pants, begging for relief. So I give it to him. I undress, leaving only my boxers on. The ground is warm under my feet, and soft. It's like I'm walking on clouds.

"Kinky," Emmett teases.

"Shut the fuck up." I groan. "Oh God. I sound like him," I grimace. "You know what? Don't shut the fuck up. Talk the fuck down."

"What?" Jax asks.

"I was trying to think of the opposite of what you say."

"Fucking idiot."

"Love you too."

"How should we do this?" Emmett asks, looking out.

"Teams or no teams?" Callum asks.

"No teams. I say we also make a wager to see who can find and fuck her first," I propose, hopping up and down. Excitement was literally trying to burst out of me. The primal and feral need I have bubbling inside of me to find her first and claim her is ravishing me. It's like it's unlocking every instinct the military beat inside of me, but on a much sexier level. Like those things I tried to push down and hide were smack at the surface.

"Sounds good to me," Jax agrees.

"Same," Callum and Emmett say in unison.

"May the best man win."

"None of us can lose." Emmett winks.

"You're right, but one of us can win more."

"Do you need to go back to school to learn how to English?" Jax says, making fun of me.

"Shut up! I English just fine."

"Ok," he says sarcastically, "I'll just go over here and talk the fuck down."

"No. You can actually shut the fuck up. I think that would be great for all of us." I lurch forward and jump on his back, wrapping my arm around his neck, making him bend over.

He's grabbing and twisting his way out of it seconds later.

"Knox is feisty," Emmett says.

"Knox is very excited," I say, referring to myself in the third person.

"May the best man win," Callum says, sneaking off to the right with Jax on his heels. If Jax were a werewolf, his eyes would be glowing right now. Eager for the hunt. I've seen that look on his face before, many times. He's as excited as I am.

I tear off down the left side, putting distance between Emmett and I. I'm going to win and I know Everlee. She's heading straight for the back and going to work her way to the front. I could wait for her, but where's the fun in that?

I'm a hunter, not a gatherer.

I go after my food, not wait for it to come to me.

That's what she was to me right now, because I will feast on her soon.

I lick my lips in eager anticipation. After the Shibari demonstration, I knew she was eager to feel my cock, our cocks, inside of her. She wasn't even off the stage when she demanded I fuck her and goddamn, it took everything I had to restrain. I have no qualms fucking in front of people, and I don't think she would either. By the end of the demonstration, she was so fucking wet. Part of it had to do with the couple in the corner. I saw her watching them several times.

There's something up ahead on the ground, so I run over to pick it up and smile.

"Everlee," I yell out. "You're playing dirty."

"I found her pants!" Jax yells out. "And her watch!"

"I have her shirt!" I return.

Jax is somewhere to the right of me, but it's hard to tell how far away he is.

So she's in her bra and panties and shoes, at most.

"I've got her bra!" Emmett chimes, somewhere behind me, between Jax and I.

I adjust the band over my cock.

"I'm coming for you Everlee. And when I find you, my cock is going to be so happy," I yell out.

Silence.

Good girl.

Don't give away your location.

I will find you without your help.

Blood pumps through my veins and I feel dialed in.

When I find her... I bite my lip again.

If I don't stop thinking about it, I'm going to blow my load before I even see her.

A limb cracks behind me. Soft. Light. Then stops.

A smile curls on my lips.

I slowly turn and move towards the center of the woods. Of course, she would be in the center and likely working her way back to the front.

But I'm not going to take the easy way to get her.

No. I'm going to hunt her down.

EMMETT - I'M A GATHERER, NOT A HUNTER

MOMENTS EARLIER...

"Come on, it's been ten minutes," Knox whines, eager to go through the doors.

"It's been four."

"Four. Ten. Same difference."

He's excited. He's hard as a rock and ready to fuck.

So am I.

Shit. Watching them on stage with her tied up in rope. I'd heard about Shibari before and never been interested in it. Decorative rope tying. Whatever.

But what I saw tonight...

It was like a fine cuisine. Prepping and preparing the meal and enjoying its beauty before feasting. The control one could exercise over her when she's tied up, and fuck me when she's suspended. The image of her swinging onto my cock over and over again, the power and control of those thrusts, makes me harder with each passing second.

My watch buzzes.

Ten minutes.

"It's time."

"Thank the lords," Knox says, throwing his hands in the air.

As soon as the doors open, Knox yells out, "Ready or not, here we come."

Here we come.

I'm not as in to this as Jax and Knox are. I can literally feel their excitement coming off of them in waves. This is probably the closest thing they've experienced to their past lives since they left. I was scared for a second this was going to trigger something in Knox, because he's never come to terms with what happened there. He just pushes it away, pushes it down, and tries to avoid it, but this. I guess this is different.

This is hunting. There are no bombs, guns, or loud noises that would trigger his PTSD.

In fact, I haven't seen him this pumped in a while. This is the old Knox.

He undresses down to his boxers, leaving a neat pile where he stands.

"Kinky," I say, pumping my eyebrows.

After some more bantering, we split up. Callum and Jax head to the right and Knox and I to the left. I'm pretty sure I have no chance of finding her. Not with Jax and Knox, so amped up and tuned in. But it's ok though. I'll hang out closer to the front and wait for her to come to me. I'm not the hunter and that's fine.

Knox takes off down the path, moving with a lethal precision I've never seen in person. His moves, his footsteps are soundless, like he's moving in a vacuum. I knew he was a good SEAL, too good, some could say. I pause for a second on the trail, watching him until he disappears.

Silence.

A bush shakes to my right. I don't know how far away. Three feet? Ten feet?

Let's explore.

The sticks crunch loudly under my feet. I'm not a ghost like Knox.

I move slowly, walking between bushes and around trees.

"Everlee," Knox yells out. "You're playing dirty."

"I found her pants!" Jax yells out. "And her watch!"

"I have her shirt!" Knox shouts back.

Jax is somewhere to the right of me, but it's hard to tell how far away, and Knox is further up and to the left.

Something catches my attention on the bush, so I slowly walk over to it. A smile tugs at my lips. She's toying with us.

"I've got her bra," I add to the conversation.

"I'm coming for you Everlee. And when I find you, my cock is going to be so happy," Knox yells out.

Silence.

I have to admit, I'm enjoying this a little more than I thought I would and my cock also wants to play. I slip out of my clothes, wearing only my boxers, and leave them beside her bra. Knowing her goal is to get to the front door, and her bra is here and her shirt is further up, she's probably making her way back.

A stick breaks just behind me.

Everlee.

CALLUM - TRAPPED

▪ ▪

"READY OR NOT, HERE we come," Knox cheers out. He's excited. Amped. Ready.

After some banter between the boys, I move to the right and start down the trail. I know I don't have a chance of finding her unless she falls into my lap, which would be most welcome, but doubtful.

She's competitive and will want to win, although part of me knows she's horny. I could see it on her face when she was doing the demo with Knox and it killed me, knowing I couldn't satisfy her. I could only watch.

The dirt under my feet shifts slightly, as the sound of sticks and leaves crumbles under each step. The attention to detail in this room is amazing.

While I'm looking down, trying to figure out if the dirt and sticks are real, Jax speeds past me, moving like a ghost. Soundless.

He's in the zone.

Him and Knox, both.

This is probably the closest they've been to something like this since they left the SEALs. Neither of them talks about it very much, but I have to imagine they're excited about the hunt. I feel something with the whole Hunter Warrior complex, but nothing like them. I can nearly feel their excitement, their arousal, pulsing off of them.

Everlee is the same. The need to win, but also the need to be hunted. I saw it on her face when she was in the room. She's excited.

"Where are you, Everlee?" I whisper to myself, veering off the path into the center.

I pause, waiting for an answer, a hint, a noise, but I'm met with silence. Aside from water off in the distance?

Suddenly, voices yell out. Knox, Jax, then last, Emmett.

Ohhh, that woman. She's teasing us.

If my calculations are correct, she's only wearing panties, but I doubt that because she's Everlee. We just haven't found her panties yet.

Leaves and sticks crunch under my feet, and then I pause, waiting to hear any sign. I'm closer to the front, and know she has to make her way past me. I don't think she has yet, at least I hope so.

I take another step and a twig breaks, so I remove my shoes. Both Knox and Jax did, so there has to be a reason.

When I stand, Emmett and Knox are rushing me.

"What are you doing?" I ask, confused.

"I thought you were Everlee."

"Did you even look at me?" I scoff.

"You were hunched down. I just saw a figure getting low," Emmett says.

"I saw Emmett rushing you, so I thought you were Everlee."

"No. She seems to be a little more difficult to catch than expected."

"We'll catch her, though," Knox says confidently before darting off again.

"We don't have a chance, do we?" Emmett asks.

"Not a chance in hell."

Emmett laughs. "Well?" He holds his hands up.

"True. Although if this is hell..."

"It won't be so bad when you arrive?" Emmett chuckles.

"When we arrive."

"Don't buy yourself long."

"Ok Knox, with your random opposite sayings."

"How else would you say the opposite of not selling your-self short?"

"Should we go wait in the room for Everlee to get back?"

"Let Knox and Jax have fun?" He scrunches his nose.

"True. We shouldn't give up. Who knows what will hap-pen?"

A bush shakes up ahead, closer to the back of the room.

JAX - TRACKER

MY BLOOD IS PUMPING so fast and hard. The feel of the warm soil under my feet, the smell of pine in the air. I'm hunting.

My eyes are laser focused and my ears listen for every breath, every movement. The way the air shifts around me and everyone else in the room.

This is what I love.

What I miss.

"I'm going to find you, Ev, and when I do..."

My cock twitches with excitement.

I undress as I run along the path, tossing my clothes along the way, leaving only my boxers on. I thought about taking them off, but honestly, I don't know if I'd be able to keep my hands off myself. Thinking about Everlee out here somewhere, watching. Waiting.

The sound of water calls my attention, so I move towards it and find something tucked behind a tree. If she tried to hide it, she didn't do a very good job, but something tells me she did a great job. She was trying to make it look like she hid it, but wanted it visible enough for someone to find.

"Everlee," Knox yells out. "You're playing dirty."

"I found her pants!" I yell out, then feel something in her pocket. "And her watch!"

"I have her shirt!" Knox shouts back.

"I've got her bra," Emmett yells out a moment later, some-where in between Knox and I.

"I'm coming for you Everlee. And when I find you, my cock is going to be so happy," Knox yells out.

Silence.

"Where are you, Everlee?"

Based on the triangulation of Knox, Emmett, and I... I'd have to say she was leading us away. She wasn't along the trail. She wouldn't do that. She's in the middle somewhere, likely waiting or working her way back to the front.

I jut off the path and venture into the overgrown center.

"Come out, come out, wherever you are."

A twig breaks ahead, and I freeze. Waiting.

Others are rushing to the sound. My breath hitches in my throat.

Then voices, no squeals. If they found her, there would be squeals and moans.

Most definitely moans.

It's the other three. It sounds like Emmett and Knox found Callum. I toy with the idea of meeting up with them to regroup and lay out a plan, but I don't. She's close by. I can feel it. Her eyes on me. Watching.

I chuckle to myself. I wonder if she would come out if she saw me stroking my cock? I know she wants it. Wants all of us. The way she was flushing and panting on the stage. She was hot and ready.

"I've found her panties!" Callum yells a moment later. He's closer to the front. She's moving. The twigs and bushes are no match for me, as I bat them out of the way easily as I pass. I'm not trying for stealth now, but for speed.

I make it back to the front and stare at the ground, looking for her tracks, but there aren't any. She's not made it back yet. My blood is pulsing through me. She's making this hard and I love it.

God, I fucking love it.

I walk back up the middle.

"I will find you Everlee!"

"Doubt it!" She yells back, and the room falls into silence. She's somewhere near the back, but she's moving. The way her voice was breathy.

With my eyes closed, I replay her delicious taunt and an image of her forms in my head and I see her moving right to left.

I smile and creep to the left.

EVERLEE - PUT A FUCK IN ME, I'M DONE

"Doubt it!" I run across the back away from the water, then pause. I can feel the tenseness in the room. Everyone, everything is silent.

When the boys first came in, I didn't have enough time to get back to the front like I wanted, so I climbed the nearest tree that had a low enough branch. At one point, Emmett was right below me and I was surprised he couldn't hear my heartbeat.

But then something pulled his attention, and I saw him, and a moment later, Knox, running towards it. But it wasn't me.

I climbed down and hugged the right wall, still covered by some taller bushes meant to hide it. I found a few rocks along the base, which must have been extras or something for the water area in the back. I picked one up, slipped off my panties, placed the rock inside, and let them soar to the front of the room, then retreated behind the bushes again and waited for a second.

This is so much better than sardines, because the no orgasms with less than three people rule. I'm pretty sure when one of them finds me, it will be game over. The sexual tension in this room is at a fifty out of ten.

When Jax runs by, I head towards the back, then hear Jax's frustrated yell. Should I have taunted Jax and the boys? No. But I'm enjoying playing the game.

I crawl through the bushes behind the trail. From up in the tree, there looked to be a flat area or a clearing this way. Even from the tree, I couldn't see the entire room, just a sizeable chunk of it. If I would have gone higher, I'd have been fine, but I didn't want to fall and break a bone. That would have ruined the night, and damnit, I want their cocks.

A twig breaks behind me and I freeze.

Silence.

The hair on the back of my neck is standing on end. I'm being watched. Shit!

I slowly turn around. My heart is beating a hole through my chest, my skin is tingling like electricity is pulsing through it.

Nothing. I don't see anything.

Perhaps I didn't hear anything, or maybe it was further away than I thought?

I take another tentative step, and then another.

My shoulders relax and I start moving with ease, but slower. I don't think I'm out of the woods yet.

HA! I can be in an intense, overly sexualized situation and still make a funny.

Go me!

Another twig cracks.

This one is definitely closer.

I'm being followed.

I don't even bother to turn around. My body is going crazy, yelling, screaming at me to run. So I do. I run, zigzagging through trees and around bushes. I'm not quite, but neither are they. They're gaining on me.

I chance a glance and there's no one there.

What in the hell?

When I look forward again, a figure is standing there and I run straight into them.

Knox.

That wily little shit.

"Got you," he says, smiling, his hands clamped on the upper part of my arm near my shoulders.

"Do you?" I twist out of his grip, put him in side control, then flip him onto the ground and run. I've not used that since my black belt test, and I think the fact he wasn't expecting it helped me out.

He's laughing behind me, and I know it's only a matter of time before he gets me again. He's trained for this and he's fast and that look in his eyes... he's also hungry.

Part of me wants to let him have me and ravage me because fuck, it would feel so good, but the other part knows it will be even better the more he fights for it and the more I try to run from it.

Confusion clouds my thinking. Knox didn't sound the alarm and tell the guys where I was.

No. He's keeping quiet.

Hunting me for himself.

My stomach tightens.

He's close again. The leaves ruffle behind me, but I don't turn around.

The clearing is up ahead and I run towards it, pushing past the bushes and trees.

A hand grips around my wrist, spinning me around. I swing my arm, but he's ready, and grabs it. His hands are wrapped around both of my wrists, and I look down at his beautifully tattooed body. I thought about kneeing him. It would be my only play, but I don't want to get away from him that badly. Plus, hurting him would hurt me.

He pulls my arms down with a gentle force, pinning them beside my hips just behind my back, and drives me backwards. My back stings as he pushes me up against a tree, his face inches from mine.

"Nice maneuver back there. I wasn't expecting it." He's panting and his eyes are wild. Laser focused.

"Thanks. And I know." I tilt my chin up defiantly.

A grumble rumbles low in his chest. His eyes are intense and focused on me. "Earlier," he starts and pauses. "On the stage." He presses his hard cock against my slick pussy and we both suck in a breath. He lifts my arms above my head, pinning them to the tree, and passes my one wrist to the other, so he has them both in his left hand. "When I said..."

His eyes penetrate mine, my stomach is in knots, and my heart is pounding.

"I meant it." He rests his forehead against mine and closes his eyes, breathing me in. Breathing us in.

"I love you too, Knox."

His eyes spring open and there's a hint of surprise, like he expected me to say something else, or perhaps nothing at all. It's gone in a flash though, as his lips take mine in an unforgivingly passionate kiss. The emotion laced through the kiss is... breathtaking. Is that the right word? His glimpse of vulnerability makes me want to wrap him in my arms and hold him tightly... after we fuck. Because, priorities and what not.

"Fuck me, Knox."

"Yes, Madame McKinley."

I throw my leg around his waist and use my heel to bring him to me.

"You've been a bad girl."

My hand slides down to grab his thick, hard cock. I slowly glide my hand along his length and listen to his breathing stutter.

"A very bad girl."

When my hand gets to the base of his cock, I continue it down further and rub them over his balls and squeeze gently. He raises on his toes a little.

"Fuck. A very, very bad girl." He hunches over, nibbling on my neck before he sucks my fevered skin into his mouth. "Trying to trick us. Tease us."

"I was playing to win."

"Too bad you lost."

"Did I?" I push him off me, then dart around the tree. I've never seen this side of Knox before. The hunter.

He laughs, standing by the tree watching me run further away from him. My heart is pulsing with anticipation. I know he's going to catch me, but this running. This running is hot.

I dart to the right and see the clearing up ahead, a small hill with grass that ends at the wall. I've run the entire length of the room and can go no further. The second I turn around, Knox is on me. He grabs me, spinning me around and I trip, falling towards the ground. He lurches forward, grabbing me as we both fall, cradling me towards the ground.

"Well, that worked out better than I planned." His hand is pinned under me and his cock is pressed into the side of my leg. "Are you done running now?"

"Do you want me to be?"

He looks at me curiously for a moment, like he's surprised I noticed how much he enjoys this. The chase.

He shakes his head slowly, like he's having a conversation with himself, and then his eyes see me again. He's back.

"These marks." He pulls his hand out from underneath me and traces the rope marks over my body. He slowly slides down my body and kisses them, trailing from the top of my neck to between my breasts. "Did you like being tied up?"

His question feels heavy. Like there's another message underneath it, but I don't know what it is, so I simply answer the one he asks, "I did."

He smiles, sliding further down my body. He leaves a trail of kisses over my stomach to the inside of my right leg, then over to the left.

My body is writhing in near pain as the anticipation of what's next tingles inside of my body. My pussy is pulsing, in need of something to fill it. He runs his nose up my center and I try not to cringe at the thought of him smelling down there. I've been butt ass naked running around in this made up forest for who knows how long. My ass has touched bark, leaves, and dirt.

Bertha is sitting in a tree eating popcorn, watching with her handy dandy opera glasses... with night vision. The green glow is illuminating her face.

He looks up at me from between my legs. Our eyes lock. He tilts his chin down, eyes still locked, and licks from the bottom to the top. His eyes roll into the back of his head momentarily before they land on me again. He does it one more time and pauses, "My favorite thing in the world is watching your face the first time I taste you."

My chest flutters.

"You do this little nibble thing with your lips and your eyes close just for a second. It's like your body is just..." he sighs. "It's the best fucking thing. Well, second to this." He dives back into my pussy with speed. Licking and sucking on my clit as his tongue fucks me.

My hands grab his head and I hold him there, my body taking. God, this feels so fucking good. I'm not shy about what I want. What I need.

A moan escapes my lips and a few seconds later, several fucks echo through the room like owls hooting on a cold winter's night.

Knox's hand grabs around my ass and pulls me towards him like he can't get enough of me, which turns me on even more. I press my palm to his head, pushing him away and quickly crawl over to him. I don't want him thinking I'm about to run again, because there's no way in hell I'm going to run.

No. Running is over. It's time for fucking.

I push him backwards, and he tumbles with ease. I crawl over his body, his cock sliding along my pussy. My eyes roll into the back of my head, as the feeling is almost too good to control. My lips find his as I give him a quick kiss, and then suck his bottom lip into my mouth. I pull away, then look at him. "I'm going to sit on your face and you're going to eat me out until I come all over your tongue and then I'll let you fuck me."

His eyes grow wide. "Yes, ma'am."

His words do something to me. Give me a feeling of power. I continue to climb up his body and plant my pussy over his face. "Bon appétit."

His hands reach up and grab onto my thighs and he brings me down. Another loud moan escapes as my back arches and my head looks towards the sky.

"Yes. Yes, Knox. Fuck. Shit. Oh, my." Words continue to flow out of my mouth as my orgasm builds quickly. "Yes."

"No," a voice whines.

My head falls back to level, but Knox doesn't stop. Emmett, Jax, and Callum just arrived on the scene. "I'll call you Hansel and Gretel. Your moans are like breadcrumbs leading us right to you," Jax says.

I smile, but it's wiped from my face as my orgasm slams into me. "Oooh," I moan out, grabbing my breasts, then reach out to them.

Jax walks over and his cock is right by my face. I grab it and bring him the rest of the way towards me, sucking it into my mouth, hard and fast.

"Fuck. She's hungry."

I bob on his cock a few times before he pulls out. "No come for you, darling. I want to unload inside of your pussy tonight. I want to feel it wrapped around my cock."

"Samesies," Callum jokes.

Knox rolls us over and flips me onto all fours. "Fucking perfect ass." He leans down and bites it before giving it a kiss. He presses his cock at my entrance and I gasp out.

"Are you going to be a good girl and take our cocks?"

I glare at him over my shoulder.

"Answer me, love, or no cock for you."

I press back onto him, sinking onto his cock. "You be good boys and fuck me like you hate me."

"Goddamn, Trouble."

"Put her on stage with a domme one time and all the sudden she's Madame McKinley," Knox says.

"If I wanted to be your domme, I'd buy a strap on and peg you."

"Would you make us peg for it?" Knox laughs at his play on words before taking my hips and thrusting into me.

I groan out. The feel of his cock driving deep inside of me is both painful yet pleasurable.

"How about this?" Knox asks. "Shut the fuck up and take our cocks like a good girl."

I press back into him.

"She likes that," Jax says.

Knox unloads with a speed he's never fucked me with before, using my hips to push and pull. Claiming me.

I look over my shoulder and see the boys standing around Knox, with the cocks in their hands, rubbing slowly, watching him fuck me. My stomach tightens even more. I swear it's like a core workout the amount of times my body clenches just watching them.

"Everlee. Your pussy." His hand runs up my back and presses down between my shoulder blades, holding me there. "Fuck. You feel so good."

"Hurry up. I'm next," Jax demands.

"You can't rush," his words are cut off as he unloads inside of me. His cock is throbbing in my pussy. "Ok. Maybe you can." He pauses before pulling out. "But for the record, it's because her pussy is a tight little honey pot, not because you told me to."

He's gone for a second before I feel Jax. He presses in and his cock feels different. He has a slightly larger girth, so I feel myself stretching around him.

"Yes." He picks up where Knox left off, with my face planted on the ground and my ass up in the air. "I've wanted you around my cock for most of the evening. And then," he pauses, seating himself deep inside of me and pausing, before he squeezes my ass cheeks together. "On stage."

He pulls out and quickly flips me over, pulls my legs up and lifts my ass off the ground and continues fucking me. "You feel so fucking good."

The pad of his thumb finds my clit, and he rubs again. "Jax," I moan out.

"That's right baby girl, moan my name," Jax rasps. He rolls my legs back so my knees are on my chest and my toes are close to touching the ground behind me. He's fucking me from on top and the pressure is almost too much, but I'm not going to say a fucking word. I love this. The feeling of him this deep inside of me.

After a few minutes, he lets my legs go and they fall to the ground, giving me more control. I press my heels to the warm, soft grass and raise my hips, fucking him back until the only sound are the wet thwaps of us colliding against one another and the moans and groans coming from us.

Electricity tickles my skin as another orgasm is coming, like a wave building in an ocean. My fingers claw and latch onto his back, holding him near me. I want more of him. My fingers slide up to his hair, locking in to give me control. I tilt his chin up to take him in a kiss, but his eyes... they meet mine and I don't get a chance to move before he does. He kisses me strong and powerful, his tongue matching his thrusts. I wrap my legs around his waist and he lifts us up in one move, so I'm sitting on his lap.

I cry out as his cock fills me deeper than it ever has before.

My hands fall back to support me and he fucks me from underneath in this new V shape. The pressure inside makes it feel like I'm being punched, but his finger on my clit is sending me reeling.

"Oh, fuck," I moan, my eyes fluttering. "Oh, Jax."

The orgasm is upon me. If I was a super religious woman, I'd start tapping the cross into my head and chest, because this one... It's intense. He grabs my hair, pulling it back so

I'm looking at the fake moon in the sky while he continues to fuck up into me, my orgasm crashing around us all.

He leans forward and takes a breast in his mouth, his teeth clamping down on my nipple, sending waves of passionate desire straight to my needy cunt. My eyes have rolled into the back of my head and there are sounds coming out of me that are a cross between and ooh and a fuck, but sound more like a troll under a bridge getting off his ass with busted knees.

Jax pulls me back up so I'm straddling him and fully seated on him, my muscles too weak to move. A devilish smile crosses his lips. He pulls out and flips us over so I'm on my knees, the way we started. He grips my hips with both of his hands, his fingers digging in and pounds into me relentlessly.

"Fill me with your come Jax," I groan out.

"Fuck." His grunts echo around the room until he presses into me deep and holds, his moans rolling in waves as his cock explodes his warm release inside of me.

"My turn," Emmett says, stepping in where Jax left. His cock fits in nicely, the ripples of his Jacob's ladder sending waves of pleasure through me. He's slow, pressing in and pulling out as he savors my heat and the feel of my pussy. "So fucking beautiful," he says in a low voice.

He plants kisses down my spine and when he gets to my ass... I suck in a breath. Nervous excitement pulses through every fiber inside of me. He swipes his tongue over my hole and I moan so fucking loud, my face sinks and melts into the ground. Never in one thousand hundred million fifty billion quadrillion years did I ever think I would let anyone's lips or tongue at my entrance. No, that is forbidden, but goddamn, the way he eats it... Fuck. Me.

He slides his fingers inside of my pussy, coating them and pulls out. A warmness- Jax's, Knox's, and mine combined releases, trickles down my leg. He takes their lubrication and rubs it over my asshole and presses a finger in. I moan again into the ground, fairly certain I bit off some of the perfectly manicured lawn into my mouth. Something to add in the future. Edible rooms.

His fingers pulse slowly in as he gets their release and uses it as lube. He's slow, methodical, taking his time. It's torture, but so welcome. Emmett is my teddy bear.

Teddy bear who loves asses as much as you do now, apparently.

He adds a second finger and works my hole; I hope prepping me for his cock. I love his cock in tight places, either in my ass or coupled with Jax's.

"Are you ready for me, love?" His words flow across my body like warm silk.

"Yes."

He lifts behind me and presses his cock at my entrance, sliding his clean fingers inside of my pussy to get more come and glides it along his cock. The sight of watching him coat his cock in our combined release is so fucking hot. He slowly pushes in at my entrance, the ring at the tip sending a shiver down my spine. He grips my hips and glides in slowly, letting me stretch around him, pausing at the tight ring of muscle.

"How are you doing, Trouble?"

"Good," I grunt out.

He slowly runs his hand up my spine as he pulls out until the tip is just left in, then pushes in again as his hands slides down. He works his way in, further and further, until he is fully inside of me. He holds there for a second and slowly pulls out, this time pushing back in a little faster.

"Oh Emmett," I moan.

He picks up speed, at the same time I push back on him. I glance over my shoulder and watch him watching his cock disappear into my ass. His teeth are scraping across his bottom lip and his hand is pressed into my back.

"I love watching your ass take my cock," he says, noticing me looking at him.

"Fuck me," I plead. The ribs of his rings ripple through my ass, sending waves of pleasure throughout my entire body.

He looks up at me, studying my face, like he's scared he's going to hurt me or I can't take more. I press back into him, swallowing his cock with my ass, and let out a growl. "More," I command.

"Fuck E, give her what she wants," one of the guys calls out.

I can feel the hesitation in his moves, so I pull myself off his cock and press back again, and again. I'm fucking his cock for several thrusts until something inside of him changes and he unleashes his power on me. His fingers clamp into my hips and he fucks me. Fucks me like he never has before.

"You're so fucking tight," he moans out in heady frustration. "I won't be able to last long. Fuck."

My head falls to the ground as I let him have control over me and then I remember I'm being fucked so now I'm pretty sure have a huge ass grass and or dirt stain on my forehead. Son of a bitch! And I can't wipe it off because I'm being fucked on my knees and the speed with which he's moving right now is not enough for one arm to hold up my body. I'd likely face plant, only making the stains on my face worse. No. I'd just have to wait.

He shifts his stance and all the sudden he's hitting some place new and I nearly buck off the ground. "Oh."

"Do you like that, Trouble?"

"I love everything."

"Yes, you do." His clean fingers move to my clit and he begins to circle and press, in sync with his thrusts.

Desire is pulsing inside of me, swirling around me, consuming me. His hips jerk up, hitting that magic spot, and I combust. I wasn't even prepared for it. I scream out at the same time he releases inside of me. I feel like my body is being ripped apart at the seams, but in the best possible way. I'm convulsing and shaking around him, my body out of control, moving and twitching. My toes curl up, pleading for my muscles to release. The orgasm lasts longer than any other orgasm I've ever had.

Once Emmett is done, he leans over and kisses my back before he pulls out.

"Are you ok?" he whispers in my ear.

"So good."

Callum steps up and rolls me over, looking at my very satiated body. "Can you handle me?" His words are free of judgement, hopefulness, irritation or any other feeling you may expect him to have. No. His words are laced with compassion and concern.

"Yes, sir."

"Oh, baby," he says softly, lowering his body on top of mine. "You seem well fucked. I don't want to hurt you."

"I need you Callum." I didn't mean for my words to sound like a plea, but they did. I wanted all of my guys. I didn't want him to see me as someone who can't handle a few fucks. Although, I've been fucking for a while, but that doesn't matter.

He kisses me softly, tenderly and adjusts his cock, sliding into me. My back arches off the ground as he presses all the way in, but he's slow, gentle. His lips press against mine and he kisses me. Soft, passionate. There's so much feeling in his kiss that I nearly melt into him and into this ground.

His hips rock softly. "You feel so good."

"So I've heard." I wink.

He chuckles and presses his forehead to mine. "You are ours; you know that?" The layer and feeling is deep in his words, like if I didn't know I was theirs, then he would burn the world down to prove it.

I nod slowly, my stomach twisting in knots.

"We've been a unit for a long time, but until you... we weren't a *unit*. If that makes sense."

I nod my head, thinking I know what he's saying.

His hips continue to thrust into me slowly, almost like he's making...

Before I can finish thinking my thought, his words rip through any wonder. Any confusion. "I love you, Everlee.

So much so that the thought of losing you sometimes feels like a dagger in my heart."

My throat seizes and I forget how to swallow.

"You... God... you are perfect in every way and I hope you know that."

I nod.

He smiles and takes my lips in a soft kiss, his tongue slowly dancing, pressing inside of my mouth. My arms wrap around his neck as I hold him to me, taking him all. His cock, his tongue and his love, and then I push him away. "I love you, too."

Tears stream out of my eyes.

He tilts his head to the side and stares at me. "Love, don't cry."

"I'm just so happy. Happier than I've ever been in my entire life. You guys... you are... words can't explain the way I feel or what you do to me. I don't know how I got so lucky and never in a million years is this where I thought I'd end up."

He smiles. "Getting fucked on your back, in some fake woods, under a fake moon, in the basement of a sex club?"

"Hopefully our sex club." I smile.

"You want it?"

I nod, "Very much."

"We'll look at the paperwork this week and if all looks good, we'll present her an offer."

Just like that. No questions. No doubt.

I tangle my fingers in his hair and pull him down to me, kissing him hard. All the emotion and exhaustion swelling inside of me until I have nothing else to give.

"Fuck me hard, Callum."

"Do you want to go to bed?"

I smile at him. I don't want to say yes, because I don't necessarily. I just want all my guys around me right now.

He kisses my nose. "I think you've been fucked hard enough for the night, but I will finish."

He presses inside of me, thrusting deep and rolling his hips. His lips move from my cheek to under my jaw. Tingles run down my body, through my nipples to my clit, causing goosebumps to spread like wildfire on my skin. My head rolls over to the side, giving him more access as he continues to glide inside of me slowly, but fully. I don't know if we've ever fucked this slowly, but it's... unbelievable. So much feeling and passion in each thrust.

My body starts to piston and thrust like a wave under his steady pace. "More," I cry out, needing to feel all of him inside of me.

He laughs, a heady laugh. "I'll give you anything you want, Everlee. You just ask."

"Anything?" I know there are guardrails on the statement. I don't know if he would give me anything, but maybe. And I don't know what I'm thinking right now, but I can't help but wonder if that includes kids. I don't want them now, but that doesn't mean in the future I won't. The longer I'm with them, the more I want mini versions of them running around, but I know what I've agreed to and I won't let that get in the way. They are enough for me. They complete me, but...

Callum's pace picks up the slightest as he's nearing completion. My fingers dig into his ass cheeks as I hold him to me.

He thrusts several more times, then grunts before he collapses on me.

"Next time you can be first, so you aren't fucking a sack of potatoes."

He laughs, propping himself on his elbows, looking at me. "You could never be a sack of potatoes, love."

We lay there for one more second. I hadn't noticed before, but the others had left, giving us our space and privacy. This felt more intimate, and it wasn't just because of the full moon.

Callum stands up and reaches his hand down to help me up. "Let's get you bathed."

"My favorite part of being with you all is the aftercare. Well, second favorite part, obviously. Your cocks are pretty great."

"They are, aren't they?"

I'm still chuckling as he scoops me into his arms.

"We're at the very back of the room."

"I don't care. I will not make you walk back."

"I could."

"Just because you can doesn't mean I will let you." He kisses my forehead.

I don't know how long we walk for, but the soft jostle back-and-forth lulls me into a deep relaxed state. By the time we're in the room, I'm in that space between awake and asleep.

"Did you break her?" Knox jokes from across the room.

"Tub is ready," Emmett says.

He's standing beside a large black glossy tub with golden feet. Its backdrop is an elegantly designed accent wall. It's a deep red color with a black trim tacked on with curves and lines. Dark, to go with the theme of Infernus, but also exquisite.

Once in the tub, I lean back and let my body relax, as the sting from the heat relaxes my muscles and soothes me into a lull. I assume Emmett added some sort of essential oil, because lavender, eucalyptus and another scent dance around me.

The boys move around the tub, and wash, massage, and in general, just soothe me. I catch Jax's eye, but he says nothing and before I can speak, my eyes are rolling into the back of my head. Emmett is massaging my scalp and if I had any moans left, I would, but my little moan box is empty.

Knox picks up my foot and I'm out.

Put a fuck in me, I'm done.

Fork.

Shit!

Put a fork in me, I'm done.

Although I guess either could really apply here.

EVERLEE - VOLITUS, VOLITUS, VOLITUS!

IT'S BEEN A FEW days since our trip to the sex club. We stayed the night and left the next morning around five, which made for a long workday. It just felt... weird. To go from the sex club life, seeing all the kinks and masks, and... everything. To just flipping a switch and coming back to my normal corporate nine to five. Part of me wants to walk away from it and fully immerse myself in that environment, but that's weird. Right?

I don't hate my job, but there's just something that seems so different there. A level of love, acceptance, exploration.

And with =D=N and Infernus, those rates were crazy. To have that kind of money to spend on sex club memberships means they have to have a lot more money, which means they are likely to have some very high-paying jobs.

Do I walk around the office now and look at all the executives who are making half a million or more a year and wonder...

Yes. Yes, I do.

Do I also have this game called match the kink?

Yes. Yes, I do.

Lizzy wanted to meet the day after, but our schedules haven't lined up, which, as anyone can guess, is driving her absolutely crazy. I'm honestly surprised she hasn't shown up on my doorstep pounding it down, but she's been fairly busy on her own with a couple of dinners with Tony and some wedding planning stuff. Some vendors are making her pick a date and I'm fairly certain she's floating June ninth, which makes my heart sing.

The one night she had free, I had a meeting with the guys and the lawyers to go over final numbers for the offer they have plans to present tomorrow. I thought it was weird to do business on a Saturday, but they all play in a different field than I'm used to. They're playing the World Cup and I'm trying to find a baseball.

Callum's taken the lead on most of the financials for this project and has been meeting with the guy's lawyers and accountants all week to dig through business records and make sure everything looks good. Last night, Callum walked us through the offer and everyone seemed on board, which is exciting.

The guys seem to be a little concerned I'm going to have issues with them owning a sex club. While Callum had initially offered for me to be a part of it, I thought it best to just let the boys own it. It's not about the long-term commitment and what not, but it just felt weird to not be contributing anything financially to the deal, but to reap the benefits. I mean, they've already given me a house and four cocks. A girl cannot be too greedy.

Lizzy is coming over tonight and the guys asked that I hold off on discussing Allure, well, the potential ownership of it. Obviously she's going to ask me all about being there since she saw me, but there are bets on if she will approach it per the rules and guidelines or if she will lose her shit and forget or ignore them. All the guys think the latter, but I bet them she will say the magic word.

The doorbell rings at ten after six. Before the door is even fully open, she's yelling "Volitus, Volitus, Volitus!" and pushing her way in.

I step back a few inches so I'm not mauled by the overactive Lizzy that's barreling through the door. "Good evening to you. Volitus," I respond. Saying the word makes me feel a little like a badass or like I'm part of some secret society. I guess I kind of am, which, again, makes me almost too hot to trot.

She fully walks into the house and then grabs her arms. "Jesus fuck Everlee! It's colder than a witch's titties in a brass bra in here! What is your thermostat set to?"

"Oh sorry. I was cleaning and got hot. I think it's set to like sixty something."

"Well, not sixty-nine. My skin can tell when it's sixty-nine. Like a seventh sense."

"Don't you mean sixth?"

"No. My sixth, aka my sexth, is knowing when you've got some. Although, I think you're trying to overload the sensor because it's always pinging lately." She bats her hand, "But that's neither here nor there. Tell me all about Allure!" She walks into the kitchen and starts rifling through the cabinets and fridge, pulling out glasses, juices, and liquor.

"Is there something I can help you with?" I love how she makes herself at home. It's been a long time since we were roommates and while I loved it, she was intense. I had moved out of her place when I thought I was taking things to the next level with Rich and then when that didn't work out, I just thought it was a good idea to have my own place. She was always going out, and I needed time to decompress and just focus on me and what I wanted.

She fixes us each a drink, then hands me the glass and walks past me, opening the French doors to the patio. "Oh, we are definitely talking out here. It's like a freaking ice box in there."

We talk about all things Allure, then order some sushi and talk some more. I can't remember the last time we talked this much. It's nice. Probably the nicest part is that we aren't talking in a crowded restaurant and I didn't have a permanent blush on my face from all the inappropriate words or hand gestures she'd be making.

"So, when are you going to move in with the boys? Like officially?"

"What do you mean?"

"You're always over there. I can tell because you hardly have anything in your house. You still haven't decorated it and it's been almost two months."

"I've been busy."

She throws her head back, laughing. "Yea. Busy fucking. Which doesn't count. I mean yes, but no. The problem is that you have been spending all your time over there. Tell me. When was the last time you slept in your own bed?"

I stuffed the second to last piece of sushi in my mouth.

"Ex-ash-ly. You haven't."

"I don't know. It's an enormous commitment."

She puckers her lips.

"It is," I whine.

She taps her chest like a singer who's about to perform, stands up and holds her hand out, "Bullll shiiiit. Bullshit, bullshit, bullshittttt," she belts as loud as an opera singer.

"What in the fuck are you doing?" I grab her arm trying to swing it down, as if it's the lever for her volume.

"I thought it was obvious. I'm calling you on your bullshit."

"Oh no. It wasn't before, but now you've really cleared it up."

"Good. Because if you didn't get it, I was going to get another round and then go for an encore."

"Man. I hate I missed it," I drone sarcastically.

"Never fear, my dear. I will give you a second round."

"Pass."

She laughs and walks over to me. "You pass on me. On my encore. I worked very hard on that song, I'll have you know."

"I could tell. The key change for the third bullshit really stretched your vocal range."

"You noticed?" She clasps her chest. "My vocal coach said I shouldn't, but I said nay. I shall push my boundaries for my boo boo."

I have no words and just shake my head.

"Have you talked to the guys about a cookout at their place on Monday?"

"I forgot." With everything going on with Allure, it had completely slipped my mind.

"Well, thank God I reminded you. It would have been super awkward to show up with a cooler of drinks and my fruit platter with no party."

"Somehow, I doubt they would blink an eye."

"What's that supposed to mean?"

"That they have found a way to love you and accept you for the gem you are."

"I feel like that was a backhanded compliment or something, but I stopped processing after you said they love me!"

"How can they not?"

"You know, I've said the same thing about all my exes. How could they let all this go?"

"Well, thank the lords they did, because you were able to find Tony."

Her bottom lip sticks out. "Aww. And that's why you're my maid of honor." She bats at the tip of my nose.

"So I guess that also means you didn't ask about the Rainbows and Unicorns party?"

"Actually, that, I did."

"Really? What did they say?"

"They loved it, and I gave you all the credit. Emmett is already working on a themed drink."

"Do I smell a taste test at the party on Monday? I mean I will test them if I have to. Plus, I just want to be at Vixen and be like boo-yah bitches, I already tried this drink, and it's the bomb. Ooh, I could walk around getting people interested in them."

"If you're working there, then you wouldn't be able to partake in the pleasures of the drink."

"True." She points at me. "Scratch that. This mama needs to drinky drink. BUT! And I say this… he needs to incorporate cotton candy in it! What goes better with unicorns and rainbows than cotton candy?"

"That's a good point. I will have to tell him."

"Excellent. Tell him I expect to have several samples to try on Monday at the party."

"That we aren't sure we're having yet."

"You kid."

I wasn't kidding.

"We can be here around sixish. That will give you all enough time to fuck or something and then get hamburgers and all that stuff prepared."

"Is there anything else you need to plan?"

"Goodness to Betsy no! This wedding is enough."

"You have a date yet?"

She winks at me.

"Oh, thank you! I was hoping you were going to pick that date."

"Girl. When June ninth falls on a Saturday, you have to get married on the day!"

"No truer words have been spoken."

A silence falls on the air as we just sit outside and listen to the night insects serenade us with their symphony.

After several minutes, Lizzy pops up in her seat. "What time is it?"

I glance at my watch. "Just after ten."

"Do you want to go get in their hot tub? Or should I say yours?"

"We can."

I pull up my phone and login to the app and turn the heaters on. They usually have it programmed to turn on at midnight in case they want to get in when they get home.

A minute later, my watch is vibrating.

Jax: What do you think you're doing?

Everlee: Lizzy and I are getting in the hot tub.

Jax: Go on.

I chuckle.
Everlee: Stop.
Jax: You ladies have fun.
Everlee: We will.
"All good?" Lizzy asks, gathering up the glasses and trash.
"Yes. Jax was just wondering what was going on."
She let out a hum, but says nothing.
"Do you need a bathing suit?"
"Do bra and panties count?"
"I'm fine with it if you are."

JAX - TO SAY OR NOT TO SAY

My phone feels like a brick in my pocket, after I send my last message to Everlee. I want to pull it back out and stare at the message or send her another one. I'm regretting not getting cameras installed before so I can watch her. Not in a creepy way. Just...

All the guys have said they love her except me and it's not because I don't. I do. She's great. Better than great. The way she is around Callum. What she's done and is doing for Knox. Emmett. He's just over the moon.

I just feel like if I say it now then it's because they did and she won't think I mean it, but now it's been days and it's beginning to be too long.

Fuck!

I fall onto the couch and lay here for a second looking up at the ceiling. What am I doing? I was not supposed to fall in love with a chick. We were going to be bachelors forever. I know that doesn't seem likely, but that was the plan until her.

"Everything ok?" Callum opens the door and walks in.

I roll off the couch and plant my feet on the floor. "All is gravy, brother."

"That good? Do you want to talk about it?"

"Nope."

"Everlee in the hot tub?"

"Yea. Her and Lizzy."

"Oh, boy."

"Yea."

Callum's eyes are like lasers, burning a hole in the side of my face. He's concerned about me, and really he doesn't need to be, but I guess he doesn't know that. I sigh, "I haven't told Ev I love her."

"Has she said it to you?" he asks, stepping a foot closer to me.

He clearly thinks he's made it past the outer barrier he says I constantly keep up. One thing he says I need to work on, but he's said that since we were little. When we moved into our first foster house, I went into it unknowingly. I thought our dad was going to find us, come track us down, but he never showed up and the couple that was supposed to watch over us were a bunch of cunt bags. They were using their home to get money and treated us like complete shit. I started running away, because I didn't want to stay and one time ran into Mrs. Mary. She was different, loving. She made me miss what I never had. Made me want it. I was terrified of getting hurt or being let down, so I built up walls and shut people out. I mean, I gave them a peek inside through little windows I was forced to carve out, but no one ever really saw the real me. It's what made me so good in the Navy.

Methodical.

Emotionless.

When I came back, Callum had pushed me to open up and talk about my feelings, but that's not me. Occasionally, when I'm with her, they come out. She allows me to let down my guard, but then I get scared. So I fight it.

"Jax? Has she said it to you?"

"What? No, but I think it's because she doesn't want to pressure me..."

"Or maybe it's because she's scared."

"You think?"

He shrugs. "You're a hard man to read sometimes."

I roll my eyes. "Same story, different day."

"Well..." He walks over to the desk and pulls out two glasses and a bottle of Blanton's.

"Why not?"

He pours me two ounces neat then slides the glass across the desk. I sit in the chair across from him and can feel the words on the tip of my tongue. I want to let him in, but I've kept him out for so long. I'm scared that once I remove one brick, the entire wall will fall like dominoes and that's not something I'm ready for, or will ever be ready for.

"This is good." I hold up the glass.

"I know. One of my favorites."

"Hey," I pause, taking another sip. "Did you ever get all the tops?"

"Tops?"

"Of the Blanton's bottles? I know when I left for my tour, you had just started trying to collect them all."

"Oh. Yea. No. I never did. I think I had B, A, N, and T. I kept trying to find the other letters, but had the hardest time. All the N's I was finding were the first one."

"Shame."

"Yea. I could have hung it on my wall up here or something."

"It would look nice. Where are the tops now?"

"I don't know. Probably in some storage case stuffed in a bedroom closet." He laughs. "I see what you're doing."

"What am I doing?"

"Getting me to talk about bourbon, so I'll stop trying to pry into you."

Busted.

"Hey." He knocks back the rest of his drink. "How about you take the rest of the night?"

"It's almost eleven. You still have three hours."

"I know. It's fine. I have Knox here."

"You say that like it's a good thing."

He laughs and knows I'm kidding. Knox is like my little brother. When he came to the house, he stuck to us like glue. To me especially. It was probably my outgoing, open personality that said please talk to me. No matter how rude I was to him, or how many times I tried to push him away, he always stayed around. One time, in school, some kids were making fun of me and my brother. Callum wasn't there, but Knox was. He stepped up in those guys' faces and ripped them a new one. He was at least an entire head shorter than their shortest guy, but he didn't care. *Nobody messes with his brother.*

Little shit stain got under my skin then, so I took him under my wing. I think it was all part of his master plan and he's playing some long game. I'm just waiting for the other shoe to fall, but it hasn't yet. He annoys the piss out of me most hours of most days, but he's the most loyal jackhole there is and I wouldn't have it any other way.

"Oh stop. He's really been stepping up lately. He was never a bad business partner, but I can tell he wants to take a more active role in all of our business dealings."

"You going to let him run Allure?"

"Well, Sammie has to accept our offer."

"It's a very attractive offer. It's going to make us a lot less liquid for the next several years, on top of making it difficult to invest in anything."

"I know."

"But Everlee wants it," I mock, repeating his words back to him.

"Yes, but it's also a great investment. Have you seen her numbers? The growth year over year, hell, period over period is crazy."

"That growth is not sustainable long term."

"I know, but why not ride the wave while he can? Plus, I think Everlee has some great ideas. Apparently, she reads lots of smutty books."

"Makes sense."

"Anyway, she thinks there would be a huge market for smutty book clubs at the sex club. Doing themed books. I'm willing to try it out. Sammie had a list of ideas she wanted to still do, and a lot of them are great."

"So we're going back into the sex club business."

"I hope so. We'll find out tomorrow."

Our phones dinged at the same time.

Everlee.

"Shit," I moan, reading the text.

Ding!

Knox. "Of course he'd be all for it."

"Looks like we're grilling out Monday," Callum cheers.

"She really has taken over our lives."

"You love it."

I grumble my response.

His phone chimes again.

"Looks like Lizzy just left, head over there. Just spend some time with her alone."

I snarl my lip at him. "Fine."

"I don't want to force you to spend time with someone you want to spend time with."

"Shut it." I set the glass back on the desk and grab my keys off the hook on the wall. "I'll see you when you get home."

"Try not to fuck her."

"No promises."

There were no promises, but it was mostly to myself. I could say that I would not fuck her and have every intention of not fucking her, but she has this way. It angers me, but then she smiles and presses harder because she's fucked in the head and loves it... and I love her.

EVERLEE - COME SPLATS ARE NOT KUMQUATS

WELL, THAT SEEMED TO go better than expected. Lizzy made me send the invite to the cookout for Monday at their house. I told her I would talk to them about it tomorrow, but she made some quip about how I would be fucking them and then forget and she really didn't want to show up with the fruit platter and no party.

Which I don't get because she hates fruit platters. She always complains about the fruit touching and how the flavors mingle.

I wave her goodbye and watch her climb into Betty's car. We chat for a bit about my brother and his cute boyfriend and how precious they are together before she takes off.

The house feels so much quieter now that Lizzy isn't here, but fortunately, a wave of exhaustion passes through me. My yawn carries me upstairs, so I take a quick shower to wash the chlorine off, then climb into bed. I double check to make sure the alarm on my phone is still set for fifteen after two. It's when I usually move to the group bed, to limit the time I'm by myself. It's too big without them, so when I move into the room like a half-dead zombie, I can fall asleep pretty quickly before they get home.

The alarm panel dings and I stir from my sleep. I grab my phone and see it's only been thirty minutes and panic courses through me. They shouldn't be home yet. Is someone breaking in? My door creaks open and an enormous figure is standing there staring at me. My heart is pounding through my chest, and then he calls my name.

"Squirt?" he whispers. "Are you still awake?"

Jax.

My pulse slows. "No. I'm sleeping. This is her night time ghost that watches over her," I whisper back.

"Dumbass," he huffs and walks into the room.

He strips out of his clothes, leaving only his boxers on, and climbs into bed, laying on his back. I roll over to face him. "Everything ok? You're home early."

"Yea," he pauses, like there are other words on his tongue, but he can't figure out a way to say them.

"Ok." We lay there quietly for a moment. He stares at the ceiling with his hands tucked under his head, his chest slowly rising.

I know he's like Knox in a lot of ways, each needing their space and their time to deal with and process things.

"I haven't said it."

It.

Those three little words.

I had an idea his distance lately was because of that. To be fair, I haven't said it either, but it's because I didn't want to push him into something he wasn't ready for. And it's fine. I'm ok with him telling me when he's ready not because he feels forced. Would it be nice to hear the words? Abso-fucking-lutely, but I get it.

"I know. It's ok." I reach across the space and put my hand on his chest.

He rolls over to look at me and in a quick move slides his arm between my legs, grabs my ass and pulls me across the space between us and nearly pulls me on top of him. My breath leaves my lungs as I look down at him before laying my head on his chest.

His fingers mindlessly move up and down my back like silk on my skin, but they keep getting hooked on my shirt. I love love love my back being rubbed and part of me is scared if I move, he'll stop. Don't you always freeze like a statue, scared to breathe if someone starts rubbing your back, for fear they'll realize what they're doing and stop?

He does it a few more times, so I risk the move. "Hold on." I awkwardly sit up from my position and slip my shirt over my head. I ignore his blown puff of air when he sees my breasts, and I lay back down, resting my head on his chest and throwing my leg over his waist.

He puts his hand on my back, but he doesn't move it and I beat myself up.

Amateur hour, Everlee. You know the rules of the back rubbing game.

Never move.

Barely breathe.

I nuzzle my head on his chest and hope my back moving ever so slightly under his touch will kick start his hand, as if it were a lawnmower needing to get started. A moment later we have movement. He continues to rub my back, but the air in the room is still weird. I know there is something on his mind, but I won't push him. He shows me more love than Rich ever did, even as he was saying he loved me. I feel like I've gotten to a stage in my life where actions are more important than words. Or maybe I have to be at this stage with these boys because of our arrangement.

After a few minutes, I can feel his cock hardening and pressing up against the underside of my thigh, like a snake poking its head out of a hole.

"Did you have a good night tonight?" I ask softly.

"Yea."

"Why did you come home?"

Silence.

I wanted to know, but I also didn't want to push. It sounded like he came straight to my room as soon as he walked through the door, like I was his reasoning for coming home. But that would be weird, right?

He shifts a little. "Did you enjoy the hot tub?"

"I did. I'm pretty sure it knocked me out. Well, that and the drinks and general conversation with Lizzy."

"That's pretty exhausting."

I laugh and look up at him, resting my chin on my hand on his chest. He cuts his eyes down at me and smiles. Fuck, he is so good looking. And mine. How the fuck is he mine?

"You like her, even if you won't admit it."

He blinks slowly, to hide his eye roll.

"It's fine. You don't have to say something for me to know it's true." As soon as the words are out of my mouth, I stop breathing for a second. I refuse to overthink what I just said. It's the truth, even if I was talking about Lizzy at the moment, it still applied to what I think is really on his mind and I wanted to let him know *it* was ok without actually saying it specifically. To let him know I feel loved, even if he doesn't say the words.

He kisses my forehead and looks back at the ceiling.

His cock has only gotten harder and is damn near pushing my leg up his chest, but he's made no move to initiate sex or said anything along the lines of wanting to. Is he waiting for me to initiate? So many questions swimming around us!

I rub my hand across his chest, which should be a universal sign for let's get our ba-doink-a-doink on.

"Are you ok with the party on Monday?" I ask.

"Do I have a choice?"

"You always have a choice."

He chuckles. "If I say no, will Lizzy still show up? Will Emmett grill hamburgers? Will there be music and laughter?"

"You sound a little like the Grinch."

He wraps his arm around me and pulls me completely on top of him. I can feel his cock at my entrance, through the very thin fabric of my thong.

"What did you say?" Fire blazes in his eyes. I guess he got my sign and decided to come to the open house.

HA! Come. So many meanings.

"I think you heard me." I look up at him then move my hips a little, so I press harder onto his cock, which has to be bursting through the band of his boxers now.

Without saying a word, he pops us up, throwing the covers off and just stares at me, rubbing my hair back off my face. His teeth are scraping over his lip as he watches me. Again, there is something about his expression. It's guarded.

"I think I need to teach your mouth a lesson," he growls.

"Good luck. She's had a mind of her own for years now. Gets me in the worst trouble."

He's speechless for a second. I know he's trying to be his dark and delicious self, but I'm also a smart ass with a filter problem, so cracking jokes at the wrong time is sort of my M.O.

"You're a dumbass."

"Your dumbass." I press my lips against his and push him back to the bed. He's not going to be the one to lead tonight. I'm going to take charge.

I break off his lips and slide down his body, kissing along his pecs and each of his tattoos, as I work my way down. His cock is still restrained inside the band of his pants and I feel bad for him, being cooped up like that. I grab the edge of his boxers and slide them over the head of his cock, freeing the one-eyed monster who thumps against Jax's stomach with glee.

My eyes greedily travel over his body, soaking in his beautiful, hard length. I love his fucking cock. Everything about it. The look, the feel, the taste. My mouth is salivating, just staring at it. When his boxers get a little lower down, Jax takes over, pulling his legs out and using his feet to push them the rest of the way down. I glide back up, rubbing my wet pussy over his cock and feel his hips buck up a bit, but he doesn't take. Like it's reflex, but he regains control and continues to wait.

When my fingers trace over one of the scars, his breath hitches, like he's nervous or ashamed. "You're so beautiful," I mumble against his skin, before gently pressing my lips to his scar. His muscles relax a bit, so I move to another one, and then another one. I can't help but wonder what they're all from, or who they're from. Was it an enemy? Did Jax kill them? A few are from bullets, but the majority appear to be knife wounds. I want to know everything about him, but I accept this may be something I never learn about. A secret in a box locked away.

"Are you going to get any more tattoos?" I ask, tracing each with my finger before kissing them.

"Yes," the single word is short, guarded.

My lips kiss up the inside of his forearm, following the lines on his tattoo, before I move over to his chest, running my hands up his chiseled torso. His tattoos are another thing I want to learn about. Where did he get them? Why? Who? What do they all mean? Tattoos are very personal. Each design is significant. I want to know what Jax's mean. Why he got them? When he got them? But he'd have to let down his guard first. I hope we get to a point where he can do that with me. I feel like we are getting closer with each passing day, but... there is something. Something that's holding him back. Preventing him from tearing down his walls.

I continue to work my way down to his cock, running my tongue from tip to base, before I grab it and suck it in without warning or finesse. It hits the back of my throat and he lets out an appreciative grunt. His legs tense under me, widening to give me more access. I pull him out and lick up the underside and around the head, coating it with my saliva. His breath shudders a little, while his hands grip onto the sheets and the heels of his feet dig into the bed. I smile, loving the way he reacts to me, how they all do.

"Yesss," he breathes out. "Your lips feel so good wrapped around me."

I pump his cock a few times, and then flick my tongue down his shaft before getting to the base where I suck at the seam of his ball sack, before I work my way back up, taking him in my mouth again. He lets out a heady breath at the same time his fingers tangle in my hair.

"You're toying with me, Squirt," he growls and pulls my hair up so my lips slide up his cock until they are at his tip. The pain quickly turns to pleasure as the dark one inside of him is coming out to play. I love Jax when he's rough. He doesn't hold back. I mean, I'm sure he does, but he definitely pushes pain to the limits. "I don't like to be toyed with."

Let's play his game and see what happens. I know what he needs tonight. He needs to let *it* out, whatever it is. He needs rough, so I'll give it to him. My eyes set on his, and my jaw clenches. "Fuck you!" A wave of euphoria passes through me as my heart is hammering in my chest.

His eyes nearly bulge out of his head in shock before he reads my face. A smile settles on his lips. "No, darling. Fuck you." He thrusts up suddenly, his ass lifting off the bed, as his fist yanks and pulls my head down.

My scalp is screaming at the same time his cock hits the back of my throat, but I try not to gag or whimper. Instead, I take it. Because fuck me, I love it. I love *him.*

"Swallow my cock down your throat, Squirt." He pulls out and shoves it in again, "Swallow it all down."

His words and actions are rough, but he's still calling me Squirt. His name for me. So that's what I hold on to. Tears sting my eyes as I fight back the urge to gag, but I take it. I take him. I know when he came home, he was feeling vulnerable. Something was bothering him. He needs a fight. He needs to let whatever it is out before it tears him apart.

My hand clamps around his shaft, hard. He shows no mercy, neither will I. I take over, sucking his cock in hard and deep. Need filling and fueling every cell, every fiber, within my body. I want his cock so badly.

I need it.

I need him.

"Fuck Everlee!" he pants, the grip in my hair loosening as the same need consumes him. I cannot get enough of his cock. I devour it. Lick it. Suck it. Just pure carnal desire. My hand grips tightly, stroking it with each lick or flick while my other grabs his balls and squeezes.

He bucks off the bed.

"Shit!"

He likes this. Likes it rougher.

His balls are tightening in my hands and I can tell he's close. He loses control and tightens his grip in my hair again, pulling me down on to him, grinding into my mouth.

"I love fucking your face. I love to feel your lips wrapped around my cock. And I especially love when I explode and you swallow it down like the good girl you are."

I smile, his words making me only want to move faster, but I can't, because he takes over. His ass is popping off the bed, while his hands grip into my hair, holding me in place. Tears are streaming down my face. "Take it, Everlee, take all of me."

My hand grips tighter on him to the point the muscles in my forearms are shaking.

"Look at me," he commands.

And I do. God, what a fucking beautiful sight. The muscles in his arms, chest, stomach all bulging as he presses into me. His eyes are watching me intently as his teeth bite into his bottom lip. So fucking sexy.

"Swallow me down." His ass shoots off the bed as his hands pull me down and he explodes into my mouth, his warm saltiness sliding down the back of my throat. I swallow as fast as I can, but it keeps coming. He thrusts a few more times before he stops. Our eyes lock again and I pull off his cock and slide my lips along it, kissing him down his shaft before switching to the inside of his thigh, our gaze never breaking. The look in his eyes is somewhere between satisfaction and curiosity, which makes me giddy with pleasure. Because hidden behind it all is excitement and lust.

"What are you doing, Squirt?" he whispers cautiously.

"Nothing." My lips curl into a naughty, wicked smile, which causes him to smile.

"You're going to be the death of me," he sighs, sitting up. He hooks his finger under my chin and lifts me, wrapping his hand around the back of my neck. He yanks me to him with force so my face is inches from his, our eyes locked. The emotion on his face is yelling, screaming out at me, but I just wait. I don't want to push him.

His fingers dig into the back of my neck and then he pulls me to him, his lips crashing against mine, his tongue pressing in. He moans into the kiss and I climb further up so I'm straddling his semi hard cock. "You're so wet," he groans against my lips.

"Mmhmm," is all I can manage to get out. I love kissing this man. The heat, the fire, the intensity behind it. It's all consuming and makes my stomach flutter and my head feel like it's in the clouds.

"Now I want to taste you." His hand moves to my hair, and he yanks hard, pulling my head back, exposing my neck. My pulse beats wildly under his lips as he peppers kisses down and sucks hard. A moan escapes as he continues to tease me, his teeth gently scraping across my skin. My hips gyrate on his lap, coating his cock in my arousal.

"You like it rough, don't you?" He doesn't wait for an answer before he bites, his teeth feeling like dull razors.

A shudder moves through my body as the idea of being marked by him shoots desire straight to my aching pussy. "Fuck," I moan out, grinding my hips into him. The need to feel his cock in me right now is overwhelming. It's getting harder, but it still isn't fuckable yet. It would do for a simple fuck, but not what I want right now. Not what I need.

He continues to work his way down my throat, planting kisses along my collarbone before he pushes me back on the bed and crawls over me like a wolf stalking its prey. A smile curls on his lips as he looks down at my chest. "Mine." He swoops down, clamping his mouth around my left breast, his teeth tugging on my nipple hard enough to make me arch off the bed and scream out. Pain turns to pleasure as he flicks it with his tongue. He kisses down my chest and plants his face on my sternum, grabbing the sides of both my breasts and quickly motorboats me, his eyes finding mine with a mischievous twinkle that makes me laugh.

Just a small window of humor in his usual serious demeanor.

He continues to the other breast, repeating. Sucking it into his mouth, biting his teeth down around my nipple before flicking it with his tongue. He runs his hard cock between my legs, and my arousal glistens all over him.

Eyes closed, I soak in all the sensations that are swirling through my body. Heat, pain, pleasure, want, need. He slips further down and gently bites on the inside of my leg, the scruff of his beard swiping against my pussy. He blows a warm breath on my clit before moving to the other side to bite again. The words 'Eat me' play on the tip of my tongue, but at this point I'm a little nervous he'd bite down and try to take a chunk out of my leg. I suppose it's my fault for watching a zombie show last night, and that's perhaps why he's suddenly bitey mcbites a lot.

But I don't hate it.

Apparently, I like pain more than I thought I did.

He swipes his tongue up my center and lets out a long, low growl before sucking on my clit. It's like a beast is unleashed because a moment later, both of his hands are scooping my ass off the bed and he is sitting up with my legs over his shoulder, eating like I'm his favorite dessert at Christmas.

"Fuck Jax." My hands search feverishly to hold on to something as desire swells inside of me. His tongue presses in like he's fucking Gene Simmons, trying to tickle my cervix, twirling it around and sucking.

He doesn't relent and I know my cunt, along with the inside of my thighs, is going to have a beard rash tomorrow, but it's worth it. He drops my ass to the bed and runs into the closet and before I can recapture enough of my senses, he's there, holding a little orange dildo and a devilish grin.

"Where do you think that's going?"

"Anywhere the fuck I want it to go." He pumps his eyebrows once, daring me to say something.

Sass pops on my face. "You think so?" I scramble to get off the bed, but he takes three gigantic steps and is across the room in a second flat, grabbing my ankle and twisting me around. I press my other foot into his arm, causing him to drop the dildo on the bed and grab my other ankle. His grip hard, biting the skin.

"Now, what are you going to do, Squirt?"

I try to fight and twist, but he's too strong.

"That's what I thought." He yanks me effortlessly towards the edge of the bed so my ass is barely hanging off then flips me, planting both feet on the ground and bending over me. His hands run up my arms, interlacing his fingers in mine, outstretching them above my head. His cock is pressed between my cheeks, his chest is on my back, and his lips are right by my ear. "Don't fucking move."

I don't listen. I struggle to get my hands free, but he only clamps them harder.

He shifts to grip both wrists in one hand, then spanks my ass hard, the sting moving through my entire body. "You don't listen very well."

"Big fucking surprise." I grind out, bucking my chest off the bed to look at him.

He chuckles low in his chest, then uses his free hand to grab the dildo off the bed. He runs it over my ass, lines it up with my pussy, pausing for a second, then slams it in with a satisfying roughness. I jerk forward as his hand comes into contact with the outside of my pussy.

"Don't. Fucking. Move."

"Fuck you," I seethe through set teeth.

"Wrong answer," he grits back.

He tosses the dildo across the room, clearly abandoning his plans in a fit of lustful rage. I feel his hard cock swipe across my clit and I whimper out with need. He pauses, keeping it at my entrance, then he punches into me, hard and fast filling me. I scream out in pain and ecstasy, but he doesn't stop.

"You like this? You like it rough?"

"I love it and I love your cock!" I slam into him, causing him to stumble backwards a bit.

He grabs my hair and pulls my chest off the bed, so I'm standing up while he fucks me from behind. He wraps his hand around my throat and uses his finger to turn my head to the side and takes my lips in a rough kiss. My legs shake with weakness. Goddamn. Can I come from this kiss? When he can't get a good enough angle, he releases my hair and quickly spins me around, lifting me into his arms and carries me to stand against the wall. He lets my left leg fall, but he keeps a tight grip on my right, and fucks me again.

Our eyes lock for a moment and I tangle my fingers in his hair and pull his head to the side and take a bite out of his neck before sucking his skin in hard and fast, not sure how long he will let me go before he stops.

It's not long.

His hand slips up between us and clamps on my nipple. I scream out in pain, releasing his neck from my mouth. There's a nice red mark, which brings a smile to my face, before his other hand grabs my chin and directs it to his lips, where he swallows my moans with his kiss.

I wrench my leg out of his grasp and press my heel to the wall, pushing us away.

He stumbles, regains his balance, then looks at me with a flicker of a spark as realization hits.

A challenge.

He's just over an arm's reach away, but I'm right by the door.

"Come get me," I command, twisting out of the room and taking off at a full sprint down the hall. I glance over my shoulder and see his tall, muscular figure step out of the room and look both ways before his eyes land on me. He takes a step, not moving with any speed, and a thrill of excitement pulses through me.

So fucking hot.

"Everlee, stop running," he growls, thick and heady.

"Make me," I call back without turning around.

He chuckles, a terrifying sound. "As you wish." His feet slap quickly on the floor and I squeal in excitement. My heartbeat is pounding and my body is electrified as adrenaline pulses through me.

Breathing heavily, I run downstairs, taking them three at a time, hand gripping on the rail, preventing me from ending this epic chase with a broken face from falling down the stairs. I get into the kitchen and fall behind the island, hugging my knees, trying to calm my breathing.

He descends the stairs quietly.

Hunting.

Silence.

Is he still moving? I strain to listen for any sign of a breath, or a foot padding across the floor, or the air moving around him.

Nothing.

It's like he's a ghost.

I fight the urge to peek around the edge of the island to see where he is, knowing that he's likely waiting for me to do that.

Silence.

My skin begins to prickle, and my pulse quickens. It's like it's hyper aware of something I'm not. I close my eyes, like that's going to fucking help me.

A low, gravelly chuckle sounds right above me.

Fucker is laying on the counter.

"Even though your eyes are closed, I can still see you."

I glance up and then roll to the side away from him, but he rolls off the counter, landing with ease like a tiger ready to pounce on his prey. Knees are bent and he's ready to attack.

Fuck!

I take a step back and he follows, like we're in a deadly tango dance. He takes another step forward, closing the distance between us. His hungry eyes rake over my body and I do the same. I fight back the moan that bubbles within at the sight of his glorious body- his thigh muscles, the curved edges of his chest and arms, and the beautiful ink spread across them all. He stalks towards me, a man in control.

A hunter.

Damn it! I need to focus. My life is hanging in the balance and here I am horny as fuck, but I don't want to let him win. At least not yet.

"Are you ready to surrender?" he asks, a mirthless grin on his face.

"Suck my dick."

His lips twitch, fighting a smile. "Gladly."

He lurches forward again and I deflect his grab and try to sweep him onto the floor, but it's like trying to trip a concrete pole. Shit ain't moving and neither is he.

He's cocky and chuckles. "Did you really think that would work on me?" His grip latches onto my arms.

"Worth a shot." I shrug. I grab the bowl of fruit to my side and swing it at him. His hand drops from my arm as he blocks the bowl and the fruit tumbles to the floor.

"You're going to have to explain that to Emmett," he says, completely unfazed. I'm losing control and panicking while he is cooler than a fucking cucumber.

I push off of him and bolt towards the stairs, but he catches me by the thighs and grabs onto me, stopping me dead in my tracks. I fall forward and catch myself on the tread as his hand slides down and wraps around my ankle and flips me over. My back arches around the stair, the riser holding me in place, preventing me from scooting away from the tower of a man lurching forward.

"Not so talkative now, are you?" He pushes my head to the side like it's nothing.

I shake my head, breath panting, neck exposed.

I'm caught. There's nowhere left for me to run, no punches to throw, nothing within grasp.

He crawls up my body, his knee positioned between my legs as his lips kiss my throat. I keep waiting for the beast to unleash his revenge, but he sucks on my fevered skin before nibbling gently.

I feel like this is the carrot and I'm a rabbit moseying into a trap.

"You're mine." His expression, the look in his eyes, robs me of my breath.

I nod, staring at him.

He presses his forehead to mine and breathes me in for a moment and then, like a switch is flipped, he's back. "Now, to finish what we started." He smiles.

He slides down my body, licking his tongue along my slick clit. My arousal is nearly gushing out of me all over the stair. Perhaps they have caution wet floor cone somewhere because they're going to need it.

While he licks my clit, he inserts his fingers, bending them in that come-hither move, hitting on all the right spots. "Fuck, Jax."

"That's right. Come for me." He continues to lick and pulse his tongue in as I come around it, my toes curling and my fists tightening in his hair. My body is reeling for this oh so glorious orgasm as my pussy continues to pulse.

"Now to fuck you, darling, so you can come around my cock."

He grabs my arm and pulls me up into his chest and stands us up with ease. My legs instinctually wrap around him.

"Are you ok?" he whispers, carrying me effortlessly over to the counter, ignoring the bowl and the mess of fruit on the ground.

I lean forward and plant soft kisses under his jawline and suck his ear into my mouth, turned on by the low growl that resonates through his chest.

"I'll take that as a yes." He sits me on the edge of the kitchen counter and my legs fall from around his waist, but hang loosely. "Are you ready for me to...how did you say it? Suck your dick?"

I blush, "Fuck me, Jax."

"Gladly."

He slides me off the counter, turns me around so my breasts are pressed into the cold granite and runs his cock up between my legs, then presses in. Feelings of pleasure radiate through my body from my pussy like a unicorn riding a fucking rainbow train.

"Yes," I moan out. I don't fight him, I don't press back into him, I just take what he has to give and God, it is good. The way he fills me. He pauses, wraps his arms around my chest and walks us over, my body impaled on his cock, to the dining room table. It's lower, so I can hinge further over.

"I can't get enough of you," he grunts out. "I want more. I want it all."

"You have me Jax."

His hands run down both my arms and he interlaces his fingers within mine while he takes me from behind. Slow at first, savoring the feel, and then he picks up speed. The edge of the table bites into my hips, but I don't dare fucking move. I need his cock in me like the trees need the sun. He pulls me back into him some, and off the edge of the table, a welcomed reprieve. I move our combined hands and press them into the table and push back into him. "Give me more," I whimper.

He pauses and then punches into me, filling me deep. I let out a gasp of air, then match his thrusts, pushing back into him, sending him deeper inside of me. Faster and faster.

Sweat is glistening on my chest, the table is rocking, making noises as it moves against the floor. It's an enormous table that isn't going anywhere far, but it's moving. There's no way it can't with the pounding that is currently taking place in my pussy.

He's getting so deep, his balls are smacking against my clit.

"Yes. Yes." Another orgasm is coming, this time slower than the last, but still coming none the less.

His hand reaches down and he rubs my clit as he grinds his cock into me. "Oh. Oh." Another string of sounds tumble out of my mouth, incoherent. "So close."

"Come for me, love."

He thrusts a few more times and my orgasm unleashes inside of me, making my eyes snap shut and my lungs stop breathing. I'm immobile, paralyzed, as wave after wave after wave crashes around me.

"Goddamn, your pussy is clenching and pulsing so hard."

I don't think he's talking to me, rather making a general statement. I hope, because I can't talk. Words are no longer coming out of my mouth. It's like a dragon puffing out smoke because they have lost their fire breath. That's me. I'm that dragon.

He makes a few more thrusts, then presses in hard and deep and explodes so hard and so fast inside of me I can feel it. His release is all over his cock, as he slides a few more times, making it a sopping wet mess. He kisses the back of my neck and pulls out. Like pulling the plug out of the ocean, our combined release oozes out of my pussy and slides down my leg.

"Where are your so-called ninja skills now?" he taunts, referring to the time when they surprised me at Easter.

"I'll have you know I'm an excellent post sex ninja." I look down at the glob sliding down my leg. "Obviously, not tonight. It's not my best work, but to be honest. I'm fucking tired."

"You like to fall asleep right after sex, you know that?"

"Usually it's four on one and you guys tire me out. But tonight!" I hold up my finger in the air. "I was asleep when you got home."

"Sounds like excuses." He whips a kitchen towel at me and I stare at it. "It's clean. I just switched them out this afternoon."

I glare at him, and he chuckles. "Scouts honor. I'd never do anything to that pussy of yours. I love it too much."

His eyes catch mine, like he's said something he shouldn't have. Still so guarded.

"Well, she thanks you. She loves you, too."

Is that what we were going to do? Was I going to be a little bitch and hide behind my pussy? Oh, my pussy loves you. Oh, my pussy wants your cock. Oh, my pussy wants to talk to you. Should I just add her to my cell phone plan and check to see if the number 697-8779 is available for 'MY PUSSY'. I was being a pussy, that was for sure.

He helps me up, grabbing my face in his hands and slowly brings his lips to mine, kissing me tenderly. "Let's go get you cleaned off. Callum's going to be pissed if you leave come-splats all over the floor."

"Sounds like a food. Come splat."

"You mean Kumquats?"

"I like come splats better. Maybe we could put it in the fruit bowl with the oranges."

"Speaking of." He picks up the fruit and quickly tosses it back into the bowl and sets it on the table. "What was with throwing the bowl at me?"

I scrunch my face.

He laughs and plants a quick kiss on the tip of my nose before scooping me up in his arms. Even though I'm exhausted and I don't think my body could literally have another orgasm, the feel of his warm skin on mine causes my pussy to tingle. Oh look. My pussy wants to go again.

"My hero."

"Shut up." He shakes his head back and forth.

A few minutes later, we're in his shower and he's washing my hair and rinsing me off. He slides the hair off my neck, then leans in closer, to the point I think he's going to kiss my neck, but he doesn't.

Even my nipples harden at the thought.

"Looks like you're going to have a mark."

"You think? You fucking bit and sucked me like you're a werewolf marking your mate."

"Maybe you are in some ways."

My stomach tightens with his words as my eyes catch his and again, it looks like the words are on the tip of his tongue, but he can't say them. Should I? If I did, would it make it easier for him? Is he scared to say it because he doesn't think he'll hear it back?

He sighs and reaches around me to grab a loofa. I step forward, closing the gap between us, and look at his neck. "Samesies."

"What?" He reaches up, swiping his hand over his neck.

"It's not something you can wipe away, silly!"

He flicks water in my face and I can't help but smile. He gives me these quick glimpses into the quirky and funny Jax, and I'll take them. All of them.

We head to his bedroom and climb into bed. I've only slept in here a few times, because usually we're in the group bed. He keeps a simple room with only a bed, a desk, and a small corner bookshelf behind his chair. His sheets are black satin and feel so smooth against my skin. I learned my lesson the first time with these sheets. Approach with caution, like you're on a safari surrounded by lions, not like a kid at a bouncy house party. The first time I slept in here, I ran and jumped on the bed and slid straight the fuck off. I was wearing a satin nighty and apparently satin on satin equals face planting on the floor. So as you can imagine... super sexy with a busted lip.

He rolls to his side and before I can even scoot over to him; he snakes his arm under my leg, grabs my ass, and pulls me toward him. My leg rests on his stomach, which is still warm and a touch damp from the shower, and my head finds the crook in his neck. "You know I was coming over here already," I mumble with my eyes closed. The sandman has loaded up my eyelids because it's getting harder to keep them open.

"I know, but I didn't want to wait a second longer." He kisses my forehead. "Goodnight, love."

"I love you, too," I mumble out against his skin, head foggy and falling down the dark hole of sleep rapidly.

EVERLEE - BUTTERFLY MEET PTERODACTYL

- -

THE CLOCK ON THE wall feels like a guillotine inching closer and closer to my neck. Sammie will be here in a few minutes and I'm running around the house like a chicken with its head cut off, straightening everything. That's not true. Callum hired a company to clean this morning, and they just left thirty minutes ago.

Four hours! They were here for four hours, but I feel like they left the house how they wanted to, versus how the guys like it, or maybe that's just me.

Knox swings into the room and grabs me around the waist and lifts me up, with my back pressed against his chest, pressing his nose into my hair. "What are you doing? It all looks great." He sets me down.

"I know. I'm just... excited? Nervous? Anxious?"

"To take ownership of a sex club? You're perfect, you know that?"

"No, but you can keep trying to tell me." A sly smile parts my lips.

"I will tell you whatever you want to hear, love." He brushes the hair away from my face and plants a kiss on my lips.

"And also, I'm not taking ownership. Remember?"

He rolls his eyes. "Whatever. You are, but if you want to think you aren't to make yourself feel better, that's fine, too."

"Knox."

He waves over his shoulder as he walks out of the front living room.

"Knox!" I yell, running after him and turn the corner running into a wall of muscle. "Jax."

"Don't sound so happy to see me."

I wrap my arms around him, inhaling his citrusy, musky scent. "I'm always happy to see you and your grimace," I say, grabbing his chin and shaking it.

He was gone this morning when I woke up, which made me a little sad, but I know he goes on early morning workouts and runs to clear his mind before he starts the day.

"Your phone was going off this morning. I went and cut the alarm off."

"Shit. Sorry."

"Not a big deal. I needed to get up and workout, anyway."

The air falls silent, and he looks at me. For a moment I think he's going to say something about last night, but he doesn't. "Are you ready for Sammie?"

"Yea, but what if she doesn't take the offer?"

He shrugs, "It's a good offer, more than she'll probably get from an outside buyer, plus we've written in the offer we'll keep all the things she has changed and try to tackle the list of her other ideas." My face contorts, so he adds, "We won't only do her ideas, we'll do yours too." He kisses my forehead. "We think that's something that will be important to her. She put in a lot of time and work into this place, really making it her own, so we want to honor that."

"Aren't you boys the sweetest?" I tease.

"Sometimes." His eyebrow quirks up, matching his devilish grin.

Flashes of last night replay in my mind, and my body instantly reacts. My nipples harden, my stomach clenches, and my pussy pulses.

"You need to stop with all that," he warns.

"With what?"

He closes the gap between us, his chest presses to mine. He wraps his hand around my neck and pulls me to him with force, with dominance, and whispers in my ear, "You know what." A tingle races down my spine as his other hand slides around to my lower back, pressing me against him.

"This isn't helping, asshole," I moan back breathlessly.

He smiles against my ear. "I know."

"Fuck you." I push against his hard chest, but don't budge. His grip on my neck and waist only tightens.

"Maybe later. If you're lucky."

I raise on my tiptoes, "Let's not pretend you're the only cock in this house I want to fuck."

A low, heady chuckles sounds. "Oh baby. But I'm the only one who will be rough with you and give you what you want and fuck you like I hate you."

My pussy quivers with excitement, and my pulse quickens, causing him to smile. Damn this man and his effect on me. Callum was close one time at Easter, but that had nothing on Jax from last night. He was rough, scary, but I loved it. I don't think I've ever been so turned on.

The doorbell rings, breaking our trance.

I move to turn away, but he grabs my arm and pulls me back to him. "You've got something there." He points at his neck.

"Fuck you," I glare hard again, my eyes not matching the smile on my face.

"We'll see." He winks and lets me go, following me over to the door, and places his hands on my hips.

I open the door and smile, "Sammie. How are you?"

Her eyes flicker from me to Jax, whose hands are still wrapped around me. "Doing well." A smile plays on her lips as she looks from my neck to Jax's. "You?"

"Great," Jax says, letting go of my waist to shake her hand before bringing it back. I can't help but wonder why he's being so overly, and more importantly, openly affectionate.

Davis is just behind her and hasn't said a word, and I feel like I can see the invisible ball gag and collar around his neck.

Bertha, of course, appears in her leather domme outfit on the sidewalk, with a whip in hand and several little elephants behind her with bright red apples in their mouths marching back and forth like a scene from the Jungle Book, only kinkier. Fuck me, what's wrong with me? Over active imagination? Nerves?

"Please come in," Jax welcomes, stepping us out of the way of the door.

"Thank you." Sammie steps in and Davis follows.

"The guys are in the office waiting for us." Jax unwraps his arms from around me and leads them through the kitchen.

"Would you like anything to drink?" I offer.

"No, thank you." Sammie flicks her hand casually over her shoulder and Davis doesn't respond.

I know we dabble in the dom/sub relationship a little, but there's no way. I have too fucking much to say. Too many opinions. Perhaps that's why Callum has never pushed me further, because he's scared it would push me away. Although, now watching them has me curious. Until last night, I would have probably said I didn't like it rough, and boy, would I have been wrong. The fight for power, control.

Yes, my head is a little tender from the hair pulling and my pussy feels a bit bruised, but it was so worth it.

"Everlee," Callum and Jax call in unison.

When I look up from the kitchen island, I see them both waving me into the room. Folding the dishcloth back and tucking it into its spot on the counter, I nod and hastily make my way into the room. Waiting by the desk is an empty seat for me beside a disappointed looking Callum to its right. I was unaware they wanted me in the room.

I've been a part of a dozen or more large client deals, but this feels different. This is real money, like personal-ish money, with a building and business changing hands. This is a lot of pressure, but I seem to be the only one freaking out on the inside and I don't have a proverbial dog in the fight or a dollar that's being spent. Everyone else is cool, calm, and dare I say collected, to finish out the idiom.

After the second look from Jax, I tuck my hands under my legs to stop myself from fidgeting and picking at my nails. Sammie sits and moves with such calm grace, so I try to imitate her, to exude the power she has. Literally, she walks into a room and you can almost feel the gust of wind that plows in after her, smacking you in the face. I walk in, and it's like pew, pew. Like the amount of wind you get from having a butterfly flap its wings in your face. Butterfly meet Pterodactyl.

Fuck.

I nearly laugh out loud at the latest smut trend I was seeing pop up on my feed. Dinosaur smut, and now all I can think about is a having sex with a pterodactyl or perhaps a Jurassic night at Allure. I cover my mouth and clear my throat. My go to for embarrassing moments, or if I need to stop laughing during meetings, I take a sip or sixteen of water. Effective for covering smiles and laughs.

Sammie inquires how the night went and our, mostly the guys, thoughts about how it looked. The changes. They discussed finances, and I tried to hold my shit together when they were talking about annual revenues and expected projections for the balance of the year, as well as for the next two to five years.

Fuckin' aye, sex really sells.

They talk some more about future plans, expansions to both the property and expanding to Texas potentially, and lots of other things, all casual. At the end, Callum hands Sammie a folder, which she immediately hands to Davis without looking at it, then stands up.

"Thank you so much for the time and the conversation. I will have our lawyers look over the offer and let you know." She reaches out to shake everyone's hand before turning to leave, then pauses when she gets to the door. "Everlee. Would you walk me out?" She glances at the boys, who all have furrowed brows, but don't speak up.

I stumble over my words, then agree, running over to meet her.

When we step through the door, Davis paces two steps behind us and she links her arm in mine. "Darling," she coos in a soft and silky voice. "These men seem to adore you and want you included. Do not be nervous, do not be shy. Take the place you have earned by their side."

I look up at her, shocked.

"They are men of power, yet they treat you as an equal. Own that darling. Few men will. Often times they're too scared of looking inferior to a strong woman and will continue to oppress and belittle you to make themselves stand taller. These men, from what I can see, are confident in every aspect of their lives. So I say again. Take your seat at the table and never back down. They clearly see your worth and value, so you need to as well. You're welcome to come to Allure anytime I'm there or call me and I'll be happy to teach you and give you the confidence."

"To be a domme?"

She laughs, like I just told a funny joke at tea time, whilst eating a crumpet or two. "Darling. If you'd like to be a domme that will take time, I'm simply talking about confidence."

When we get to the door, Davis runs around and opens it for us - her. She pauses, pulling her arm out of mine. "It was lovely getting to chat with you. I look forward to any future chats we may have. Ta-ta."

"Ta-," I start then stop, "Good bye."

I close the door, then press my head against it. She's like a sorceress, weaving her fingers through my mind to control me. I was close to saying yes ma'am, a few times and then damn near said ta-ta at the end like I'm some sort of English aristocrat. I don't know if that's what they say, but they might and that's what I'm going off of right now.

EMMETT – LEOPARD PRINT THONGS AND DONGS

<hr>

FIFTEEN AFTER FOUR. LIZZY and Tony are going to be here in fifteen minutes and the baked beans aren't finished yet, potato salad still needs to be mixed and the hamburgers. Shit! Where are the hamburgers?

I throw open the fridge and shuffle through all the shelves and drawers in a slight panic.

"What's going on in here?" Everlee asks walking in wearing a white eyelet dress with puffy lace sleeves. Her hair is put up in a sloppy bun on her head and she looks damn delectable. I don't know what you call them. Fashion was never my strong suit. The fact I know it's an eyelet is amazing and really, that's only because she was running around the house earlier yelling something about finding her eyelet dress. Last night, Knox was in her room and I think he thought it'd be funny if he hid it from her. But Everlee, being the cunning little fox she is, started crying, saying that it used to be her mother's and she wears it on this day every year... it's a tradition yada yada... Knox felt bad and gave it back to her. She wiped her crocodile tears away, popped up, and slipped it on in the middle of the living room. When Knox went to apologize, she told him she was kidding and then threatened him for future shenanigans.

Knox was dumbfounded and the rest of us were rolling on the floor laughing.

He's potentially met his match with her. We all have in some way or another. It's interesting to sit back and watch the family dynamic now that she's here and how she molds to each of us so completely, yet so differently. If I was a religious man, I'd say she was created for us, because that's the only thing that could explain how perfect she truly is.

Her arms wrap around my waist and I feel a calmness surround me. When I turn in her arms and hug her back, she presses her cheek against my chest. "I can't find my hamburgers. I marinated them and was ready to roll them into patties, but the meat is all gone."

"Not the meat," she teases. "I do love meat, especially yours."

I chuckle, rubbing my hand over the top of her shoulder, knocking her sleeve off.

"Emmett," she warns cautiously, her eyes meeting mine. Her pupils are completely blown and her breath is shallow. God, I fucking love this woman. Always so eager and ready to take and give. My cock twitches in my pants, even though I know it's not the right time.

"What? I'm not going to do anything," I say, leaning in and planting a kiss on her neck.

"Emmett." She fidgets her hands pressing up against my chest, but not pushing me away.

"I hear you," I say, trailing kisses down her collarbone.

"Fucccckk," she sighs out, her head falling to the side, giving me more access.

The doorbell rings. And then rings again. And again.

Three times back-to-back.

Lizzy.

"Sounds like Lizzy is here," she mumbles, but makes no show of moving.

"Saved by the bell," I sigh and pull away.

As she's walking towards the front door, she calls over her shoulder, "I rolled your meat in my hands earlier, then took it upstairs. Callum and Jax have it in the kitchen up there and are waiting on your go-ahead to grill."

"Next time you pat my meat, make sure I'm there!" I shout after her, a stupid smile spread across my face.

I listen for the front door and hear Lizzy shout something and, in typical Lizzy fashion, calls out the fact Ev looks like she's just been fucked. Only she's wrong, because she's five minutes early. Which I doubt would have been long enough. I enjoy taking my time with her and making her moan and come all over my face and my cock. The way her voice squeaks ever so slightly at the start of her orgasm or the way her hands grab her breasts when she comes, drives me wild.

Stop Emmett. Stop thinking about her delicious pussy and start thinking about this food. I pat my crotch, trying to tap down my growing erection.

They walk into the room and Lizzy is flipping Everlee's hair and looks at me. "Oh. Sorry I cock blocked you."

"All good," I chuckle.

"I brought this delicious display of fruit, cut and melon-balled it myself, then arranged it in this beautiful design." She holds it up and some of the fruit shifts. "Son of a bitch!"

Tony takes the dish from her and walks it over to the counter, while Lizzy runs around to the sink and washes her hands to fix the pieces of fruit. It was a flag with blueberries in the upper left corner, and red and white stripes of apple slices, honeydew, strawberries, raspberries, bananas, and watermelon.

"I told her it was too much fruit, but she insisted it was needed when going up against you."

"Going up against?" I laugh.

"Well, not competing, obvi! But I can't bring some janky ass dish over here with basic cut pieces. You're a fantastic chef and soon to be Michelin star. No. It needed to look balla... melon balla that is."

"You're an idiot," Everlee chimes in, plucking a piece of fruit.

Lizzy tries to quickly take it back, but Everlee plops it in her mouth.

Lizzy warns, "You better be lucky there are other people around or else I'd go in there after it."

Everlee pumps her eyebrows playfully.

"I mean, I don't mind. Just sayin'," I mumble, also taking a bite of fruit, and Tony shrugs and smiles.

"You heathens! The whole lot of you!" Lizzy fixes the fruit and grabs the dish. "I'm taking this upstairs, so excuse me," she huffs playfully. When she gets to the first platform on the stairs, she turns back. "Emmett, I hope you have some samples for me to try for Rainbows and Unicorns night. And I hope one involves cotton candy."

"Yes, darling. I will have some samples for you."

"Excellent, good sir."

"I'm going to go supervise and make sure she stays out of trouble," Tony smiles. "Do I need to take anything up?"

"Yea. If you don't mind." I hand him a carrier full of condiments and a tray of toppings for the burgers.

Tony nods and heads up the stairs.

"Your friend," I simply state.

"She grows on you."

"She's great. I love the energy and the fact she is... normal."

Everlee clenches her stomach and bends over in laughter. "Are you... you ... are you fucking with me? Normal," she continues to laugh.

"Well, like with us. Not pretentious or judgmental."

"Ok. I will take all of those, but I vehemently reject normal."

"Vehemently?" I close the gap between us and wrap my arms around her. I absolutely love touching her and holding her in my arms. It's like I'm addicted to her. "Does Tony know?"

"I don't think he's expressly been told, but I assume he has an idea. Probably should have said something to him before today. Could be interesting."

"What?" Jax walks downstairs. "Ooh an Everlee sandwich. My favorite kind to eat." He presses up behind her and wraps his arms around me, squishing her between us.

"You boys and your filthy words and sexiness!"

"You love our filthy mouths," Jax retorts.

"I do." Her hand slides up between us and she grabs my chin and gives me a kiss, then turns around and gives Jax a kiss before ducking under our arms.

"Want me to take anything up?"

"No. I need to finish a couple of things and then we'll bring it up," I say turning away from the now awkward embrace with Jax.

She blows a kiss, then disappears.

"What's up?" I ask Jax, who clearly has something on his mind.

"Nothing." He takes a seat at the bar and watches me continue to cook and prepare the side dishes. "I had to get away from Lizzy because I can only take her in small doses. She needs to burn off some of her excitement and energy before I can go back up."

Pouring the beans into a serving dish, I laugh, because I know what he's talking about, but that's one of the things I like about her. Unafraid to bring her entire self to any environment. It's probably liberating. "Is that all? I noticed you were home early on Friday and the kitchen was in a disarray."

"Disarray? It was spotless." He folds up the towel on the counter, his mind clearly somewhere else.

"Maybe disarray is a bit much, but there were things out of place. Not to mention the-" he points to his neck, "on each of you. And… you've seemed more relaxed. Did you tell her?"

"Tell her what?"

"How you feel?"

He shakes his head and starts looking around the room. His tell-tell sign he really doesn't want to talk about it. Almost like he's an animal terrified of being locked in a cage. So I change the topic. "I saw the lawyers brought by some paperwork this afternoon. Have you looked at it?"

"No, but Callum said it's a go. There are a couple of other things that were called out, but they're minor. He wants to review with us tomorrow around two, then have the lawyers over at three."

"Does Everlee know?"

He looks at me, then up the stairs. "No."

"Are we going to tell her tomorrow at two?"

"I guess we have to because lawyers will want her signature, too."

"Do you think Callum talked to Sammie after the meeting and requested she make it part of the deal?"

"To make her an equal owner? Possibly, probably. He knew Everlee wouldn't go for it since we already tried once, but coming from someone else." Jax laughs. "Seems like something he would do."

"Do you have a problem with it?"

"Not at all. As far as I see it, she's ours. We can't marry her to make it official, but…"

"We can buy a sex club with her?"

"A contract is a contract, I suppose."

"Yea. So then, couldn't we have some contract created tying us together… like a marriage?"

His eyes widen.

"I'm not saying now, but sometime. In the future. More symbolic. I don't know. It may be kind of nice."

"You're only saying that because you're knee deep in Lizzy's wedding plans."

I shrug. It's something that's always weighed on me to some extent. The want and desire to get married and have kids. It was never an option before, but that was before her. Before us. She makes things so easy. "Look, don't say anything to anyone about this."

"My lips are fucking sealed. Don't want her getting her hopes up for something that can't happen."

"But it could be nice though," I dream.

"What would be nice?" Knox bounces down the stairs gleefully.

"Your ass in a thong. So tight and perfect," Jax chides, not missing a beat.

"Don't pretend you haven't seen me wear my leopard print banana hammock thong. I know it's your favorite," Knox remarks.

"No, the fuck it's not."

"Then why is there a picture on your phone?"

"No, there's not."

Knox raises his eyebrows.

"What the fuck did your dumbass do?" Jax yanks his phone out of his pocket and begins flipping through the pictures.

My hands are tingling with anticipation. I can tell by the look on Knox's face, he put pictures of himself in a thong on Jax's phone. And the fact he didn't know and literally walked right into that setup is fucking hysterical.

When Jax finds them, he's going to lose his shit, so I move around the island, closing the distance to Knox, so I can run interference.

"You son of a-," Jax seethes. He holds his phone up and flips through twenty or so photos of Knox posing in a thong. A few are of him looking over his shoulder with his fingers pressed to his lips like he's keeping a secret, more of him laying on the bed with his leg propped up, another of him reading a book at Jax's desk. "You're dead!"

Knox tears up the stairs in a fit of laughter, with Jax following.

"I guess I'll get all the food and take it up," I mutter to myself.

I'm still chuckling as I walk up the stairs a few minutes later.

EVERLEE – UNDERWATER ORGASMS

- -

THE COOKOUT WAS A success, well, aside from the thirty minutes of Jax chasing Knox around the patio with a look of intent to kill fused into his face. Knox couldn't stop laughing and kept talking about a thong, so one could only imagine what was going on. Tony seemed mildly concerned while Lizzy was cackling hysterically, trying to figure out what exactly had happened. When she found out it was pictures of Knox in a leopard print thong, she suggested he get the photo printed and blown up. She shut up real quick when Jax cast daggers at her.

Fortunately, Emmett came up and informed us it was about time to eat, so Callum started cooking the hamburgers. I was able to get ahold of Jax and pull him into a corner and talk him down. So after that, the rest of dinner went fine. However, we all thought it best to keep at least two people between Jax and Knox. We weren't trying to terrify poor Tony.

After dinner, Emmett let us all sample the three finalists for his rainbows and unicorns drink for the upcoming costume night. It was interesting being able to see this side of the parties. Historically, I'd always just showed up to them, but this time I was getting a peek behind the curtain.

The cocktail that we all unanimously agreed on was a vanilla vodka martini that tasted like cotton candy that had a piece of the rainbow treat on top. It was simple enough, too. Put a piece of cotton candy in a glass, pour the vodka over top and watch it melt, then top with the fancy rainbow colored cotton candy. Sweet and delicious. I thought Lizzy was going to pass out when she saw him make it.

He saved it for last, which was equal parts smart and funny because Lizzy was working herself up, thinking there was no cotton candy. Emmett is so good with her. He's patient. Like very patient. All the guys are really, but Emmett more so than the others.

After drink sampling, we played a few rounds of pool and darts in the game room and then Tony and Lizzy called it a night and took off. I helped Emmett wash the dishes and talked with Callum a bit about the dinner. Jax had retired to his room and Knox was still hiding. He was fairly certain Jax didn't unleash beast mode because we had guests and once they left, so did his protection.

I knock softly on Knox's door and he calls out from somewhere in the room; I assume the bathroom, since it's slightly muffled. When I walk in, his sheets are pulled down on his bed, causing a small pang in my chest.

No group sleep tonight. It's probably the right idea, because the house as a whole is still not sure if Jax would kill him while he slept. I didn't see all the pictures, but the few I saw were fantastic. I tried not to laugh because I didn't want to exacerbate the problem.

Knox slides out of the room wearing only a pair of boxers with wet hair. "Have you come as a Trojan horse?"

"Nay." I laugh.

"I see what you did there."

I wink and move across the room. "I was just checking on you."

"I'm still alive."

"What were you thinking?"

"I don't know. I think I was drunk. Honestly, I don't remember. It's been months."

What he isn't saying is this happened when I'd left. He'd been drinking and acting recklessly.

"Honestly, I'm surprised he hadn't found them before tonight." He lifts me in his arms and spins me around.

"Do you want some company tonight?" I offer, not out of pity or guilt, but something else. Something I can't place. Knox has been coming out of his shell more, but there's still something inside of him that makes me want to just hold him and love him.

"Let me think about it. Hmmm. Yep. One hundred percent."

"Let me run to my room and take a shower, and then I'll come back."

"Or," he grabs me again. "You could take a bath here, with me?"

My eyes narrow at him and he tosses a lopsided grin my way.

"Twist my arm."

"Never. That's Jax's kink." He's chuckling as he walks into the bathroom. A moment later, the boxers he just had on are flying out of the door landing at my feet.

I've only been in his bathroom one other time. It's similar to mine, with the biggest difference being the fresh bouquet that is always showing up. The floor is an industrial concrete gray with wooden accents. In the center of the floor is a white porcelain tub, because Knoxxy baby loves him some baths.

Knox is already sitting in the bath, with the steam rolling off the top, by the time I get over to him. "You seem to be wearing too many clothes."

"You're very observant."

"It's one of my special skills."

I roll my eyes, smiling as I slip out of my dress, letting it fall to the floor.

"Getting warmer."

I slip off my bra and underwear and toss them on my dress.

"Smokin.'"

My fingers wrap around the cool porcelain tub as I dip my toe in, testing the heat. It burns on the skin for a second, but my body quickly adjusts.

"Here." Knox motions for me to sit in front of him with my back against his chest. "I was going to do bubbles, but thought that may be over the top."

"This is perfect." The water sloshes a bit as I settle between his legs. This is a large tub, but we fill it up almost all the way. His knees are bent, pressing on both sides of the tub, while I sit nestled in between, with a small bend in my knees.

"I put some lavender fragrance in here, though."

I look over my shoulder and use my fingers to guide his lips to mine. "Thank you."

He wraps his arms around me, and I fall back, resting my head on his shoulder. "This is what you see every day?"

"What are you talking about?" I moan out as relaxation sets in.

"Your tits, your body, your pussy. You just look down and voila."

I pull my neck to the side and see him looking down at my body and smile. "Yes, this is what I see, and you too, lately." I snicker.

"Perfection."

"How much did you have to drink?" I tease.

"Nothing. I didn't drink, well, aside from the samples of Emmett's drinks. I just appreciate the finer things in life."

I snake my hand behind me and rub his cheek affectionately.

"Do you want to wash your hair tonight?"

"Probably not."

He grabs a bottle of body wash from the wooden tray beside the tub and squirts some into his hand and rubs them together, working up a rich lather. It smells like him, eucalyptus and mint. He lifts each arm and rubs his hands up and down them a few times before he moves to my neck.

"You know I can do this myself?"

"I know, but I want to do it for you," he whispers, like his thoughts are far away from this conversation as he rubs his hands along my neck, massaging the muscles behind. I naturally lean up to give him more access and moan. God, I love massages. Especially from hot naked men in their bathtub.

His hands shift from my back and wrap around either side as he loops them under my arms and swipes them over my breasts. He kneads them, swirling his fingers around my nipples, causing a light moan to escape. I love his hands on me, rubbing, massaging, kneading. He's delicate, but intentional. My back arches, pressing my breasts into his hands, needing to feel more, causing a low groan to vibrate in his chest as his hard cock presses into my back. Light pants of breath fill the space between us as the warmth envelopes us. Every sense is amplified right now, it seems. Even the small stream of suds trickling down between my breasts cause goosebumps to appear on my skin, making my nipples harder.

"Knox," I moan out, letting my feet rub against his.

"Shh," his finger glides up to my chin and turns me towards him, taking my lips in a slow and passionate kiss. His tongue swipes at my bottom lip before pulsing in.

His hands continue to rub through our kiss, working their way down my chest to my belly. My head tingles a little with anticipation and excitement because I hear the O train off in the distance, but she's a' comin'.

His hand slides further down as he rubs the inside of my thigh across my hip bone to the other side. My hips shift, trying to close the space between my pussy and his hand, causing him to chuckle in my ear.

"Patience, love."

I groan out, and he continues to chuckle.

His hand rakes back up my body, and I swear I can almost feel my pussy frowning. He runs his fingers over both my breasts, then slides down and brushes them over my clit.

Ding! Ding! Ding!

Jackpot.

"Is this what you wanted?"

"Mmhmm."

He rubs the outside of my pussy, occasionally brushing across my clit, taking his time. He's toying with me. Teasing me. My hand slides on top of his and guides him where I want him to be, which he does, but then stops.

"I want you to finger yourself so I can watch."

Desire pools in my stomach when my eyes land on him. I want to give him what he wants. I yearn for that look of satisfaction in his eyes while he watches me, teeth biting down on his lip. My hand slides down my body, dipping below the water's edge, and curls around my pussy. My finger circles my clit a few times before dipping inside of me. First, one finger, then two.

His hands grab and rub my breasts, squeezing each time I push inside, in perfect unison, like he can feel my pleasure flowing through me. My head rests on his shoulder and my eyes close as I savor all the sensations boiling up inside of me- the feel on my pussy, his hands on my breasts and the feel of his cock against my back eagerly waiting to push inside of me. As my orgasm edges closer, my fingers pick up speed, riding the wave that is nearing. He leans down and presses his lips to my neck, his tongue and hot breath send shivers down my spine. The palm of my heel plants firmly on my clit while I curl my fingers inside of me, bucking my hips slightly.

His fingers pinch on each nipple, sending pain and pleasure through my stomach, straight to my pussy. "Ahh," I groan out.

"I want you to come for me," he softly commands, then grabs my hand and removes it from my pussy. "But not yet."

I turn to look at him dazed and bewildered. My orgasm was right on the edge. "You ass."

"It will be worth it, love." He pushes me off of him then commands me to turn around.

I spin, drawing my knees to my chest. He grabs my legs and guides them over his thighs to each side of him. "Beautiful," he says, staring at me. "Now, scoot back." He gently pushes me, so my back hits the edge of the tub. It's much colder than the water and causes me to clench and suck in a breath, but the sting is gone as quickly as it came.

He leans forward in the tub, his hands pressed to either side, his biceps bulging as he leans down. "You know," he whispers, with a smile on his face. "There are certain skills required to be a SEAL," he pauses, hovering over my body, his lips near my ear, "Like holding your breath for at least two minutes."

My stomach tightens at both the idea and the image in front of me. He's doing an equivalent of a diagonal push up on the tub, his elbows bent at ninety degrees, his feet pressed against the back of the tub, and the tip of his cock dipping just below the water. All I can do is moan and nod my head, because I'm on sexy sensory overload.

"Have you ever been eaten out underwater?"

A mangled noise escapes my lips and I'm pretty sure tears of joy are trickling down my face. I'd reach up to check, but my arms are currently pinned to my side by Knox's and I'm scared if I move I'll wake up from this dream.

He pushes up a little, then back down and plants gentle kisses on my neck, lowering his body and working down to my collarbone. His cock brushes between my legs and I tell myself not to move, but fuckin' aye. Pussy wants what the pussy wants. She bucks up to rub along his cock, causing him to blow out a breath. "I need you to behave and wait."

My eyes squint because my head is nodding yes, but my body is saying fuck no, and my brain is hoping we aren't caught in the lie.

"Good girl."

I whimper.

Straight up, dog whimper.

His knees sit between my legs as he works down my body, taking my breast in his mouth, planting soft kisses and flicking his tongue around my nipple, before repeating on the other. He moves down my chest to my stomach, his chin dipping under the water. I tilt my hip up, but he presses it back down, cutting his eyes up at me. My brows pump in apology, but I don't think he notices.

He takes a few deep and slow breaths.

Oh fuck! This is it! This is it!

It's like riding on a roller coaster and inching up to the top slowly. You see the end in sight and know you're about to fall and fall hard.

He slowly dips under the water, smooth like glass. Barely a ripple or a bubble.

His lips kiss on the inside of my thigh, then trail over to my pussy and I try as hard as I can, not to buck. I focus on the faucet and blow out a slow and steady breath as my head falls backward onto the edge of the tub.

Holy fuck. This sensation.

He readjusts his hands, scooping under my ass while his tongue licks up my center. I'd say it's fucking wet, but that would be an understatement since it's under water. I don't know if it's because I was so close to coming before, but this feeling... it's so intense.

"Ooh," I moan out, tilting my head back, grinding my neck into the side of the tub.

His tongue moves with such precision and the fact I'm trying not to move I think is only intensifying the sensations. This is so much worse than sitting on his face scared

I'm going to suffocate him, because it's that, but add water. Death by drowning whilst performing cunnilingus. Great way to end up on an episode of dumb ways to die.

But he's not dead. He's still very much alive because fuck, he's eating the hell out of me. The closer I get to the edge of my orgasm, the more my hips buck and my legs try to wiggle free, but he keeps them pinned down. Suddenly, he slips two fingers inside of me while he sucks on my clit.

Fuck. I'm like a bucking bronco, raising out of the water. Fucking Free Willy, jumping over the rocks. Give me orgasm, or give me death!

He bolts out of the water, taking in a large gulp of air, but lifts my ass with him, pulling me on top of him. Shit. I can't sit on his face *in* the water.

No. Can't do it.

That's a line I can't cross.

I *think.*

Fortunately, I don't have to decide. He slides back and lifts my legs out of the water and plants them on the edge of the tub, and slides forward. I raise up and grab the edge, so it looks like I'm crab walking around the tub. This has bad idea written all over it, but before I can say anything, he grabs my ass and brings me to his face.

He must have sensed my hesitation, because he pulls away briefly to say, "Don't fall." He's chuckling when he dives back in, but the laughter is soon replaced with groans. My head falls back as sensation after sensation rips through me. It's like my body is a live wire, and one touch is going to send me sparking. My nipples are so hard from arousal, coupled with the cool air on my warm skin, I'm fairly certain they could cut glass right now, but –

"Knox," I moan out, fighting the instinct to latch onto the side of his head and ride his face until I come. He doesn't relent and seconds later, I'm losing all control. My legs and arms grow weak as my orgasm tears through me, splitting me open. "Fuck, Knox!" I continue to repeat his name over and over again as wave after wave passes through me.

He lets my ass go and I collapse in a spent heap into the bathtub. Water splashes out and sloshes around me -us- as I fully submerge.

I pop up immediately, gagging and spitting water out and Knox is there, grabbing my arm, helping to hold me up.

"You weren't supposed to do that, goober," he coos, pushing my wet hair out of my face. Our eyes lock and emotions swell. "I love you so fucking much it hurts," his voice nearly quivers with a rawness that cuts through to your soul.

"Knox."

It's like time freezes around us, every sound fades away, every wave of the water ceases to splash. The veil he lives behind is down, if only for a second, and behind it is a boy scared of getting hurt. Scared of not being loved.

"Knox," I breathe out and crawl over to him, pressing my forehead against his. "I love *you* so much." I curl my forearms around the back of his head and sink onto his cock, each of us blowing out a breath.

"That first thrust inside of you always feels like heaven, like home. My home." Knox groans.

Fully seated on him, I grab his cheeks and tilt his head up to kiss him, slow. Passionate. Every gentle grind is full of so much emotion it aches. My heart aches, feeling like it's about to explode. His hands slide to my waist and he holds me there, as my hips rock slowly, grinding onto him. The pressure inside is on the verge of painful, but if I could take him deeper, I would.

Our tongues move faster, as do our hips. I moan out through the increased friction and speed of our thrusts. By this point, half the water is already out of the tub, so it's not sloshing around as much.

"You feel so good," he groans, taking my mouth with his again, his tongue fucking my mouth as fast as his hips. I'm hovering just above him so he can fuck me from below, his need overflowing.

"We need to get out of this bathtub." His words were frantic.

I nod quickly and pull myself off him and climb out, moving towards the bedroom. I don't know if he thought I was running from him, but he grabs me around the waist and carries me to the bed, pushing me over so my chest falls on his comforter. He grabs me around the waist and plunges into me deep for several thrusts, then with speed, pulls out and flips me over. He nods his head up and I promptly scoot up the bed.

"I need to watch you while I fuck you," he smiles. He presses his lips to mine again and slides his cock in. "So good."

He runs his hand down my right leg and lifts it straight up, and plants kisses down as far as he can go without pulling out. He holds it tight, my ass slightly lifted off the bed, while he continues to drive into me faster and faster. His pants are getting shorter and shorter and then he yells out and I feel his cock pulsing inside of me before he stills. My leg falls to the bed, and he crawls over the top of me and plants soft kisses around my breasts and under my jaw.

"Do you mind if I go to sleep with my cock in you?" There is a soft need or ache in his voice that pulls at something inside of me.

"Not at all." I push him, so we roll over and my legs flank his thighs. I lay my head on his chest and listen to his heartbeat slow down as my fingers dance around lightly on his skin.

His cock softens inside of me with each breath until the darkness creeps in and we're out.

EVERLEE - TOO LEGIT, TO QUIT

WHEN I WALK DOWN the stairs from sunbathing, I find the guys huddled around the kitchen bar with a folder sitting in front of them. They stop talking when I walk into the room, looking at me with their mouths open. A smile pulls at my lips. One way to shut up a group of men... walk in from outside, completely nude.

"What are you doing?" Jax chomps out.

"Getting some water. The fridge upstairs was empty."

Glancing at the paperwork spread before them, I know they're discussing the counteroffer Sammie had the lawyers bring by yesterday. Only Callum had briefly glanced at the paperwork because Knox had been driving him crazy, wondering what Sammie had said. Callum said all looked good, and she accepted the offer with a small contingency, but he wouldn't say what.

"This is perfect timing," Callum says.

Knox grabs the dishtowel off the handle on the oven. "For the love of our cocks, please put this on. I can't focus with you like... that." He throws his hand in the air.

"Sorry. I didn't mean to interrupt. I was just going to grab a water then go back up."

"We need you to stay," Callum says, clearly working through something in his head.

"I can stay, but I don't think I need to. I don't want to get in the way."

"You could never get in the way," Emmett says, licking his lips and moving around the counter to stand behind me.

"I seem to literally be in the way right now of you and the paperwork you all need to discuss. Had I known you were in the kitchen, I would have put clothes on."

"That would do everyone a disservice," Knox chimes, pumping his eyebrows up and down.

"We need to focus," Jax says, bringing everyone back to the topic at hand.

"I don't want to beat around the bush because the lawyers will be here within the hour to potentially finalize this."

"Potentially?" I ask, curiosity peaked. As of last night, it sounded like a done deal. "I thought she accepted with a small request."

"We all think it's small."

"Ok, so?"

Jax blurts, "She countered, you need to be part owner. Equal owner."

"Wait, what? Me? Why? We've already talked about this."

I try to ignore the look on Knox's face. He's been so excited about getting Allure back and right now he looks like a kid who's just had their ice cream stolen.

"We just got off the phone with her and she had a long explanation and honestly, we stopped listening because we were sold before it was even a condition of hers. Simply put, she stated a female's perspective is vital to the success of the club. She said that for so long, women have been forbidden to take pleasure in sex. They were purely repro-ductive instruments. A place for a man to stick their cock and a place to carry his child. If the woman couldn't do that, she was expendable. Sammie believes that while we have evolved leaps and bounds from where we were, women are still subconsciously held to those standards. A man who bangs a lot of women is a baller. A woman who bangs a lot of men is a whore."

I couldn't argue with that and it sounds just like something Sammie would say.

"She said it's really important to her to have a female perspective at Allure, to ensure women feel safe at the club. Safe and confident. Confident to explore what drives them, what satisfies them. She wants to do a monthly get together or something for all the women of the club, but she was still working out the details. She wants to empower them to take their sex back. I think that was her working motto."

"Wow. So..." I pull up a seat and let all the words seep into my brain. "So, in order for this deal to go through, I would need to agree to be an equal owner?"

Knox walks around to stand beside Emmett and starts placing kisses on my neck.

"Knox, you aren't playing fair," I moan as my body betrays me, giving him more access.

"What?" he whispers, his lips barely brushing along my neck.

"Do you want to be an owner with us?" Jax asks, rubbing circles on the counter.

"I do, but."

"But. I don't like buts," Knox says, stepping back a foot from me. "Except for yours. I love yours, but-"

"Shut the fuck up, Knox," Jax commands. He was still a little cross with Knox for the whole thong dong pics. Knox has been avoiding Jax as much as possible today for fear of an attack.

"What? Sorry. You know I ramble when I get nervous."

Jax face softens and he just rolls his eyes.

"I don't have the capital to contribute to this very large offer. It's unfair for me to be a partial owner without giving anything."

"Ev. We don't care about the money."

"I do," I snap, then quickly correct so they don't get the wrong idea. "I don't want you to ever feel like I'm taking advantage of you. The fact you gave me the house." My arm flings into the air towards the direction of my house, which admittedly, I'm hardly ever at.

"You're paying us rent," Callum says.

My hip pops up and my head falls to the side. "I know I'm paying you rent." I also know he's just funneling the money away into a bank account for me. He doesn't think I know, but I saw it by accident when I was looking for some paper in the office a week or so ago.

I glance at the clock.

Fifteen minutes.

"Fine."

"Fine?" Knox chirps, stepping closer to me.

"Fine, but–"

"Fucking buts!" Knox cries.

I reach out for him and bring him into me, placing his hand on my bare ass.

"So dirty, but I love it. But." He laughs at himself.

"It wasn't even a pun. Or a joke. You just said but, twice, but not even the right but."

"You just said but three times."

Jax shakes his head. "Seriously, shut the fuck up."

Knox's eyebrows rise on his forehead as his lips twist.

"My condition is that I don't get paid. Any money I would get goes back towards the loan to help pay for my portion of it. Once it's paid off, then I will accept a paycheck."

Without hesitation, Callum agrees, and then I see it on his face. This was going to happen all along. He had already played out all the moves, like a chessboard. I just got check-mated.

I narrow my eyes at him, and he gives me a sly smile back. I mouth 'you ass', at the same time Knox pulls me up into his arms, jumping up and down.

"You may want to get dressed, unless you want to meet our lawyers like that?" Emmett reminds.

"Shit. Right. Put me down, Knox," I say, quickly patting his chest.

Five minutes later, I'm racing down the stairs in a knee length green and white polka-dotted dress with a pair of flats on and my hair in a low messy bun just as the lawyers are walking into the kitchen. The man looks to be in his late thirties, with short and spiky light brown hair, a chiseled jawline, and a broad chest that fills his designer suit perfectly. He screams wealth, power, and confidence. Goddamn. Beside him is a younger woman with long brown hair pulled back into a low ponytail, wearing a knee length white and black pencil skirt with a dark blue silk blouse. She carries herself nicely, back straight, but I can see she feels slightly uncomfortable, even if she doesn't know it.

"Preston, Eliza, this is Everlee. Everlee, this is Preston and Eliza, part of our team."

"Nice to meet you." I slide to a reserved stop beside Knox, clasping my hands behind my back. I don't know why I just got nervous suddenly.

Because this is a big fucking deal. You're going into business with your men. You will be on a legally binding document with them, tying all of you together, my subconscious chimes in.

Shit. She's right. That's stupid. She's always right because she's me.

Fuck. Focus Everlee.

Knox's hand slips around my back and his fingers slip into mine. Nothing sexual, just encouraging.

He gives me a small smile and a wink, and it calms me almost instantly.

"Nice to meet you as well." Eliza smiles.

"Should we begin? This should be fairly quick, assuming all things are in order?" Preston asks.

Callum looks at me, waiting a beat, giving me the chance to back out, I realize, before nodding. "Yes. We're all in agreement."

"Excellent. We will get your signatures here, and then we'll head to Allure to get Sammie's. It feels like yesterday I was just helping on the documents for the sale to Sammie."

"And now you're the one owning it." Callum nods.

"We can handle business here at this table. The office will be a little too cramped."

"Perfect," Eliza and Preston echo in unison.

Preston pulls another set of documents from his briefcase and lays them out on the table. There are colorful tabs jutting out all around the document, all pointing to places where signatures are needed.

Knox gives my hand a light squeeze before he drops it and stands beside Callum.

Thirty minutes later, the last document is being signed.

It's done.

I'm officially a partial owner of a sex club.

I'm legally bound to my men. It's just a sex club, but... I take a deep breath, letting the moment pass before it swallows me. Do the men know that? They sign contracts all the time.

Knox is walking Preston and Eliza to the door with Callum.

"What's wrong?" Emmett asks when they leave the room, walking over.

"Nothing."

"Ev," he scolds.

"That was... just... we are bound together through this club."

He smiles. "I know."

"You know?"

"Yes. You didn't?"

"Well, I mean I did, but I didn't really realize..."

"We love you, Ev. We want you to be in every part of our lives."

When I walk into his arms, he squeezes me tightly, and a moment later, I feel Jax pressed behind me.

"My favorite kind of sandwich," he says with his nose pressed into my hair. "You smell like the sun and coconut."

"I was sunbathing an hour ago. Wait. I was sunbathing an hour ago."

"I feel you intended to say something different, but it just sounded the same to me," Emmett says.

"She was sunbathing an hour ago, E," Jax teases.

"Yes. I get that, but I'm also not getting it."

I press my lips to Emmett's and then turn to give Jax a kiss. "You guys are a bunch of assholes. I was sunbathing an hour ago and now I'm a partial owner of a sex club. You somehow worked your voodoo magic on me."

"Is that what you think?" Jax says, sliding his hand up my leg.

When he sighs, I let out a laugh.

"No fucking panties."

"I had little time! Putting some on would have wasted time, and I needed my hair presentable."

"Do you hear yourself?" he quips.

"Yes. Do you realize your finger is inching ever closer to my clit?"

"Yes. We have to celebrate."

"Did someone say celebrate with an exposed butt of our girl?"

"You just had to slide but in there, didn't you?"

Knox runs over to the cabinet and pulls out five flutes, while Callum grabs the champagne from the fridge.

Jax's finger lightly brushes along my clit at the same time the cork goes shooting across the room, making us jump. He pulls his finger away, letting my dress fall, as he walks over to the bar.

"Are you fucking kidding me right now?" I pant, body on fire with need. He was so close...

"To the first deal with the five of us," Callum says.

"You are ours, we are us," Emmett says, pressing his lips on my head.

"Now we celebrate," Jax says.

"But-" Knox starts, then stops when Jax moves towards him.

"How does it feel?" Callum asks me.

"The same? I feel like it should feel different."

He smiles. "I get that. When we first bought the property for Vixen, it didn't feel real for a while. Just give it a few days."

"I want to give as much as I can to make this place a success. I have so many ideas and thoughts already."

"I know you do." He kisses my forehead. "I can't wait to do this with you. It's the first of many."

"Many?"

"You are ours. We are a team."

JAX - A PEEK BEHIND THE CURTAIN

THE LAST FEW WEEKS have been a clusterfuck. I suppose the more politically correct term would be a whirlwind, but that would not accurately reflect the amount of bullshit I've had to deal with. And don't get me wrong. I'm not so much complaining, but simply stating it's been a lot.

It started two weeks ago when we finalized the deal for Allure.

It still feels weird saying we own a sex club again. A very profitable sex club, at that. More like a sex machine. We're tied up for a few years financially because of this, but we all think it's worth it and in some ways I'm glad we have her back. Almost like it was meant to be.

Everlee is definitely discovering she has kinks, so this has, and will continue to be fun.

We've been finalizing the date and decorations for our Rainbows and Unicorns party. We thought it was the perfect theme for pride month and I've been so lucky to have Lizzy's input and opinions.

I'm lying.

But I guess it hasn't been that bad. It's just a lot of extra Lizzy time.

If forced to tell the truth, I'd have to admit she has been *some* help. We settled on the seventeenth because Everlee got really excited about the numbers. Something about six plus seventeen equals twenty-three... so 6.17.23. Which then, of course, Lizzy got excited and was talking about fate and stars aligning and other random bullshit. It's a tighter deadline than we've been used to, but she managed to pin down all the decorations and order the costumes for the servers. She, of course, found out about Allure, so just two words.

Holy and shit.

She... I know this will be a shocker, also has a ton of ideas for that too. One of her best was actually apparel and toys and such at Allure. For the themed events at Vixen, we could do tie-ins or something at Allure. It would definitely be a one-way street. Allure members could know about Vixen, but not the other way. We're still flushing through the legalities of that and what it would exactly look like.

I glance at my watch.

Three after five.

The sun is hot on my face as I stand beside the car outside of Everlee's work. I want to surprise her tonight with a special dinner for just us. I still haven't told her I loved her, which I think is irritating me more than her. Sure, I've said it in other ways indirectly, just not directly. Not those three little words that refuse to come out of my mouth.

Every time I try to say them, my throat seizes and I feel like I've swallowed a fish. Which, yes, I have done. Not my best story from my time with the SEALs. It was only for a second, but fucking Knox saw and fished it out.

Ha. Fuck. That was a slip.

When she walks out of the building, the smile on her face dances in her eyes.

She jogs the short distance between us and gives me a hug and a kiss on the cheek. "What are you doing here?"

"I thought I would take you out to dinner. Just the two of us."

"Really?"

"Is that ok?"

"Yea, yea, of course!"

She slides into the passenger seat when I open the door for her, tossing her bag in the back. We've started doing things more one on one with her. We didn't want her to think she had to be with all of us all the time. Between the clubs, work, and home, we didn't want to wear out our welcome, as Ms. Mary would say.

When the car starts, I press play and Romantic by Stanaj starts playing. I had thought about going with the NOTD Remix because that's the one I usually listen to, but decided to go with the original. It's slower, but feel it will really say the words I can't.

I recently found Stanaj and love a lot of his music, but this song really spoke to me. I hope she sees the meaning behind the words in the song and will know I love her even if I can't say it to her.

My hand drifts to her leg and I give it a light squeeze as I hold her gaze, watching her as the words dance around us. I wait until she reaches the moment of realization that this song was picked for her, then pull out onto the road. My plans were to take her to a nice steak house tonight. It's one that recently opened up. I've been wanting to try it and I know she loves her steak, so win-win.

When we get to the light, I quickly glance at her and see her eyes are glassy, so I flip my hand over and she interlaces her fingers in mine. When the song ends, I turn off the audio and we sit it silence. Admittedly, not my best idea. Should have thought past the song, because now I feel like there's an awkward silence in the car. Or maybe that's just me.

Ten minutes later, we're at the bar inside of the restaurant. We still have a few minutes until our reservation, so we decide to get a drink. She squeals when she sees they have Luxardo liqueur to make Emmett's old fashion, so we give the directions to the bartender and order two.

We get to our table and talk about any and everything, but mostly about my time at Ms. Mary's and which school I went to. We determine we had to have crossed paths at some point growing up because we lived so close to one another. Perhaps we were at some of the same festivals or fairs. She and Beckett loved going to them, and Ms. Mary usually had a booth setup selling her homemade jams and chow-chow.

We talk so much it's hard for us to eat our food, but we do. We decide to split a twelve-ounce wagyu filet so we can order more sides to try as many as possible. The steak is perfectly cooked and seasoned, and we order a side of spinach, mushrooms, brussel sprouts, potatoes au gratin, and asparagus. It's a ton of food, and we devour most of it, but have to bring a few boxes home of the sides. The boys, mostly Emmett, will be happy he gets to try them.

Even though we're stuffed, we order dessert, because why not? We get a flight of chocolate cake, cheesecake, and a raspberry and lemon sorbet. As soon as Everlee sees the chocolate cake, she attacks with a ruthless ferocity I've never seen from her before and that's saying a lot since our latest trysts have been... well, more intense. She refuses to give me a bite until I threaten her with vanilla sex. I was only teasing, but you would have thought I threatened her life.

We wrap up our three-hour meal and head to the car.

"Do you want to go home?" I ask.

"Not yet. This is nice." She interlaces her fingers in mine.

"This is." I lean over and kiss the top of her head.

"But we can't do anything super active because I feel like you could literally roll me around right now, I'm so full. I shouldn't have had that last bite of cake."

"You could have shared it with me. The one tiny little bite you gave me was the equivalent of a crumb."

"Yea, I suppose I could have."

She doesn't say anything else and I'm all smiles.

"I have a spot I used to visit when we first moved here."

"Really?"

We get in the car and take a thirty-minute drive to an abandoned area of town. The buildings are empty and have graffiti painted all over the walls. I lead her around to the back of one of the buildings and we climb the stairs, all the way to the top of the building.

"How many flights of stairs was that? Fuck." She bends over at the top and grabs her knees.

"Seems like more than I remember, but this view." I walk to the edge and just stand. It's like a wave of memories come rushing back to me. Memories and feelings of when we first moved here. The excitement, the fears, and the pain from all the bullshit I left overseas. The loneliness and loss of purpose. I fought for a long time with the feeling of duty to go back, while also having the desire to be home. I missed Callum and Emmett. And Knox. We were together in the same unit, but I saw him drifting further away and at moments, it was like he wasn't even there. We talked and decided to come home, but I still miss it. And parts of me always will. I get my fill every once in a while, when I go on random missions with Dufrey, but it's not a life I can go back to again. Not with Ev here now.

"You can see the downtown lit up from here. That's what, like an hour away?" she asks in her light singsong voice, pulling me back to reality.

I laugh. "With traffic, maybe a little longer, but we're about twenty miles away. When we first moved here, I would come here and just sit on the edge and stare at the city. Part of me wanted to live there, but the other part didn't. I was torn with what I wanted, because around the same time we were expanding our business, or at least talking about it, as well as, debating if we should live the poly lifestyle."

"Why did you?"

"You know... I don't really know. It just sort of happened. I don't really want to get into the details because that would mean I'd have to talk about the girls at the beginning. I know they are in the past, but if the roles were reversed, even though I know you're with me, with us, I would hate to hear about you being with other men. Even seeing dickface-"

"Rich? I've moved on from calling him dickface because I have no feelings for him anymore. No love, no hate. He is nobody. I feel like calling him dickface, still implies I have feelings."

"I'd give you a cookie for all that, but I know you're stuffed. I'll still call him dickface because I have many emotions I still feel about him. Mostly hate. But a little gratitude, because if he wasn't such a fuckup, you would have never left and never found us. So, there's that."

She smiles and walks over to me, looping her arms around my waist. I pick her up and her legs instinctively wrap around me. We walk over to the edge, and the closer we get, the more I can feel her tensing and clamping around me.

"Are you ok?"

"Umm, sooo, yea, not really. I don't like edges of buildings."

"Heights?"

"No. I'm mostly ok with heights, but the edges of building specifically. Like that wall barely comes to your knees, you could just tumble and flip over. I guess I'm so clumsy..."

She shudders in my arms. "I will never let you fall. Ever." I take three steps away from the edge and press my lips to hers. She wraps her arms around my neck and the kiss deepens.

I fucking love kissing her sweet lips. They're soft like clouds and so damn delectable. I could spend my days with her in bed with my lips pressed to hers or anywhere on her body, really.

She stays, wrapped in my arms, for an immeasurable amount of time as we just silently look out at the cityscape in the distance. We eventually head back to the car and she grabs my phone unexpectedly.

"What are you doing?" I question, chuckling.

"Sorry," she holds my phone in her hand, staring at me, eyes wide.

"I don't care you have it. I was simply wondering what you're doing."

"You don't mind me looking at your phone?"

I chortle, "No. Why would I care? You're welcome to touch anything of mine you want." I toss a quick wink at her and watch as the blush tinges her cheeks. The guys and I find it hilarious that after everything we've done and been through together, she still blushes at the slightest hint of anything sexual. Do we say things on purpose to watch her blush? Yes. Yes, we do.

"Wow," she whispers, then looks down at the phone and begins flipping through songs it looks like. I really don't care what she's doing. I have nothing to hide from her... well, feelings wise maybe, but I'm getting better, and that's when I realize it probably wasn't like that with dickface. The thought of him causes my body to tense and grip the steering wheel, but I take two deep breaths and try to let it go.

She looks over at me. "Sooo... since you played a song for me, I have one for you. I heard you playing Stanaj a week or so ago. I think it was the Sweat song and when I heard it and saw you working out, I nearly orgasmed and probably would have, but I had an early morning meeting. So that was the only thing that stopped me from jumping your bones right there."

A smile spreads across my face because I remember the day she's talking about. I was working out doing lunges and weight lifts, and when I looked in the mirror, I saw her by the door with a flush across all the parts of her body I could see before she darted. I meant to ask her about it later and then completely forgot.

"So anyway, I found the song and also started listening to his other stuff and really liked his music. And then there was this song that stuck out to me." She presses play and Love Me, the acoustic version starts playing. I can feel her eyes on me and then when it gets to the second verse, I feel those words - her words - on so many levels. I grab her leg and can't help but feel this overwhelming emotional connection to her. It's like she sees me and understands me on a level I don't know if I understand. She doesn't ask for more than I can give and accepts it and meets me on that level. She only said she loved me the one time, and I think that was only because she was half asleep. She doesn't push or try to overwhelm or even guilt trip. She simply accepts what I have to give and I love that.

When we get home, the lights in the house are off, except for the under-counter lighting in the kitchen.

"Are they gone?"

"I guess they went out and got their own dinner."

"What do you want to do?" she asks in a cutesy voice, twirling her hair.

I smile, shaking my head from side to side. "Run."

She stares at me for a moment, then squeals, bouncing up and down in her spot.

"I'm going to count to ten."

Her eyes grow wide with excitement.

"One... two... three..."

She darts out of the door.

I grab a piece of paper from the office and jot down a quick note. *Meet us in our room.*

EVERLEE - LUNCH WITH LIZZY. ENOUGH SAID

THE SUN IS SHINING on my face and I'm happy. Like walking on clouds happy. Beckett and Will get in tonight for the Rainbow and Unicorn's party at Vixen tomorrow. Things with the boys are going amazeballs, and I'm getting my feet more wet with Allure. Knox and I have taken part in another two Shibari demonstrations and have had a private lesson with the teacher with all the guys. It's been a couple of days, but my breasts are still a little sore. They had me suspended and when I tell you it was worth the pain...

Holy shit.

They could swing me onto their cocks. I felt like I was on a merry-go-round of dicks. Amazing!

The door to the restaurant opens the same time I get up to it and the kind gentleman holds it open for me. Before I can thank him, a tornado of a woman is hurling herself across the floor, yelling my name.

I nod quickly at the guy and his worried glance flickers between Lizzy and me.

I'm pretty sure he nearly ran down the sidewalk out of fear of that crazy, shouting woman.

She wraps her arms around me. "Are you so excited?"

"For?"

"For? Rainbows and Unicorns tomorrow night!"

"Right."

"What else could there be?"

"I don't know. With you it's a crap shoot. Could be a party, could be a new pen."

"I do love pens."

"I know you do." I smile, shaking my head. "Yes, I'm excited about the party and happy that Beckett and Will are able to come."

"What time is their flight landing?" she asks, linking her arm in mine walking us to the hostess stand. She flashes two fingers and we're sat in a booth near the front, which is the absolute worst place for her to be.

"They land at six."

"Are you going to the airport?"

"No." I raise my eyebrows. "Betty is."

"That Betty."

"God love her."

"So what's been going on? Has mister tall, dark and cranky said those three little words to you yet?"

I blow out a breath. "No. Not exactly, but that's fine."

"Men. I know he does... so why not say it?"

I shrug. "He tells me through songs. He'll send me songs to listen to that say what he can't."

"That's the most bumblebee transformer shit I've ever heard."

"What?"

"He's bumblebeeing you."

I'm still confused.

She sighs like I should be getting this reference.

"Bumblebee, the bright yellow car. His voice box was messed up, so he communicates through his radio. Jax is bumblebeeing you."

"Maybe, but it's nice. He'll say it when he's ready.

She smacks her lips. "So Tony and I are headed down to South Carolina this weekend to look at some wedding venues."

"You're getting married at home?"

"I don't know. We're still up in the air about here, or at home, or even on a remote island with a few close people."

"Does Emmett know?"

"Yea. I'm pretty sure I've been talking to him more than you lately. It's just under a year which is crazy to think. There's so much planning left to do."

"I know. But as much as you have talked about this since we were little, I would have assumed you had it all planned out."

"Yea... but now it's real. Emmett said he will go wherever I need him to go. I then jumped into his arms and told him I loved him. He laughed and sat me back down. He's a good one, kid."

"Kid?"

"Well, being engaged makes me feel like I'm adulting more. Do you think the guys would propose to you?"

"Lizzy. We've been over this before. I can't exactly get married to four guys," I whisper the last part.

"They could still put a ring on it. Fuck, put four. OMG I would be so jealous. Not really, but maybe a little. Just kidding. I wouldn't be. I don't think. It's hard to say. I'd have to see the rings first."

"Are you done now?"

"Yes. I suppose I am."

We order our food and talk about Allure and theme nights to get more business, especially more female clientele. Lizzy loved my themed book club sex club night. She called it book sex club squared, or BSC squared, or BCSC. She rambled for at least five minutes on the possible names.

"You know what bothers me?" she bursts randomly.

"There are so many things, it's hard to say," I answer, deadpan.

She narrows her eyes at me. "This." She holds up her drink.

"Your drink bothers you?"

"No."

"I'm so confused."

"Why can I drink a drink, but I can't food a food?"

"Oh, is that where we are today?"

"Yes."

"I see." I pinch my lips together in a hard line.

"Well?"

"Well, what?"

"Do you have an answer?"

"I do not, but I'll propose this. Which is silent in scent? The s or the c."

"Son of a bitch. That's good."

I can't help but laugh at her. She's so funny and random. "Hey. Back to your wedding."

"Go on."

"Where would you go if you went away?"

"I don't know. A big part of me just wants to have it here. Traveling, even back to South Cakalacky is going to be a pain. Most of our friends are here, Bo's is here. I think I'm just going to do it here." She nods like her mind has been made up.

"Here? That's it."

"Yep. It's about time I make some decisions."

"So, are you still going home?"

"Yea. It will be nice to show Tony around some more and see my mom. If you recall, I didn't have time to go at Easter."

"Yes. I recall that day and our conversation vividly."

"As you should all of our conversations."

"If you see my parents, will you say hi to them?"

"Yes, I'm going to see your parents. They're on my schedule. I need some of your mother's exquisite cooking."

"Just remember not to say anything..."

"About what? There are so many things with you now. The fact you have your own little harem, the fact you are part owner in a kinky sex club, the fact you love being tied up with ropes. Really, I feel like the list keeps growing and growing."

"Shut up."

She zips her lips and throws away the key.

"If only your lips were zipped for real."

She gasps dramatically.

Our food comes and we eat while we continue to plan out places she can call to book for her wedding. When I get back to work, I send out a few more emails before the bosses come in and tell everyone to take off the rest of the afternoon. Said they wanted to start summer hours, effective immediately. So we basically get Friday afternoons off, now through Labor Day.

It's nice to get off a little early because it gives me a chance to get home and clean up some before Beckett and Will arrive.

EVERLEE - BECKETT AND WILL, SUSHI AND CHILL

<hr>

JUST BEFORE SEVEN O'CLOCK, my doorbell rings. I jump to my feet and race across the floor, throwing the door open.

"Hello sister," Beckett says, peeking his head in.

"Hello brother. What are you looking for?"

"Your men."

"They aren't here. They're at the club."

"Which one?" He shimmies his shoulders playfully.

He just found out a few nights ago about Allure and has been giving me shit nearly non-stop through texts ever since. "Vixen."

"Are we going there tonight?"

"Do you want to? I figured since we were going to be there tomorrow night, you may want to just relax here tonight. We can order in some sushi and hang out on the guy's roof."

He pulls his face. "I don't know. What do you think, babe?" He looks at Will.

"That sounds great to me. I had a long shift last night and didn't get a ton of sleep, and I'm fairly certain tomorrow is going to be a long night."

"Your first pride party," Beckett says, making a heart with his hands and tilting his head to the side.

"So sweet." I clasp my hands under my chin.

"Shut it. Only I can be a smart ass." He shifts his bags in his hand. "Show me to my room, servant maid."

"One, kiss my ass. Two, it's the same room as last time. And three, I'm not showing you anywhere. I'll be here waiting when you come back down."

When the boys are walking into the kitchen ten minutes later, I hand them each an old-fashioned. I'd gotten pretty good at them since Emmett's been working with me and I got all the right ingredients.

"Is this what I think it is?" Will asks.

"It is."

"I've missed these since our last time here."

"You mean a few weeks ago?" Beckett snarls.

"It's been over a month. Don't be dramatic."

"All I'm saying is that I've seen you more in the last two months than I have in the last two years. I can only take small doses of you and this is really pushing it."

I shove his shoulder and his drink sloshes, but he does some maneuvering to not spill any. He laughs, "I'm kidding. Of course." He looks away and whispers, "Maybe."

"I hope you don't mind, but Lizzy is coming over. She said she has to see her beau FF."

"Beau FF?"

"Beau friend forever?"

"She called me that? I love her."

I turn my head to the side. "She was talking about Will."

"What the fuck?"

Will steps forward, excuse me, "Make way for the Beau FF."

"She's dead to me."

The doorbell rings and Beckett holds his arm out. "I'll get this."

A few minutes later, Beckett is walking back into the room with Lizzy on his back. "Let me koala youuuu!" she whines.

"No! You're dead to me."

"Boo boo brother. Say it ain't so."

"It ain't so."

"What?" She tries to crawl over his shoulder to look in his face.

"You said to say it, so I did."

"Aren't you a funny?"

"Yes. I am a funny."

She crawls off his back and pats him on the butt. "Thanks for the lift fire daddy."

"Ooh fire daddy. I like that," Will says, setting his drink on the counter and walking over to hug Lizzy.

After the hug, she pats Will on the butt. "Firm. I can tell you've been working out." She chuckles, then grabs Beckett's drink off the counter and walks away with it.

"What the hell?" he calls after her.

"I thought you made it for me."

"Yep. Sure did."

"I'll be on the roof waiting for you. We've so much to discuss," she taunts, walking away.

"I'll go with her," Will says, jogging away.

"Traitor!" Beckett yells after Will.

After I make Beckett another drink, we head over to the guy's house and walk up to the roof.

"What are you two talking about?" Beckett asks, stepping onto the roof.

"Her wedding."

"Ooh, fun. Fun. Go on. Let's hear the deets."

We spend the rest of the night eating sushi, talking about Lizzy's wedding, and planning a summer vacation with everyone. Somehow Lizzy had gotten us to agree to a week's vacation at the beach and was already looking at houses to rent. She found a huge one with seven rooms, two full kitchens that's on the beach. Will and Beckett were all in, but I needed to get the guys on board, which should be an interesting conversation.

JAX - UGHH

THE MUSIC IS THUMPING, and the club is packed. When I walked by Lizzy and Everlee's table ten minutes ago, they still weren't here, which is a little concerning. I'm sure she's fine- they're- I'm sure they're fine. Emmett and Knox have been telling me I should be inclusive of the group, but really, all I care about is her- Everlee.

"You ok?" Knox asks standing beside me looking down to the main floor.

"Yea."

"Did you hear we're going to the beach? Apparently, Lizzy is planning it all."

I cut my eyes at him, causing him to laugh.

"What? It could be fun. We've never done anything like this before."

"Probably for good reason. Can you imagine being stuck inside a beach house with Lizzy for seven days? Waking up and going to sleep with her there." My insides quake at the thought.

A hand slips over my shoulder. "Are you talking about me, you big hunka meat?"

I slowly turn and find Lizzy dressed in a silver sequin top with a rainbow-colored tutu, wearing a unicorn headband, with Tony beside her, shirtless, wearing a pair of tight rainbow-colored pants with rainbow fur around his ankles. The fact Lizzy has found someone to match her energy and is confident in his sexuality enough to wear that outfit is amazing.

I know I talk a lot of shit about her, but she's a pretty good chick. Just still need her in limited doses.

"Good evening Jax. Sorry we were late. Your girl couldn't decide what to wear."

I look around, trying to find her. "Where is sh-" My words are cut off when I see her walking up the stairs.

Fucking Everlee.

"Excuse me," I snap and push past them.

I grab Everlee by the arm and lead her across the floor into our office.

"What's going on?" she huffs.

"What in the fuck are you wearing?"

"What do you mean?" She looks down at herself.

"You're wearing a bra and a tutu. Are you insane?"

"It's a decorative rainbow bra that's bedazzled, and a rainbow tutu. And what's insane was that Beckett had the same outfit, but I convinced him not to wear it. Thought it would look super weird, so he opted for the white unicorn leotard with rainbow leggings."

A string of sounds leaves my mouth as I try to process before I get out what I want to say. "You can't wear that."

"The fuck I can't." She recoils in shock.

My hands are clenched at my side as rage boils within.

A moment later, there is a beep at the door and we both look to see Emmett walking in. "Thank fuck. Will you?" I throw my hand in Everlee's direction and walk away for a moment.

"Hey love," I hear Emmett say and turn to see him sliding his arm around her. "Lizzy said you may be in trouble."

"I'm fine. I can handle this brute."

"You look delicious." He slides a finger over the top of her breast, then lifts the tutu. "Underwear? I'm impressed."

"I couldn't get too crazy."

"No. You just had to wear that outfit," I snap.

"It's no less than what I usually wear and not the skimpiest thing on the floor by a long shot. I saw some chick wearing the equivalent of a strap with furry rainbow patches in three key places." She crosses her arms, puckers her lips, and raises her eyebrows. God, I could just kiss her right now. Her sass is such a turn on, making me want to show her who is the boss. Put her in her place, but I can't. I need to stay strong.

"I don't care about anyone else! I care about you!" I shout back.

Emmett steps forward, but Everlee holds her arm out and closes the distance between us. She grabs both sides of my cheeks. "I care about you too and I can handle myself if anyone tries to get handsy. Plus, you should look at it this way. Guys will be looking at me, but it won't matter because they aren't you all. They aren't the ones I'm going home with. Plus, like Emmett said. I'm wearing underwear."

"Small miracles," I huff.

"I wore them for you."

"So, you *were* thinking about me when you put this on?"

"Yes. You were the first person I thought about."

"And you still did it, anyway?"

"Did you want Beckett wearing it?"

"I don't give a shit what he wears. If–"

"No ifs. I will not wear a potato sack to make you feel better. Trust me when I say I only have eyes for my guys and no one else. Plus, between Lizzy and Beckett... they're like two Rottweilers by my side. No one is getting close to me."

I pull her hands down and grip the back of her neck, bringing her lips to mine. "You're damn straight."

She looks up at me, her eyes twinkling, "You mean compared to my brother?" She laughs. "Straight. I'm straight... he's gay..."

I can't with her. "Get." I point to the door.

She gives me a quick peck on the lips before she heads to the door. She flips up her tutu, showing me her ass just before the door closes and my fists clench. It's taking everything in me to not chase her down, rip off that fucking fabric and bend her over this desk and make her come around my cock. I take a deep breath, then look at Emmett. "You watch her tonight."

"Nooo. Any job but that," he teases.

I push past him and walk out to the club. I glance at their table and Lizzy offers me a thumbs up like that's supposed to be encouraging. Everlee's talking to Will and Beckett, no doubt telling them what the drama was all about. I usually try to stay away from anything one could call drama but her. Ugh! Wait until Callum sees that outfit. He'll lose his shit.

"Our girl is smokin' tonight. Have you seen her?" Knox bounces up behind me a few minutes later.

I simply cut my eyes at him.

"I'll take that as a yes," he whispers, holding his hands up and backing away.

How in the hell am I supposed to concentrate when I know she's walking around wearing... ugh. My cock twitches and I want to spank it. Not spank like codeword for jack it off or rub one out. No. Literally spank it for reacting like that. I know it's an extension of me and what I want, but clearly, we aren't synched up and jiving right now. Because he should not be getting hard thinking about her.

I smile as a wicked thought crosses my mind. Perhaps we could have her dress up in this outfit and take her to Infernus. I've always wanted to hunt a unicorn.

"Why are you smiling? What's wrong? Who did you hurt?" Callum asks, walking up.

"Shut up. You make me out to be some apathetic asshole."

"You said it, not me."

My lips twist. "I was just thinking about taking Everlee to Infernus wearing the outfit she has on."

He looks over his shoulder and I realize he hasn't seen her until just now. He takes a step, so I grab his arm. "Stop. It's a wasted effort."

"Wasted?" His blue eyes have turned from crystals to flames as his fingers clutch the hem of his jacket.

"I've already pulled her into the office and read her the riot act. She, of course, bucked and essentially told me to fuck off."

"Sounds like our girl," he says, blowing out a breath, realizing I'm right and confronting her will do nothing.

"Lizzy and Beckett won't let anyone near her, and Emmett's watching her tonight as well."

"While he runs the bar?"

I shrug. "I'm also watching her. I swear. If one person so much as looks at her the wrong way, I'm serving them their fucking eyes on a platter."

"That may not be good for business." He looks over at me with a cool glance.

"Fuck the business. It's Everlee."

Callum stares at me without speaking for a moment. "You know. If you told her how you feel, maybe you wouldn't be so stressed."

"I'm not stressed. I'm great."

He lets out a low chuckle. "Brother. You've been more stressed in these last few weeks than I've seen you in years. Do you need to see Rhonda again?"

"My therapist? No. I'm good."

"Do you know why you haven't told Everlee you love her? Because I know you do."

"She knows it too. I send her songs saying as much."

"Songs are great and she probably knows it, but it would be nice for her to hear it."

"Why are you pushing this?"

"Sorry. I don't mean to. I just... I'm scared you're letting fear win."

"Fear?" I scoff.

He shrugs. "Look. You say you're good. I'll believe you. I'm going to go say hey to our girl."

"Careful," I warn.

He's chuckling as he's walking away.

EVERLEE - CALLING PANTY PATROL, AISLE FUCK

"I FOR SURE THOUGHT you were going to get a fuck from the way he dragged you into that office," Lizzy says to me when I get back to the table.

"Gross. I'm right here," Beckett chimes in.

Lizzy shrugs, "Next time I'll call earmuffs, but it was a legit thought."

"I think Will and I are going to go dance."

"I may join you in a bit." I wanted to give Jax a chance to calm down because I knew this outfit was likely to set some of the men on fire. Jax was at the top of the list, followed closely by Callum. But I also wanted them to know they can't control me. I'm wearing underwear and it's really no different from wearing a bathing suit. Speaking of, what are they going to do in the summer when we go to the beach? Walk around with a towel around me?

I asked them about the beach this morning and showed them the house Lizzy had found. The guys seemed on board, even though they didn't give a firm answer. I'd have to get that tonight because the house looks amazing and it's right on the beach. I don't want anyone else to get it.

Lizzy, Tony, and I watch the boys head to the dance floor. I know Will's new to the lifestyle, in terms of being out publicly, but he seems to be doing a good job with it. Tonight, he wore a white tank that had the word LOVE splashed across it in rainbow colors with matching rainbow shorts. I don't know if it's easier for him here since he doesn't know anyone or because we're just accepting. Whatever it is, I'll take it. He seems to fit Beckett's personality well, and conversely, I would say Beckett probably helps to bring him out of his shell some.

"Darling," a voice coos behind me.

When I turn around, Callum is standing there looking down at me. I stand to give him a hug and his arms slide across my back and he lets out a low hum.

"You look..." he pauses, trying to find the right words.

I smack my lips and roll my eyes, causing him to chuckle.

"You'll have to wear this again... in private."

My stomach tightens and goosebumps race across my skin. "How mad is Jax?"

"Jax? Mad?" He shakes his head. "He's just concerned."

"He has nothing to worry about with me."

"Not you love. He trusts you. It's the others here."

"I can handle them, too."

"That's probably true, but Jax... he can't handle it."

"Well, he better learn."

"Yes. I suppose he will, won't he?"

"I did wear underwear, though." I smile, batting my hair playfully.

He chuckles and brings me in, pressing his cheek against mine. "That's a shame. It will make it more difficult to fuck you in this outfit later. Because I can promise you, before you leave here tonight, I will have had my cock inside of you. And I doubt I'll be the only one."

Where's the fucking panty patrol when you need them? It's like a fucking geyser down there right now. "Thanks," I moan back. "Now it feels like I've pissed myself because of the amount of arousal that is pooling in said panties."

He lets out a low hum in my ear.

"You better go ahead and fuck. You'll both be useless until you do," Lizzy suggests.

"Lizzy!" I snap.

"What? It's the truth. I can practically hear his mating growl from here. His eyes have even darkened with hunger."

"Are you just quoting random lines out of my smut books?"

"He's smoldering now. He's potentially burning for you. Hurry before he ignites into a lust filled inferno and brings this whole place down."

"Lizzy." I have no other words to say.

"Oh Everlee, your skin is glistening, glowing, even. Ready to take a thick cock." Lizzy continues and Tony seems to enjoy Lizzy's monologue.

"Lizzy!"

"Fuck. I know that's my name. I was born with it. You don't need to keep repeating it."

"Well, stop saying things."

"Your lady only speaks the truth. You can thank me later." She pointedly glances at Callum, who looks like he's about to implode.

I shake my head and walk over to their office to get away from her for a moment. Her fading cackles echo through the bass that's pumping and I realize I don't have a key. I really need to get one. I was already hot after my encounter with Jax and now with Callum. I need to just get away. Find a corner and just... be.

Callum presses up behind me a moment later, swiping his card.

"Callum," I breathe.

As soon as the door buzzes, he pushes it open and looks at me. "I really wish you hadn't worn this tonight."

The door closes and I just stare at him as he drinks me up with his eyes.

"I like this outfit."

"So do I. Just not here."

"I can take it off." I pull down my tutu and panties at the same time and step out of them.

"Fuck... Everlee." His hand swipes through his hair.

"You just said not even five minutes ago that your cock was going to be in me by the end of the night. Do you think it's fair to have me going around the entire night wondering when that's going to happen? I sure as fuck don't."

"Damn it, Everlee. I wasn't..."

"You weren't being serious? You were just trying to toy with me? Get me all hot and bothered? Pay me back for wearing this outfit? Guess what? Two can play that game." I shove him back against the door and run my hands up his chest and slip his jacket off his shoulders.

"Fuck me..." he moans.

"I plan to." I smile, leaning forward to nibble on his neck.

"This isn't a good idea." The words don't match the look on his face or the growing bulge in his pants.

"You're right. It's a great idea. But I'll never admit it to Lizzy. I'll never hear the end of it."

He lets me guide him towards the couch where he falls, legs spread. "Take your pants off," I command, unclipping his buckle. He's sliding out of his pants a moment later. I grab them and throw them across the room and take in the sight of his beautiful hard cock, with the hints of tattoos playing under his shirt near his hips. I climb on top of him, lining him up with my pussy and sink down, taking him fully. The first thrust in is like heaven. I grind down on his cock as I fully seat myself on him. "This will be a quick fuck. You have work to do."

"Yes, ma'am."

"Call me Madame McKinley." I wink.

"I see. Madame McKinley."

I grab the back of the couch behind him, lift off his cock before pressing back down, moving faster and faster. "You feel so fucking good."

"I want to feel your breasts."

"No. This bra is a pain in the ass to put on. If it comes off, it's not going back on and I don't think we're at the right club for that tonight."

"No. We are not."

I lift off his cock some and hold it there, "Now that we agree. Fuck me."

His hands grip into my hips, and he unleashes, pummeling my pussy with his cock. I sit up straight, arching my back, as pleasure sizzles through every vein in my body. "Touch yourself." He nods to my clit, so I obey, pressing my finger and swirling it around.

"Oh my god!" I scream out.

My hips thrust of their own volition as we each battle to control the pace. I wanted him to fuck me, but I'm so close. When he presses up inside of me, I push down, taking control back, grinding my hips on him, while I rub my nub of pleasure. Fucking Lizzy and her book words! At least I haven't thought about his cock being steel wrapped or encased in velvet.

Moaning out his name, I grind harder and harder, moving my finger faster and faster until my orgasm unleashes inside of me and I'm pulsing around his cock. The fullness of him sends me over the edge.

"I love when you come around my cock."

"Samesies," I hear behind me.

Jax. When did he get in here?

"Lizzy said you needed something, but wouldn't say what."

"I need you. Here. Now. Pants off, on the couch."

Jax just stares at me but doesn't move.

"Now! Y'all have work to do."

When he arrives at the couch, I climb off Callum and sink onto Jax. I'm so wet I slide on easily and hear a low rumble escape from Jax's chest. Callum is slowly rubbing his cock while he watches us and I find it so incredibly hot. I glide up and down Jax's cock a few more times before I climb off and put my hands and knees on the couch. "Jax. Fuck me from behind while I suck off Callum."

Their eyes pulse wide for a second, listening to my demands, but eventually do as I say. Callum's hard cock is still slick with my wetness as I pump him a few times before sucking him into my mouth. At the same time, Jax grips his fingers into my hips and punches into my pussy, causing me to scream out, before Callum's cock quiets me.

Callum lets out a groan when I suck him in again, hollowing out my cheeks and letting him hit the back of my throat. My fingers tighten around his cock, before I slide them down to his balls, where I press my thumb at the place where they meet.

"Ow," he cries out.

I pull back scared I've hurt him, but he's holding his stomach.

"Your horn tried to impale me."

While he removes it with care not to mess up my hair, I roll my tongue around the head of his cock, licking up his arousal and then down his shaft. I can tell he's close. He was close before Jax came in, but I didn't want him coming inside of me because I'd have to feel them dribbling down my leg the rest of the night.

"There. That's better."

Jax punches in again, working through his irritation with me. Sucks for him because I like it when he's a little rough, so I decide to egg him on a bit. "No, Jax. No."

His eyes set on me and he grumbles before fucking me harder, sending Callum's cock into my mouth, who lets out a sigh of appreciation. I feel like a queen between both of these men strangling Jax's cock with my pussy while Callum thrusts wildly into my mouth, taking what he wants.

Moaning.

Groaning.

Begging for more.

I am theirs, and they are mine.

"Everlee." A puff of air escapes between Callum's lips.

He pummels my mouth with need, so I suck him harder and harder, my body sizzling with pleasure and arousal as I can feel another orgasm spoiling up.

"Fuck," he sighs out before his fingers clamp onto my shoulders, holding me in place while he unloads into the back of my throat. I swallow him down over and over again until he pulls out and takes my lips with his. "I love you," he whispers, swiping his finger over the bottom of my lip.

"I love you," I whisper back, feeling a slight ache in my chest for saying it in front of Jax, but he hardly reacts. "Now go. I'm sure the floor needs you."

He hesitates looking at me and I give him another nod of assurance. As soon as he leaves, I turn towards Jax, whose eyes are staring at me, with his teeth clamped over his bottom lip. He is all sexy and god-like right now and the whole business on the top half and party on the bottom half has me all hot, too. Like a dirty CFO. *Chief Fucking Officer. Hello sir, I'm here for my internship.* I clear my head.

"I'm sorry... for saying-"

"Do you want me to put my cock in your mouth to shut you up?" he lashes out, then adjusts and says quietly, "You have nothing to apologize for." His dark one fighting to come out and play.

"I want you to finish in my mouth. I can't have your come dripping out of me tonight," I tease, trying to lighten the mood.

He bites and with a hint of humor in his voice, he says, "Maybe I want to unload my come in your pussy because I want everyone to know you're taken. You're mine."

I glance over my shoulder at him and see his dark eyes glowing with desire.

"Stand up," he commands, pulling his cock out of me.

My pussy clenches and weeps with his absence.

"Bend over and grab the back of the couch."

His words control every fiber inside of me, making me hotter with each command. He rubs his hand down my leg and when he gets to my calf, slowly starts to lift it higher and higher, so I pivot at my hip to balance.

"How flexible are you?"

"I haven't done my daily fuck me stretches, so I may be a little tight, but I guess we're about to find out."

He looks at me, the serious tone on his face dropping for a second. "Dork."

I smile even harder, bubbles bursting inside of me. I love this side of him. The part of him he tries to keep hidden. My goal is to keep cracking his tough exterior slowly but surely until it shatters and the real Jax is standing there without his armor.

He lifts my leg up to his chest. "Now, I'm going to fuck you like this."

I nod, too excited to speak.

He plants his hands firmly on my stomach and back and fills me to the hilt with one thrust causing a tingle sensation to shoot across my body. A scream escapes as he hits a new depth. I'm pretty sure I just got a cock punch to the lung.

He pulls out slowly and pushes in again, then moves faster and faster.

The door buzzes, and I tilt my head to look.

Emmett.

"Lizzy said you needed to show... me something? Well, hello."

Fucking Lizzy. Is her plan to keep me holed up in this room all night fucking my men? I mean, not the worst idea, but shit.

Emmett distracted me long enough for Jax to get to the point where his body has taken over. He's like a runaway freight train, no stopping him now. "Ev. Can I?" His words are short and nearly pleading.

"Yes." Claim me. I will deal with a sloshy vagina for you.

He punches inside of me one last time before he comes to a stop, his cock pulsing. He kisses down my leg before he lets it fall.

I wanted to shout next, but that seemed wrong.

Twenty minutes later, I'm walking back out to the floor with Emmett and Knox behind me, well fucked and sore. Yes. Lizzy found Knox too, who bounced into the room looking jollier than a Christmas elf on Christmas Eve.

Lizzy and Tony were on the main floor dancing, and Beckett and Will were just coming back upstairs to take a break, which was fortunate. They didn't need to know I spent the last forty minutes getting my brains fucked out.

"You been dancin' sis? You look tired."

"How is it down there?"

Callum places a drink on the table and I nod a thank you. I pick the small piece of cotton candy off the top and then tilt back the drink. Fucking delicious. Every time. Emmett is a master behind the bar, kitchen, and me. We didn't have sex, but he spent his time making sure I had another orgasm, eating me out and licking me like a fucking lollipop. My skin flushes, thinking about it again. That man is a master with his mouth.

"Drink good?" Beckett asks.

"So damn good."

"Oooh, it's my drink. I'll be back!" Lizzy shouts, running over to the bar.

Tony slides into the booth opposite of me and gives a slight nod.

So fucking embarrassing, although I guess no less embarrassing than seeing him and Lizzy at Allure. Apparently, he has a kink for costume play as well. I try not to look for them when I'm there because I want to give them their privacy, but he doesn't seem to care.

"Scoot over!" A hand is pushing on my shoulder.

"Fine." She looks at the seat first, then sits down, then looks at me. "What?" I had to make sure it was clean.

"Lizzy." I smack her arm.

"I see we're doing this again." She holds up her hand to get the table's attention. "Tonight, call me Seraphina."

"Why?

"Because it has a lot of syllables and isn't so easy to say. You'll get tired of saying it repeatedly."

I shake my head in disbelief. "If you wouldn't say certain things..."

"You act shocked every time I say something. Like Ev, you should... know me by now," she sings the latter words, then continues changing the song to a more modern pop song. "This is me! Look out 'cause here I come." She leans over and whisper sings in my ear, not quietly enough. "But not as much a Everlee."

"How much has she had to drink?" I ask Tony. "We don't usually get karaoke Lizzy until three or four drinks in."

"I'm not drunk. Just happy. Overjoyed. Ecstatic. I have all of my favorite people here with me tonight."

"How many drinks until overly sentimental Lizzy?" Beckett asks. "It's been a while since I've seen that."

"Shut up, asshole!" Lizzy lashes out.

"Whew. Our girl's back! Thought we lost you there for a minute," Beckett teases.

"Did Ev tell you I helped come up with the drink tonight?" Lizzy shakes her shoulders.

"No, but you have, like thirty times," Beckett says, before quickly sliding out of the way of Lizzy's smack.

A moment later, Emmett is over with a tray of his cotton candy delight. "Is everyone behaving over here?" He looks between Lizzy and me, pointedly.

"Of course... not." I smile and he winks at me, melting my insides like goo. I love that man with every part of me.

Lizzy grabs a glass, gently thrusting it at the rest of us so we all pick one up and hold it in the air. "I have prepared a haiku for you all this evening."

"This should be good," Beckett chimes.

She rolls her eyes at him and clears her throat, counting the syllables on her fingers while she speaks. "You're all my bitches. Let us drink the night away. And I love you big."

"Here queer!" Beckett salutes, tossing back the drink.

JAX - CONFESSIONS

SHE FUCKING DOES THIS to me on purpose.

Everlee.

Her and Lizzy knocked back one of Emmett's drinks after Lizzy gave one of the weirdest toasts I've ever heard. She should probably hire someone for her wedding day, because what I overheard sounded horrendous. A haiku? Really?

Regardless, they both went to the main dance floor, and right now Everlee is spinning in a circle with her hands up in the air while Lizzy is fluffing up her tutu, both laughing carelessly. If her ass wasn't on display for the whole goddamn club to see, then I may actually smile too, because her happiness is infectious and I love her laugh. It has the right amount of pitch to not be grating and the right depth of a belly laugh so it doesn't sound like a staccato'd grunt. Is staccato'd a word? Fuck if I know.

"The rail did nothing to you." A hand gently curves around my shoulder as Knox walks into view.

"Shut the fuck up," I snap back.

He holds his hands up. "Don't shoot the messenger." He looks down at Everlee and Lizzy who have just stopped spinning. Everlee's arms are latched onto Lizzy's shoulders while they talk, no doubt ensuring she doesn't fall face first onto the floor. Lizzy nods and smiles before pumping her eyebrows. A tell-tell sign they're up to something.

A man, in some sort of gold Spanx with straps looking get up, in the corner of the room spots them, and starts making his way towards them. An electricity slashes through me as every hair on my body stands on end. This man is literally pushing through the entire crowd to get to them.

To her.

Knox grabs my arm when I turn quickly from the railing. All hint of humor dropped from his voice. "Take a beat. You can't go down there all bull in china shop. She can talk to other people. It doesn't mean anything."

I snatch my arm out of his and head for the stairs, brushing shoulders with several guests. I'm trying to calm my breathing because this shouldn't be me. I'm not the overly jealous type.

Protective, yes.

Jealous, no.

Lizzy spots me coming and quickly taps Everlee's arm to get her attention away from the guy who is super chatty and smiley. Ugh.

"Jax!" she squeals, turning to me before I can even get to them. She knows. She can see the fire in my eyes and she meets it with a cool glaze and a hug. "This is Larry from work. I told him about this place and he came here tonight with his boyfriend!" She waves to a man wearing a unicorn onesie in the corner the man just came from.

Knox, standing at the railing, grabs my attention and I roll my eyes. He walks away, clearly sensing I'm not about to lay some guy out on the floor.

"Hi, Larry from work." I try not to sound like a complete dick, but from the look Everlee is casting at me, I know I failed. Tough shit.

What is wrong with me right now?

Larry's eyes grow wide for a second as he nods, before he leans over to Everlee and does that whole fake whisper thing I find so grating. Or maybe just super grating right now because as the night has gone on a stick- no, a tree, has lodged itself up my ass. "You didn't tell me how hot he was."

"I think he's taken Larry," she pats him on the chest.

My arms twitch, but I try to push the monster raging inside of me down.

Yes. He is taken. He is very much taken.

By her!

The anger I was feeling before is now replaced with a blinding frustration. Frustration with this lifestyle and that we can't take her out publicly and do the things we want to do. Should do. She's so fucking understanding, but I see all these couples out here on the dance floor dancing and... who knows what else, and she... she has to dance with her best friend, because heaven for-fucking-bid.

Fuck it! Fuck this! The guys are probably going to be pissed, but I don't care. I'm tired of hiding.

"Yes. I am taken." I wrap my arm around Everlee and bring her to my side, planting a kiss on her head.

"Shut. Up!" Larry whisper screams, panting and flapping his hands in the air.

"This just got interesting," Lizzy says, smiling.

Everlee tentatively puts her hand on my chest, so I look down at her and wink.

"If you will excuse us," I say without waiting long for a response.

Grabbing her hand, I pull her across the dance floor, through the small hall near the bathrooms and swipe my keycard at the next door. I push it open and she ducks in, her brows furrowed.

"What's going on?" she asks.

The latch clicks and I grab both of her cheeks and push her backwards against the door, pressing my lips to hers. The need to feel her lips on mine, taste her sweet kiss, is all-consuming. My fingers dig gently into the back of her neck as my tongue pulses in and around. The muscles in my legs are weak, my heartbeat is erratic. My body presses against hers, holding her to the door and my head feels like I'm swimming and my body... fuck.

She melts into my kiss like she always does, her hands falling from my chest and tucking themselves into the back of my pants. A light moan whispers in her throat, like she's trying to hold it back or hide it from me, but she can't hide anything from me. I know her better than she knows herself- what makes her moan, what turns her on, what she tastes like, what she feels like just before she comes.

I know her.

I love her. Fully, with every thing in my body. Every beat of my heart, beats for her.

I pull away from our kiss and put my forehead to hers, breathing her in and catching my breath. The silence between us lingers and grows to a deafening sound. My thoughts are muted by the pounding of the heartbeat in my ears, my stomach twists in knots and my muscles tighten.

"I..." I pause and try to ignore the catch of her breath. The words get stuck in my throat and despair creeps in. "Don't hold your breath for me," I sigh, shoulders dropping.

Her shoulders relax and I swear I can feel a wave pass from her to me. Like I can *feel* her emotions. Her disappointment.

"Ev," I start again, swallowing the knot in my throat. "I'm not a good person."

Her forehead doesn't move away from mine, but I feel her eyes shift to my face. Even though she doesn't speak, the words she wants to say are clear. *No, Jax. You aren't a bad person. You're not the monster you think you are. You are good.* She's only gotten glimpses of the pieces of him that come out in the bedroom and even then, he's restrained.

"I don't deserve your love."

"Jax," she breathes out my name like the wind floats across a flower field, a stark contrast to the intensity in her eyes. She grabs my cheeks and looks me square in the face. "Stop. Just stop." She shakes her head as frustration builds in her tiny little frame like a spaceship trying to push its way through a stick of dynamite. "You are so worthy of *my* love." Tears form in her eyes and I can see there are emotions and thoughts bouncing around in her head, words that she won't say. "You think you aren't worthy of love, but that's bullshit." The hesitant look in her eyes turning hard.

She pushes me away and pokes her finger hard in my chest. I guess I was wrong. Once again, she surprises me. My little fire cracker.

"You are scared. You're scared of getting hurt. You're scared of letting down your guard. Of letting yourself be loved."

She keeps her finger in my chest, slowly pushing me across the room as her words feel like lashings against my skin.

"You aren't unworthy of my love. You are just scared of it. Well, fuck you. You're willing to let your fear- fear from the past, fear of the future control you. Your life. The man I know shouldn't be so willing to let fear control him. Fear puts you in a box, makes you small, makes you-"

"Shut the fuck up," I sigh out, wrapping my hand around the back of her neck, bringing her to me. I stare at her for a moment, her eyes wide with shock before I crash my lips to hers in an unforgivingly hard kiss. When her muscles relax, I pull away and look at her.

"Did you just kiss me to shut me up?"

I shake my head slowly, defeat creeping in. Staring her in the eyes, I whisper, "I love you, Everlee. I fucking love you so much it hurts. You are right. I'm scared. I'm scared of loving you and losing you. I'm scared you will see the man I really am, and leave. I'm scared-"

"*You* shut the fuck up." She wraps both of her arms around my neck and jumps onto me, wrapping her legs and arms around me tightly. "Just shut up and kiss me like you love me." She smiles, her face beaming.

"I can do that." I kiss her softly, letting the emotions and the feelings- the fear- flow out of me. I don't want to let fear control me. It's not gone, but I feel infinitesimally lighter.

When I stand her back up a minute later, I see a tear just under her eyelashes, so I wipe it away with the pad of my thumb. "Damn you," I mumble.

We both stand looking at one another in silence for who knows how long. Seconds? Minutes? Hours? She takes a few quick puffs of air and jumps up and down, shaking her hands like a boxer getting ready for the ring.

"We better get back out to the floor before the others think we're fucking again."

"Not a bad idea," I smirk.

"Jax," she smacks my chest. "Maybe tonight." She winks and walks her rainbow tutu'ed ass out of the door.

Standing there in the room's silence, I take everything in. She's giving me space, not trying to crowd me. She knows me. God, does she know me. Most women would stay here and want to just dance in this feeling of bliss, but she knows what it took for me to say those words. The feelings pulling and ripping inside of my chest, even now.

I'm exposed.

Vulnerable.

My hands stretch and flex several times before I move towards the door. The loud thumps of the bass pulse through me, charging me.

I did it.

I said the words.

I've never said them to another person before and meant them like I do so fully with Everlee. My love for her consumed me before I even said them. Perhaps that's what I found so scary. The fact I feel like my feelings for her, my love, is on a runaway freight train. I need to be in control, and that part of me is not.

However, maybe telling her gives me back some of that control...

EVERLEE - MY MEN

MY BACK PRESSES AGAINST the wall outside of the room Jax is in.

He just said he loved me.

That moment. It was intense.

I feel so raw. So charged.

The music pulses through me, pulling me down the hall. I know Jax will be out in just a second, and I don't want him to see me like this. Not after all of that. I don't know if he was planning on telling me he loved me. I don't think he was. He looked so... scared after he said the words. I could see it in his eyes. It's why I left. Part of me, a big part, wanted to stay, but the other part knew I needed to get away. I needed to allow him time to process. He's like a wild animal, and I didn't want him to feel like he was caged or trapped. He needed space to breathe.

When I get to the dance floor, Tony and Lizzy are dancing, rather grinding. I feel a set of eyes on me and look up to find Callum's blue eyes staring at me. His face looks puzzled and then a moment later, his eyes shift and his face changes.

Jax is walking along the side of the room before he ducks into another nook.

Taking a deep breath, I walk to the stairs to head back up and find Callum at the top, waiting for me.

"What's wrong? What happened?" He asks, his words laced with worry.

"Nothing is wrong."

"What happened?"

My head falls to the side. I know we don't keep things from one another, but for some reason, I find myself wanting to hold on to this piece of information, at least for a little while longer. I don't think Jax would care, but...

"Everlee?" he presses.

"Everything is fine, but I don't want to talk about it right now." I throw my arms around him, giving him a quick hug and whisper. "All is great. Trust me."

He turns his head lightly and breathes in my hair. "You smell like Jax," he murmurs.

"And now I will smell like you." I gently place my hand on his chest and push him away.

He lets out a low hum. "Your brother was looking for you." He nods towards our table.

"Thanks." I place a quick kiss on his cheek.

Beckett and Will are cuddled in the booth, smiling and talking about something when I walk up, looking so cute and cozy.

"Which of your handsome harem were you with this time? I mean, really... how do you keep up with them all?"

My head falls to the side.

"What?" He laughs innocently.

"I was downstairs dancing with Lizzy, then talked with Jax."

Beckett sits up. "Everything good?"

"Great." I sit down and fiddle with a half-wet napkin that was sitting on the table. "What were you two talking about when I walked up?"

"Our forbidden love nest vacation."

"What?"

"This summer. Us, Lizzy and Tony and you and your harem."

"We're doing it?"

He laughs out loud. "Come on. Lizzy is planning it. Of course we will, whether or not everyone knows it. I'd be surprised if she didn't already reserve that house we were looking at."

He wasn't wrong. She has a way of making things happen. If you look up GSD in the dictionary, her picture would be there because she is the queen of getting shit done. "I don't think she would. It was expensive. A house that big on the beach…" I ball up the napkin.

Beckett rolls his eyes and smacks his lips dramatically. "Place a bet?" He nods to her, walking up.

The gambler in me wants to take him up on the bet just to bet, while the other part of me knows Lizzy. Could I really make the bet knowing the kind of person she is?

"You better hurry. She's getting closer."

I sigh. "I can't take the bet."

He laughs. "Probably a good idea. Let's find out for good measure." He doesn't wait for an answer before he shouts out to Lizzy.

"Yes, my love?" She dances over like a little fairy and pushes me further into the booth so she can sit.

"You book that house yet?"

"What house?"

"The beach house."

A sly smile lifts the corner of her lips. "You know I did."

"Lizzy?"

"What? We're going."

"I haven't gotten a definitive answer from the guys."

"They're going."

I stare at her, causing her to laugh.

"If we don't go, which is not an option, I only lose two hundred if we cancel more than a week out. The only reason it was available was because someone just backed out. Their loss, our win."

"That is true," I concede.

"We don't have a ton of time to decide. So you need to get on it." She laughs. "Not their cocks. I think you've done enough of that for one night. Or not?? I don't want to know. Well, not completely. Maybe just a little. No. I don't. Final answer. What were we talking about?"

My eyes drift up to Tony, who is standing at the end of the booth, with his hand propped on the chair behind her.

"But seriously," she continues. "If you want to go, they will go. And I know you want to go... so henceforthwith we are going."

"I don't think henceforthwith is a word. Henceforth or forthwith..."

"Tomato, tomato."

We spend the rest of the hour talking about plans for the beach trip like nights we will cook in, nights we will go out, what we need to buy food wise to keep in the house, breakfasts, snacks, and drinks. By the time we leave the bar, I'm excited and pumped about our upcoming vacation and am cussing myself in the car ride home.

Fucking Lizzy strikes again!

Vixen should close within the hour, so I pad into the bathroom and turn on the shower. The oversized rainfall shower head unleashes gallons of water on me, relaxing my muscles. I just stand there and try to figure out how I'm going to tell the boys we have a vacation coming up in a few weeks.

There's no way. Especially with picking up Allure.

Shit!

Sadness creeps over my skin like an infection because I had let myself get lost in the dream for a moment too long tonight. When I finish up, I climb into bed. I must have fallen asleep because I feel the bed shake what feels like minutes later, but the guys are home and freshly showered, smelling like heaven.

Jax lays down to my right and plants a soft kiss on my head. A light moan escapes as I curl into his chest, at the same time another arm wraps around me.

"I love you," I say out loud. I don't qualify it with a name because I don't have to. My guys have said it to me, and I've said it to them. There's no more hiding or whispering. No more hidden messages in songs. Just love. Open love. Free love.

They all say it back to me. Even Jax mumbles it against my skin before he presses his lips to my neck and my heart swells with emotion.

My guys.

My life.

My everything.

"We're going to the beach... in a few weeks. I'll give... you the details tomorrow."

Darkness creeps in and swallows me up before I can hear them respond.

Afterword

To all of those good girls who waited... hopefully you've been edged long enough. Find your favorite toy, go back to your favorite scene in the book, prop up your device or book and enjoy. Come so hard that it registers on the Richter scale.

What's coming next

Hopefully you ;)

I have at least 3 more planned books in this series, maybe more, plus a spin-off for Beckett and Will and I think it would be a huge issue if we don't see Lizzy's wedding. I love these characters. Writing them is so much fun so, I can easily see me writing more and I am working as fast as I can.

Thank you to everyone who shares these books on social media, on your smut groups, and to your friends. It means soooo much to me, because I wouldn't be where I am today, without you.

Knowing that people love my books enough to share them gives me the inspiration and motivation to write more books and get them out to you faster.

About the Author

Hi lovelies! Follow me below for all the updates, behind the scenes and bonus content!

You can always email me at authorsnmoor [at] gmail.com or message me below. I do rely more on facebook, Insta and TT for most of my communication.

Etsy Shop AuthorSNMoor
Tiktok@authorsnmoor
Instagramsn_moor
FacebookSN Moor Author — Author SN Moor Fan Group
GoodreadsS.N. Moor
Amazon

Also By

I have a ton of ideas for books, I just need more time to write.
But if you like paranormal spicy romance fairytale retellings, I have Snow Hunted out. It does end on a cliff (I will be finishing it), but truth be told, I think it could be better than it is now and it's going to be part of a larger standalone interconnected series like 10+ books. I will be rewriting (tweaking) Snow Hunted and making it 1 book with no cliff. Other books in the interconnected series will look at Peter Pan, Hook, Little Mermaid, Huntsman, Red Riding Hood, Alice in Wonderland, and more!

www.ingramcontent.com/pod-product-compliance
Lightning Source LLC
Chambersburg PA
CBHW020747190726
48285CB00006B/1921